PATIENT ZERO

A MEDICAL THRILLER

FRITZ GALT

PATIENT ZERO

FRITZ GALT

Sigma Books

PATIENT ZERO

A MEDICAL THRILLER

ISBN: 9781521227435

Sigma Books

The orchid weeps to know your scent is gone.

From "Heyang Poem" by the Tang poet Li Shangyin
Translation by Mark Obama Ndesandjo

Contents

CHAPTER 1

First Victim

They called him the General.

Seated comfortably in First Class, General Gavin Peak felt the Boeing 787 Dreamliner hit turbulence over the Sea of Japan. The sudden bumps and intense juddering triggered memories of similar flights in medical transports to Iraq.

Like many Americans, General Peak was born to serve his country. He had joined the Reserve Officers' Training Corps as a pre-med student, and the U.S. Army had paid for medical school, commissioned him as a captain, and shipped him off to the Gulf War. There, he ran a Mobile Army Surgical Hospital on the front lines treating horrific casualties inflicted by Saddam Hussein on coalition troops.

Over the ensuing decades, Gavin augmented his surgical skills with further education and poured all his energy into biomedical research at the nation's top biological and chemical warfare laboratory. That work was gradually taken over by administrative duties, and he steadily rose through the ranks to major, lieutenant colonel, colonel, and finally brigadier general.

It was while running the bio warfare lab, however, that Gavin became slowly seduced by the corporate world. As he signed multimillion-dollar deals with contractors, he saw lucrative opportunities available to him in the private sector. And as time and more deals passed, he quietly dreamed of one day sitting on the other side of those negotiations.

In line for promotion to installation commander at Fort Detrick, the nation's top bioweapons research facility, he was passed over by a rising star in the U.S. Army Nurse Corps. Well, he hadn't put in thirty years of service as a doctor and scientist just to be "commanded" by a nurse. It was time to change horses. But, rather than seeing it as a bitter break with the past, he regarded his decision to retire from the army as an opportunity to pursue more lucrative options.

Switching easily to a business suit, Gavin Peak transitioned quickly from government service to barefaced, unabashed capitalism. He spent the next few years making up for a career of low government wages by jumping from one corner office to the next. As a highly sought-after hired gun, he helped firms sell vaccines to the Pentagon for nearly a decade as he watched his savings turn into a small fortune.

Now, at sixty years of age, he made yet another career transition to become the new CEO of FutureGenetics. The young American company had a few vaccines in the pipeline and was eager to become a major player in the U.S. market. But he had been surprised to learn Chinese investors recently acquired a majority share of the firm, which radically changed his role.

Leaning back in his soft leather seat, he ran a hand through his military-style haircut. Then he allowed himself a smile of satisfaction. He had really done it. Before stepping on that long L.A.-Guangzhou flight, he had packed up and stored away everything he owned. As CEO, he was relocating to Southern China where he would preside over FutureGenetics' newly established headquarters. For someone who had fought hard for the American team for so many years, serving the global market felt new to him. But the world of public health and corporate sales knew no borders. And he was fully prepared to enjoy the expatriate life wherever that took him.

General, doctor, CEO. Many told him these represented conflicting mindsets. His army buddies warned him he couldn't bring all three approaches to one job. And even though he disagreed and viewed his past experiences as an asset, his new business acquaintances also cautioned him that military, medical, and business forces would always be in conflict, no matter where he found himself.

A mid-autumn sunrise peeked through the window shade, and Gavin began to wonder what China held in store for him. He fully intended to prove his friends and business colleagues wrong. But would he garner the same respect he felt while striding through top-secret laboratories in the United States?

Everything about him still evoked the rugged and persnickety character of a military commander. His jaw was square and he had a broad forehead and strong nose. His skin was fair and his steel-blue eyes were handsome. His slate-gray hair still had a stiff brush cut. With broad shoulders and a deep chest, his torso was fit and firm. Behind his dry lips, even rows of white teeth flashed in a fulsome display whenever he smiled. His rigid posture commanded attention. And his square hands, large feet, and wide stance exuded authority. He was used to giving orders and expected people to carry them out.

Who would carry out those orders next? What was the majority Chinese owned company like? He had reviewed the organizational chart, showing a thin layer of management and many laboratory technicians, and read the firm's business plan, which called for vaccine development and eventual sales within a year. But what would he find once he looked under the hood?

Then the low hum of air recirculation filters was overlaid by someone clicking on the public-address system.

It was a bad sign when an announcement had to interrupt everybody's sleep.

A trembling female voice came over the speaker. "Is there a doctor onboard?"

It was even worse when there was a medical emergency. Gavin hoped it was minor and a doctor would rise to the occasion and attend to the situation promptly. That didn't happen, as a minute later the same voice came over the intercom. "Captain Conklin has made a special request."

Gavin closed his eyes. He remembered running into the plane's tall and trim, white-haired captain as he had entered the cabin. Captain Stewart Conklin was a familiar, friendly face from the earliest days of flying medical missions over the deserts of Iraq.

"The captain has requested if there are any medical doctors onboard that they make their presence known to a flight attendant. Thank you."

Eyes closed, Gavin had been unsuccessfully trying to ignore the flickering light of his video monitor. He glanced across the cabin of fully reclined seats, and there was no response to the plea for help.

But there were hundreds of passengers in the rear cabin. Surely one of them was a physician.

The intercom clicked on again. This time, the voice was more desperate. "Do we have any EMT or person with medical training onboard this aircraft? If so, please make your presence known to a flight attendant."

They never said what the problem was. It reminded him of the calls for "Code Blue" in hospital corridors. In those days at Walter Reed, he would drop everything and respond, reaching for surgical gloves as he ran for the elevator.

He sighed. It had been ages since he performed surgery. He had traded all that in for pressure suits in a Biosecurity Level Four lab. Years after that, it had been smart business attire.

"We have an urgent request for medical assistance."

Jeez, this was getting bad. He heard it in her voice.

Where were the doctors and nurses? Healthcare workers made up nearly ten percent of the workforce. Surely several people onboard were shirking their responsibility.

He wondered what the problem was. Heart attack? Choking? Flight attendants knew how to handle such emergencies.

He listened for activity. But the curtains behind him and the white noise of air conditioning muffled anything that might be taking place.

The next voice was from the cockpit. "This is the captain speaking. We need medical assistance immediately. Will Dr. Gavin Peak kindly make his way to the midsection of the aircraft with all deliberate speed?"

Gavin's face flushed. Captain Stewart Conklin was talking directly to him.

No longer a practicing physician, Gavin had no malpractice insurance. And he had been warned of the possible lawsuits that could arise outside of the United States, where ordinary civil protections did not apply.

He placed a hand on his snug seatbelt, but firmly resisted pulling up on the buckle.

He had no medical kit. And how close were they to a hospital anyway?

He had a biotech firm to run, where thousands of lives depended on his boardroom decisions.

At that point, the First Class flight attendant, a well maintained woman in her fifties, slipped through the curtain behind him and grasped the back of his seat.

"Dr. Peak?" she said firmly, her voice directed straight at him. "The captain would like to speak with you."

Just then, the curtain that blocked off the front galley flew open and Captain Conklin came striding through the cabin.

Damn it.

Gavin slipped the seatbelt off and leaned over to tie his wingtip shoes.

"Stewart?" Gavin said, standing up and facing the taller man. "Who's flying this crate anyway?"

The captain stopped at Gavin's seat and steadied himself against a sudden updraft.

"I get it, Gavin. I get it. I've known you for how long? Before the stars, that's for sure. And now you're double deep pockets. And press shy to boot. But there are Good Samaritan laws. The airline will protect you. Shit, man, *I'll* cover your ass. But we have a woman that's badly hurt. You swore an oath. You may be a general, but I *am* the captain of this bird last I checked. And I am officially requesting you, *doctor*, to do your goddamned duty and head aft. Now, if you please, sir."

"Well," Gavin said. "That was a fine little speech. Did you rehearse it?"

The captain was in no joking mood.

So Gavin about-faced and told the flight attendant, "Lead on."

"This way," she said, and held the curtain open for him.

The next cabin was calm and dark, with the combined smell of brownies and stinky feet.

In the dim light, he made out flight attendants hunched over a body that lay prone in the aisle.

To the left and right, Western and Chinese passengers stirred anxiously in their seats.

"What do we have?" Gavin asked the flight attendant under his breath.

"She tripped on a blanket that was wadded up on the floor," the woman said. "She didn't see it in the dark and fell down hard."

"Okay. Don't move her," Gavin said, rolling up his shirtsleeves.

He still wasn't sure he should offer medical advice, much less touch the patient. He could see a tort case in the offing.

Two female flight attendants pulled away from their fallen colleague to give him a view.

All he saw was a slim, inert form on the floor.

"Where is she hurt?" he asked.

"Looks like her back," one woman said.

"Any movement?" he asked.

"She's afraid to move."

"Okay. Keep her flat."

He stopped short of offering further assistance.

But the ensuing silence meant they were waiting for their next instruction.

Gavin sighed. "What's her name?"

"Alice," one said. "From Texas."

"Okay, Texas," Gavin said gruffly, and heaved to his knees beside her. "Can you hear me?"

There was a young, wincing "Uh-huh."

"Where does it hurt?"

"My back."

"Okay, Texas. Lie still. Are you comfortable?"

He looked at the blankets wedged under her to hold her in place.

He glanced suspiciously at the averted faces in the adjacent seats. Who had been so careless as to leave that blanket in the aisle?

The plane bounced some more, and he put his hands on the carpet to keep from landing on the victim.

What the hell was he supposed to do? His mind raced back through similar cases in which he had been involved. Never a back injury without X-ray equipment. He reached even further back to his medical studies. There was one lesson on vertebrae injuries that had been followed up by a visit to the orthopedics and spinal surgery unit.

He remembered the MD who had trained the callow students about spinal injuries. "In the absence of an X-ray, feel the firmness of each spinal vertebra."

Gavin reached out over Alice's back and paused before touching her. A mental image of his company's head lawyer, complete with a disapproving expression, loomed in his imagination.

With a sudden updraft, the floor rose momentarily. Alice groaned, and Gavin's hands landed on her shoulders for balance.

With that, he began to test each vertebra from the top of her slender neck downward. "Atlas and axis are fine," he said under his breath. "C3. C4." The bones were firmly in place. "C5. C6. C7."

He breathed a slight sigh of relief. The cervical vertebrae were the most delicate, and their damage could cause the most harm.

He moved his thumbs down her dress to the wider thoracic spinal bones. He resumed calling out each vertebra he found.

"T1. T2. T3."

He could sense Alice's co-workers relaxing.

Then his thumbs probed lower. The bones were bigger, but they were also buried deeper in the small of her back.

"T11, T12."

He inched lower into the lumbar region…and found nothing. There was only a mushy spot in the small of her back where a vertebra should be.

That was all he needed to know. Based on his medical school lesson thirty years ago, he decided on his diagnosis.

"We need to immobilize her back and limbs and offload her at the nearest airport. She has a possible broken lumbar vertebra."

The news hit the crew like a hammer. He had always had poor bedside manners. In fact, he remembered proudly flunking that class. But that was the military, where bluntness was a virtue.

"I'll inform the captain," the First Class attendant whispered.

"You'll be fine, Texas," Gavin said, trying to correct for his insensitivity. "They've got good hospitals around here."

Now, that wasn't a lie. But there was nothing to substantiate the claim.

The fact was, he didn't know what city was nearest.

The next thing he heard was a flight attendant's voice over the intercom. "The flight deck has informed me we will be landing shortly. The captain has requested that passengers take your seats immediately, fasten your seatbelts, and return your tray tables and seatbacks to the upright position."

Gavin felt the wide-body jet roll left with an accompanying drop in altitude.

The altered flight plan was going to delay Gavin's arrival in Guangzhou. Would his new office and house staff still have the red carpet rolled out for him?

He patted Alice on the shoulder and rose to his feet.

He had made the call. Now everyone onboard would have to live with it. But he was sure it was the right call, and they could whine all they wanted.

As Gavin was returning to his seat, Captain Conklin's voice came over the PA system.

"This is the captain speaking. We are diverting this flight for an unscheduled stop at Beijing Capital Airport due to a medical emergency. On behalf of the entire crew, I would like to personally thank for his prompt medical attention, Dr. Gavin Peak."

"That's *General* Peak," Gavin muttered under his breath.

The unplanned delay in Beijing meant the crew's flying hours would be exceeded if they flew on to Guangzhou. Since there was no backup crew in Beijing to replace Captain Conklin's crew, all passengers were told to deplane and go through immigration, rebook, and switch to domestic flights.

Once a Chinese medical team carried Alice off on a stretcher, Gavin joined the inconvenienced passengers shuffling off the plane.

He saw Stewart Conklin standing outside the flight deck apologizing to passengers as they left. When he reached the front of the aisle, Gavin leaned in close to his old friend. "You owe me one, buddy. That one was for you. I just wanted to hear you cuss."

Conklin's face emitted a wry grin. "Yeah, you're one pill pusher that can make me do that."

"And also, that's 'General' Peak to you."

"Hey, I forgot. You weren't wearing your chest candy."

"See you in hell."

"Where are you posted now?"

"Totally in the private sector. Shipping off to Guangzhou."

"Hey, that's my normal layover. Next time I'm in town, I'll buy you a Tsingtao."

"What's that?"

Stewart looked at him more closely. "It's beer, Gavin. I'm sorry, somehow I just can't picture you living in China."

Gavin didn't know how to take that, and left his old friend with a feigned sucker punch to the gut.

Several minutes later, Gavin got a sense of what Stewart Conklin meant about China when he got a strong "fish-out-of-water" feeling. He stood in a long line in an enormous hall that was illuminated only by the orange glow of air pollution outside the windows. It made the early morning feel like dusk.

An hour later, a chunky man with a poor crewcut and an ill-fitting suit re-ticketed him on a noon flight direct to Guangzhou.

How to switch terminals was unclear to the first-time China traveler. But Gavin kept his cool and got through the maze in time to check in again, find his gate, and board the flight.

The modern airport was impressive, but even more so was the double-decker Airbus 380.

Three hours later, he emerged in Guangzhou onto a bright, hot tarmac, where buses waited to take passengers to the terminal.

Several passengers, young and old, stopped and ran back to take selfies with the A-380.

Gavin was sweating when he reached the inside of the airport, where a long, snaking conveyor belt emerged from an exterior wall. He could hear baggage handlers dumping his flight's luggage onto the belt just outside.

The new-smelling airport was surprisingly empty, giving him a mixed message about the financial prospects of the large Chinese city formerly known as Canton.

But once he had his bags, he could leave security with no need to show his papers. He made a mental note on the ease of movement for people within the communist country. How did the government know where everyone was?

A mass of people with hand-printed signs waited outside baggage claim. It reminded him of a recent trip to New Delhi where his company had acquired another biomedical firm. Guangzhou was a bit disorderly, but no hawkers or stray cab drivers tried to snag him.

Then he saw a handmade sign for "FutureGenetics" held by a small Asian man with a big smile. Around him stood a cluster of long-limbed young Chinese women in black business suits. They were all of a height and all had, from what he could tell at first glance, identical round, pale faces.

Gavin signaled the wiry young man and rolled his bags to the end of a shiny railing where passengers joined the masses.

The man tucked the sign under an elbow and extended a hand to shake. "Mr. Peak, it is a great pleasure. I am your personal assistant."

"Mr. Liu?" Gavin had expected a more imposing figure to represent his company.

"Just call me Billy."

Gavin wondered if the entire country was that informal, or if it was just his employee trying to act American. He took the jaunty handshake with "You may call me 'General.'"

"Yes, General. You will very like meeting the staff at your villa."

Gavin watched the young women grab his luggage and roll it out the door.

His company owned a fifteen-passenger minibus. It proudly sported a modern logo merging an aqua blue "Future" with an apple green "Genetics."

"Now we drive to Orchid Mountain Villas."

The drive was an uncluttered toll road with leafy bushes in the median, and green hills on both sides of the highway. It wasn't the paddies he had expected to find in southern China.

They shot through a tunnel that bored straight through one of the steep, jungle-covered mountains, paid toll, and got off the highway. A few turns later, they entered a shaded compound with a guard shack and a gate that had to be raised by hand. The guard wore a dark, police-like uniform and saluted them.

They drove past a rectangular swimming pool and a playground at the base of a road that twisted up the mountain.

The minibus took them past larger and grander villas as it labored up the slope.

"See the orchids?" his man said.

The delicate white flowers hung from trees and swayed in the gentle breeze.

At the top of the curving road, a white stucco villa stuck out from the others with a grassy front yard and a pull-through driveway.

Just by the pillared entrance, a semicircle of people in smart, tan blazers stood waiting. "Who are they?"

"Property management. This is a traditional greeting for big fish."

Gavin emerged from the air-conditioned vehicle to a hot whoosh of chlorophyll-scented air.

He went down the line shaking hands. First were the gentlemen: a corporate representative of the real estate owner, the housing manager, the head of security, and the clubhouse manager.

"We have an outdoor swimming pool, clubhouse, exercise room, restaurant, snooker table, table tennis, badminton, a convenience store, and a coffee shop."

Extravagant didn't cover it.

Business cards were offered with a formal two-handed flourish. Gavin dug into his trousers for his own cards and found a few, but decided against handing them out.

Ahead were the ladies, but the greetings were momentarily interrupted by a phone call.

Gavin had already noticed the one who stood out in the line. She was shorter than the uniform height of the rest, and her dark hair had a chestnut-colored tinge. She was a professional woman, striving for respect among her peers. And she would have remained just one of seven hundred million Chinese women except for something unique and sad about her face. She seemed uncomfortable, as if she didn't belong there. Perhaps she had other concerns beyond the mundane workplace. But it was her phone that belted out the Backstreet Boys: "Get down. Get down. And move it all around."

"Oh, excuse me." She reached for the phone in her shoulder bag and quickly squelched the ringtone.

He wasn't sure from the way she turned away and talked softly into it if she was aware of the odd juxtaposition of the song with the workplace. But it made a touching scene.

The phone call settled, Gavin started down the row of young maidens, the flower of Orchid Mountain's staff. The first was an overly smiling and ingratiating sales rep who seemed pleased to have landed him as a tenant. Then a matched pair of club receptionists welcomed him with white-gloved handshakes.

Gavin's eyes fell on the woman who had received the phone call. She wore her tan blazer as if it had been forced upon her. It was cute how she stood on her tiptoes to meet him eye-to-eye. A breath of wind blew strands of her gently dyed hair out of its bun and across her thin eyebrows and darting, deep brown eyes.

He caught her look and held her gaze long enough to admire her.

She returned his attention with a deeply empathetic look that came from somewhere beyond common greeting.

She may not have been the prettiest blossom on Orchid Mountain. But for the first time in the enormous, busy country, he saw vulnerability, and felt a common humanity.

"Your name?" he asked.

She stood as tall as possible. "I am your personal liaison with Orchid Mountain." She enunciated the words with a sophisticated, slightly British, accent that threw him. He had always been a sucker for British accents, but this one came, intriguingly, from a lovely Asian face.

She handed him her business card and he observed the smoothness of her slender young fingers.

"Yvonne?" he read from the card.

She bent and twisted in a half-curtsy, half-cringe as she heard her name read aloud. "People call me 'Eve.'"

"I like 'Yvonne.' *Parlez-vous français?*" he asked with a broad smile.

"*Mais oui,*" she replied. "*Et vous?*"

"*Moi aussi*," he said, not sure where that French had come from.

She was blushing. "Please call me directly for any problems or requests."

He would call her again, if only to make the song play again.

"I hope to make your stay happy," she said.

"I'm sure you will," he replied, and slipped her one of his business cards. Her accent, foreign language ability, and worldly eyes had put him instantly at ease.

His fingers trembled with excitement as he pocketed her card.

Then he moved on to the front desk manager, a woman built like a battleship who held out a large basket under plastic wrap.

"What's this?"

"Fruit for you."

He caught a whiff of something. "Are these mangos?"

The woman beamed proudly. "Yes. They are from our local trees." She held up a hand and pivoted around to the surrounding verdure.

He saw small yellow blobs of decaying fruit scattered along the sidewalk.

"Mango season," he muttered.

"Yes. The end of summer."

With that, he said his good-byes and the diminutive Billy took him inside.

He was met by the cool smell of marble. The house was extravagant, a hotel-sized edifice that descended, room-by-room, down the steep hillside. It ended in a lofty living room with floor-to-ceiling windows that framed the western sky.

There certainly were perks to being a big fish. He'd have to mingle more with the golf-playing crowd than the local staff. Then he remembered reading an article that China had closed its golf courses to appear less materialistic. He'd have to find the right people at some other type of watering hole.

He stood alone in the foyer and looked more closely out the three-story windows. He had a panoramic view of the valley and its surrounding forested ridges. And deep in his garden was a private swimming pool complete with waterfall.

A large flower arrangement sat on the round table before him. He set his fruit basket beside it. Someone had left an Orchid Mountain calling card on the table. He picked it up and checked the name. It read, "Yvonne Yang. Liaison."

He smiled as he remembered the young, blushing woman. Now he had two of her cards. It seemed to be a sign.

It was 3:50 p.m. when young U.S. diplomat Matthew Justice crawled awkwardly into the back seat of a taxi at Guangzhou Baiyun International Airport. He wiped the sweat off his brow, pulled in his suitcase and long legs, and asked the driver to take him downtown to the U.S. Consulate General.

An energetic officer with freckles and a mop of red hair, Matt tried to settle down by looking out the window.

The city hadn't changed much during the two-week drug-interdiction symposium he had just attended in California. But that wasn't always the case. He had traveled to the United States frequently during the first year of his two-year tour in China, and he noticed new construction sites or grand openings whenever he returned.

He had come a long way from Evansville, Indiana. Yet still it all seemed written in the stars.

Looking back, he hadn't known what to expect three years earlier when he graduated from Yale with a degree in Economics. His interests changed from day to day.

But he came barreling out of Commencement ready to put his knowledge to work and give back to the forces that had gotten him out of Indiana. He owed something to humanity in general and wanted to do right by every country in the world.

And there stood China: big, flourishing, modernizing. Just like he felt toward the rest of the world, he seemed ineluctably linked to her destiny.

The dust and construction trucks were just signs of a work in progress. The country was new in the same way that he felt newly formed.

He dug out his phone and switched SIM cards to the China Mobile network.

He thumbed through his local contacts from consulate buddies to delivery places until he reached the bottom of the list.

He smiled when he saw her name. Although she was buried in the alphabet, she was the one that mattered most:

Yvonne Yang.

He clicked on her name and the phone began to play horrible, synthesized music.

Eve would be at work at Orchid Mountain.

"*Wei?* Matthew?" Her voice sounded crushed by some torture device.

He was going to ask if she had brought her umbrella.

"It looks like–"

She cut him off before he could finish. "I can't talk now."

"And 'hi' to you, too."

"Hi. I have to go. We have a VIP moving in."

"Who's moving in?"

She hung up on him.

It must be a very VIP. Matt hadn't spoken with her in two weeks, and this was the kind of reception he got?

He tried not to take it personally.

Even that small bit of conversation brought a smile. Eve wasn't the most organized person in the world. Her being flustered was true to form, and he cherished her for it.

He looked out the taxi window at the clusters of large apartment buildings. The cab had reached the straight, wide, tree-lined streets of the city's newest expansion to the east.

As he predicted, it began to rain. Umbrellas magically sprouted everywhere, covering people on the sidewalk to those riding bicycles and scooters.

The street was awash in red, yellow, and green taxis, sleek black sedans, and the muted tones of executive minivans.

Then the sun broke out behind the trees. He put on his sunglasses.

Soon he was perspiring through his clothes. The tropics weren't a logical posting for someone with hyperhidrosis, an excessive sweating disorder. But the State Department had pressing needs and given him limited options. It had been either São Paulo, Tijuana, or Guangzhou. Any of those places would have reduced him to a puddle. So he learned, day after day, to rely on the prescribed antiperspirant, mop up the residual sweat, and laugh at life's cruel ironies.

For someone in the Foreign Service, he had another major handicap. He was also cursed with a terrible sense of direction. Having grown up with a smartphone to get from place to place, he barely knew how to read a map. So he navigated by landmarks and often got lost in the vast sameness of the city.

He had been there a year, and he still couldn't place where he was.

But the traffic congestion told him he was nearing the consulate.

Then an entire city block opened up. Compared to the surrounding office towers that soared over a hundred stories in the air, the three-floor American Consulate might have seemed insignificant. But its modern, sweeping design and generous, landscaped grounds lent the building its own grandeur.

The cabbie pulled over and set the handbrake.

Matt opened his wallet. Thankfully, he still had some renminbi, or yuan as the currency was commonly called in China, to pay his fare.

The cabbie had "neglected" to start the meter, so Matt had to ask for the price.

The driver pulled the number "*jiushi*" out of his hat. "90."

Matt grimaced. Normally it cost 50 yuan, but they had taken a longer route, possibly because the driver didn't know the way.

Matt handed him a hundred and got five yuan back.

The driver might have been able to fool a tourist, but he couldn't fool an officer with an Ivy League degree.

Matt waved the bill at him and asked for another five.

The driver laughed at his own "mistake" and peeled off another five.

Matt thanked the guy, grabbed his suitcase, and slid out of the cab.

He was back where tipping didn't exist, but haggling was the norm.

He was happy to be back in Asia.

"I need to introduce you to someone," Billy Liu told Gavin Peak in a confidential tone. "Come with me."

He led Gavin out of the villa by way of a sliding glass door.

Outside, Gavin stopped and gazed toward the end of the valley, where tall buildings penetrated the city smog. The only sounds he heard came from the drone of a distant jet plane, the splash of his own private waterfall, and palm fronds knocking against each other in a lofty breeze.

He was led down to a terrace, complete with a patio table, umbrella, and cushioned chairs. From there, a stone trail led down further to the clear, blue water of his swimming pool.

A young man stood stiffly under the umbrella.

"General Peak, this is our chief operating officer."

"Vincent Fong?" Gavin said. He had spoken with Vincent several times over the phone since taking charge of the company.

"Yes, sir," the svelte young man said, his faint eyebrows lifting curiously as he offered a handshake.

Gavin recognized the low, controlled voice he had heard over the phone. But he had been expecting a Harvard MBA, not an overdressed suck-up from a Chinese night school.

"Why are we outside?" Gavin asked.

Vincent closed his eyes and shook his head slightly. "These walls have ears."

Gavin gave a flinty look back at his big, modern house. Was it riddled with bugs? The need for privacy seemed overblown, and he decided not to step out onto the patio every time he needed to talk business.

"What can be so important?"

Billy disappeared into the garden as Vincent spoke.

"We just had a containment incident at the laboratory."

Gavin was jolted back to reality.

"Containment incident?" Aware of the dangerous viruses developed at his lab, he had to take the news seriously. "When?"

"Yesterday morning at 10:40."

"China time?"

"Correct."

"More than twenty-four hours ago," Gavin observed with relief. Whatever had happened, it no longer required immediate remediation. "What exactly went down?"

"Do you want to know the details?"

"Give me the whole story."

"One of our laboratory technicians was in a virus production lab when the power went out. The suit lost oxygen and the room was under very low pressure. The door lock was electronic and we needed to get the worker out."

"Makes sense," Gavin said. He was intimately familiar with the ultra-low air pressures required to prevent air from escaping a cellular level laboratory.

"We were faced with a forty-minute deadline to get the lab tech out before suffocation."

Gavin winced. He knew full well the implications of a power outage. "What about a backup generator?"

Vincent shook his head. "We have no backup generators."

Gavin couldn't believe it. Any such lab needed a backup power supply to ensure constant refrigeration, pressure control, and ventilation.

"The city has rolling blackouts, but never for this long. We had no recourse but to cut into the laboratory."

"With what?"

"There was no power, so we used sledgehammers, axes, and saws. The police arrived and volunteered to blow a hole through the roof, but we told them that charging the roof with explosives was extremely reckless. Eventually we turned to our welder with his acetylene torch."

"Jesus. What was in the lab?"

"I'm no scientist," Vincent said. "But I was told that it was a new virus."

"…in fragile glass tubes no doubt."

"At first, everything went well. The welder cut through the lock and we were about to extract the technician when the power came back on. There was an explosion in the biohazard refrigerator."

"What caused that?"

"Later we pieced together that in the excitement of getting the lab tech out, our worker with the cutting torch didn't completely close the gas valve. There was an acetylene build-up in a corner that wafted into the body of the biohazard refrigerator. The electric motor to the refrigerator compressor spun up when the power came on, and sparks in the motor's brushes ignited the gas."

"A complex series of events," Gavin said, thoughtfully.

"It wasn't a huge explosion," Vincent said, "but it happened in a critical area. It tore a hole in the roof and sent virus vials everywhere. And with no negative pressure, a hole in the roof and the airlock doors open…"

"What happened to the specimens?"

"Many tubes were broken. They caused minor injuries to our trapped worker, the maintenance and office staff helping out, and the policemen on site."

Gavin sat down heavily on one of the patio chairs.

"How many people are we talking about?"

"Directly hit by flying glass?"

Gavin nodded.

"A dozen."

"And how many breathed in the viruses?"

The man shrugged. "The lab is in a fairly secluded part of the city, made up mostly of large complexes for corporate headquarters and high-tech manufacturing."

Gavin was aware of the general purpose of the area, known as Science City, designed to incubate the sciences and pipeline research into products. It might be lightly populated, but it sat on the fringe of Guangzhou, in a metropolitan area of forty-four million souls. "How many people were exposed?"

"Thousands, I'm sure."

"Well, this is unacceptable."

"Yes, sir. I agree."

"What emergency efforts are underway?"

"Emergency?"

"Yeah. How's the city responding?"

"They withdrew their policemen."

"I mean, what evacuation procedures are underway?"

"Evacuation procedures?"

Gavin was stunned. "Have we at least isolated those at the site?"

"No."

Gavin stared dumbfounded at his young operating officer. Where was the rule of law in this country? The guy would be facing criminal charges in the States.

"Who's our safety inspector?"

"Eric's away at a seminar."

"Do you mean to tell me that our own company is guilty of not following biohazard contamination protocols?"

"We've been waiting for you."

Gavin looked around at the nicely manicured garden and peaceful setting with an ominous black cloud on the horizon. "What kind of two-bit circus is this?"

The young man looked unfazed. "We're glad you're here, General. Welcome to China."

Just inside the entrance to the American Consulate, Matt ran into Patrick Kind, the United States Consul General, heading down the stairs on his way out of the building.

"Welcome back, young man," said the tall, slightly paunchy diplomat with gray hair and discerning eyes.

Matt was flattered that the guy kept track of the comings and goings of the hundred-plus officers stationed in Guangzhou. The consul general might not remember everybody's name, but he did recognize faces, and that was good enough for Matt.

"How did the 'China white' thing go?"

The consul general even remembered that Matt had attended a conference on new forms of Fentanyl, a synthetic opioid created in China that was rapidly replacing heroin in the United States, with deadly consequences.

Matt stooped over and set his suitcase down for a moment to talk. "I learned a lot, and came back armed with new tactics."

"Excellent. Keep me informed."

"By the way, I thought you should know, we have an American hero here in Guangzhou."

That got the senior diplomat's attention.

"His name is Dr. Gavin Peak. As we were flying from L.A. to Guangzhou, a flight attendant fell down. He diagnosed a fractured back and diverted the flight to Beijing."

"Interesting. Are you talking about *General* Gavin Peak?"

"The pilot addressed him as 'Doctor.'"

"Huh. I wonder what Gavin's doing in town. Well, I'm off to the Foreign Affairs Office."

Matt watched the consul general leave the building for his waiting bulletproof Cadillac, then sprinted up to the Marine Security Guard booth.

There, he gave a civilian salute to Sergeant Kyle Ortman, the Kansas-born Marine on duty, and got a complimentary buzz through the door into the offices.

First stop was reporting in to Bart Parsons, chief of the economics office that oversaw Matt's duties as an environment, science, technology, and health officer.

"You're back just in time," Bart told Matt, who stood in his office doorway. "This is going to be a busy few weeks."

Matt set his suitcase down and stepped fully into his boss's office. "Okay, what do we have on tap?"

"Aside from your health and science duties, I need you to help the office report on immediate economic issues. How would you like to cover the Canton Fair?"

Matt was used to being "volen-told" what to do.

"…and possibly, the Boao Forum."

"What? That's supposed to be held in the spring."

"Not this year. The Chinese are scrapping the old schedule and moving it up. They probably want to get a jump on the World Economic Forum in Davos."

Matt sat down wearily on an office chair. "Leave it to the Chinese to try and upstage the big winter event."

The chief didn't disagree, and kept mum as if the host country was listening. Which, of course, it was.

Matt didn't care. America's attitude toward the Chinese was no secret.

"So what's the schedule?" he asked.

The chief slid a calendar toward him.

Matt had been gone during the Chinese National Day holiday, but there were plenty of events lined up that would hinder his preparations for the fair and forum.

According to the calendar, the American Chamber of Commerce Fall Ball was to be celebrated the next day, followed by the Marine Corps Birthday Ball on Friday of the following week. The Canton Fair would begin the week of the Marine Ball. As if that weren't enough, the week following that would be the Boao Forum for Asia, held hundreds of miles away on the southern island of Hainan.

"Whew," Matt said, and handed the calendar back. "What about my day job?"

Matt's environment, science, technology, and health brief covered all of southern China. That encompassed various consulate districts and everything from the Vietnam border to the Taiwan Strait, and along the heavily industrialized Pearl River down to Hong Kong.

For the past year, Matt had concentrated mainly on key issues of health concern to the United States, namely Zika, AIDS, Hepatitis, Avian Flu, methamphetamines, Fentanyl, and air and water pollution.

He saw no time in the coming weeks to focus on that portfolio. But he could see his boss's rationale for bowing to the heavy pressures of economics.

In fact, there was no better post for an econ officer to be than China. And if one served in China, one either had to be in Shanghai for the business deals and heavy manufacturing or Guangzhou for its old money and export-related manufacturing.

"And, I want you to maintain your health duties all along."

"What?" Matt stared at his boss.

Bart Parsons was completely serious.

"This is crazy."

His boss gave him an evil grin. "It's flu season. Tomorrow, I want you to check the city's quarantine facilities. I want you to count the number of beds available in case of another deadly flu epidemic."

"Someone else did that last year, and there was no outbreak."

"Memories are short. I was here during the SARS outbreak, and Guangzhou had no isolation units at the time. They had to take over hotels. They created some isolation units in the meantime, but I'm worried that those have been converted back to normal hospital rooms."

Matt was still fired up from the conference on countering imports of illegal heroin substitutes. "When do I get started on tracking down the Fentanyl labs?"

"That's Friday."

Matt stared at the calendar crammed with events for the next few weeks. "I guess the race is on."

"Gentlemen, start your engines."

Matt could see a late night of work ahead, followed by another long taxi ride before he finally returned home to Orchid Mountain.

Muted sunshine told Gavin Peak that it was time for his first day of work in China. And the first day would consist of damage control.

Sitting in his captain's chair inside his gray minivan with Billy Liu at the wheel, Gavin briefly took in the countryside between home and work.

After passing through a long tunnel, the South China Expressway burst out onto a hilly landscape of dusty white apartment buildings, half-built bridges and spinning construction cranes. Ahead lay a sea of slick sedans and boxy minivans that jockeyed for position in slow-moving traffic.

Gavin swiveled from the view and concentrated on the task at hand. In the absence of his safety inspector or any employee with a reasonable sense of caution, he had to oversee the biohazard problem in person.

His minivan was more like a moving executive suite. He had his own WiFi hotspot, laptop, smartphone, printer/scanner, and mini fridge.

It was a Thursday morning. Everyone should be at work. He found Vincent Fong's mobile number on his phone and dialed.

"Has this ever happened at our lab before?" Gavin asked.

"Not that I remember."

"How long have you worked for our company?"

"Eight months."

Gavin would have to seek out someone with longer institutional memory than that.

"But the city is prepared for this sort of thing, right?"

"I'll look into it, General."

Okay, besides not knowing the business, the guy suffered from a complete lack of initiative.

"Where's my safety inspector?" Gavin continued on the phone.

"I believe Eric's still in Boston."

"But he's on his way back?"

"No. He's in training."

"Okay, his backup, then."

"General, we don't have redundant positions," Vincent said with pride.

Gavin was going to personally seek out whoever had run this facility before him and strangle him.

"At least you can tell me where our lab technician is, the one who was trapped in the lab."

"We had an ambulance transport her—"

"Her?"

"A young woman with a biology degree from Sun Yat-sen University."

"Where did they take her?"

"To a city hospital."

"City...? And just dumped her there?"

Vincent didn't seem to catch the irony in Gavin's voice.

"I want to see our laboratory director in my office as soon as I arrive."

He clicked off the phone and stared at it. Oh yes. There was one more thing.

He reached for Yvonne Yang's business card. It should be office hours at Orchid Mountain.

The phone rang on the other end.

A sleepy, "*Wei?*"

"Is this Yvonne?"

"*Wei?* This is Eve."

What he had in mind wasn't the most romantic conversation topic, but he had left a soapy mix of beard bristles floating in an uncooperative sink that morning.

"Look, this is Gavin Peak. My bathroom sink is clogged. Could you get it fixed?"

"Yes, of course, Mr. Peak."

"You can call me 'Gavin.'"

"Of course, Mr. Peak."

"Thanks."

That had gone well. His housing liaison understood his instructions, even though she failed to catch the hint to use his first name. Maybe he should have called her "Eve" as she had requested the day before.

He vowed to try her nickname the next time he broke the plumbing.

FutureGenetics was located in Science City, a half-developed subdivision of high-tech firms. The company's headquarters consisted of a modern brick-and-concrete building set off from a wide, empty street.

Once again, a semicircle of top management stood outside for the meet-and-greet.

Gavin Peak knew some of them by name, and now began to put faces to the names. Fortunately, all the employees had Western nicknames: Violet, Hank, Opus, Homewood, Scarlet, and Winston were easily submitted to memory, though not necessarily with the gender he would have associated with those names.

How many of them had been infected by the recent "containment incident?"

Word had preceded him, and all called him "General," with half-welcoming and half-fearful smiles.

Then they waited expectantly for him to speak.

He stood, legs apart, and ignored the temptation to wipe the back of his neck as the sun baked the group in the brick courtyard. Birds chattered in surrounding camphor trees, sounding much like birds in America.

"Thank you everyone for this nice welcome," he said. "This is the start of a new future for FutureGenetics."

He uttered a few more puns, jokes, and clichés and headed for the shade of the entranceway. There he paused for a moment before the smoked glass doors. Should he be prudent and don a surgical mask? Did anyone really know how much of the released viruses still hung in the air?

This was a leadership moment. Caution told him to cover up, and institutional responsibility told him to ignore the danger to his person.

Despite the health risk, he set foot inside without requesting a mask and presented a broad smile to the occasional, preoccupied employee he passed in the hall.

For the first time since arriving in China, Gavin felt at home. As Vincent Fong led him toward his office on the third floor, they passed labs with scientists bearing down on their work.

The smells and activity of a laboratory were instantly familiar to him and excited his creative impulses.

His employees were so engrossed in their work that they seemed unaware of Gavin's presence in the building.

Within a week, he vowed, he would make his presence felt.

His office wasn't showy like his villa was, but he had a tranquil view of a forest running up the side of a steep ridge. That led him to wonder what wildlife had also been infected by the viruses, and which way the wind had been blowing at the time.

A small, beefy Chinese man in a white lab coat followed Gavin vigorously into his office.

He came right in and stopped short of the desk. There he bowed politely.

Gavin just stood there, his hand half extended.

"Allow me to introduce myself," the man said. "My name is Dr. Chen Xuejiang. I am your chief scientist and laboratory director."

What was Gavin supposed to do…serve tea? "Grab a seat and tell me what was in that laboratory we blew up."

Dr. Chen sat on the edge of the chair opposite the desk and pursed his lips in a tight smile. "I like you. You're blunt."

"What was in the lab we blew up?"

"We had a working virus stored there as part of an ongoing project. It wasn't the master virus. It was a production run."

"An experimental virus?"

"That's correct, General."

"Plant, animal, or human virus?"

"An influenza strain developed from viruses exclusively found in birds."

Gavin held up a hand to stop the scientist. While getting up to speed on the firm, he had learned that his labs principally developed influenza vaccines, hoping to contribute to the huge stockpiles in the United States, Canada, Australia, Japan, Western Europe, and now China. But experimenting with deadly forms of viruses was dangerous business. "Is there any sign that this bird flu had jumped to human hosts?"

"That was precisely the experiment. We took avian influenza viruses and looked for genetic mutations that might cause them to circumvent human resistance."

Gavin felt his breathing stop altogether. Experimental viruses that could slip past a body's defenses were a danger of the highest magnitude. Who approved such risky work? Who would want to perform it?

He was looking at such a person.

Dr. Chen, his chief scientist, had to be fearless to look for the world's deadliest viruses.

"Were you fishing around for genes, or was there a theoretical basis for your work?"

Dr. Chen studied him with mild curiosity.

"Don't worry," Gavin assured him. "I'm well-versed in human resistance to animal viruses. What theories were we working on?"

"Principally, we studied H5N1 strains that might allow airborne human-to-human transmission."

"Why H5N1? So far H5N1 has only been transmitted to humans by close contact with infected live or dead birds or the consumption of poorly cooked meat, not through the air. And it's not easily communicated between people."

"Despite our country's culling of poultry populations over the years," Chen replied coolly, "we've seen a steady return of outbreaks in the human population every six years."

"So you aren't culling or cooking adequately."

"And the outbreaks have proven more lethal every time since first discovered in 1997. In the last outbreak, the mortality rate for humans was sixty percent."

"Okay, so something seems to be changing." Gavin remembered

alarming figures from recent cases in Africa, the Middle East, and Asia. "But does it have to be genetic? The change in mortality rate could be accounted for by poor reporting and statistical error."

"True," Chen said, "but the last outbreak would have become a pandemic if we hadn't isolated the victims in time."

"So you're saying the next wave might be more deadly and widespread?"

"We already know that our new strain is more deadly and more contagious."

"How can you assert that?" Gavin asked, a shiver of fear going down his spine.

"Using gene editing, we synthesized the next generation of H5N1 based on antigenic drift observed in Egypt and elsewhere."

That set off alarm bells of the first order.

"You created the new virus in this lab?"

"Yes."

"The lab that just blew up?"

Dr. Chen nodded. He was clearly proud, but oblivious to any criminal or ethical ramifications.

Gavin's lab had created a new disease, perhaps the deadliest influenza virus ever, and they had just released it into the teeming masses of China.

"Are you telling me that we created the next generation of avian flu?"

"Of course."

"How deadly is it?"

"We based it on its ability to bind to cells lining the human airway and subsequently replicate within human cells."

"In the respiratory tract?"

Chen nodded.

"Lungs?"

A long, confident nod and a smile. "Progressing quickly to severe respiratory illness that usually results in viral pneumonia."

"Viral pneumonia can be serious, but it's rarely fatal," Gavin countered.

"In this case, it's fatal."

"How so?"

"Cytokines," Dr. Chen said. "With so much immune system stimulation, far more than we ever see in normal H5N1 influenza, we begin to see dangerously high levels of cytokines."

Gavin's support for his chief scientist was beginning to waver. Gavin didn't like that the lab was pushing the ethical envelope, but he also didn't see how the new virus could be deadly.

Cytokines were a broad spectrum of tiny proteins produced by the body for cell signaling during many processes such as infection, inflammation, trauma, cancer, and reproduction. Some cytokines were secreted by the immune system to assist in the attack of cells invaded by viruses. But he saw cytokine production by the host as a normal response by the immune system when challenged by a viral infection.

"What's so dangerous about cytokines?"

"Tumor necrosis factor," was the simple answer. "TNF is a protein that can signal the immune system to destroy the body's own cells."

"Yes, cancerous cells."

"Healthy cells, too. TNFs are present during a viral infection when there is no cancer present."

"So," Gavin concluded, "the more these TNFs spearhead the attack on cells in the area of an infection…"

"…the more cytokines are generated."

"Creating a feedback loop."

Chen nodded. "It creates a 'cytokine storm.' So if the virus doesn't kill you, the body's immune system will."

Gavin was familiar with the concept. "And the healthier the immune system…"

"Like in the 1918 Spanish Flu epidemic, the healthier the person, the more likely he or she would die."

That was a scary prospect on many levels, including personally. Gavin had been in close contact with diseases in the lab for years and understood the risks well.

Okay, the virus was deadly. "But how contagious is it?"

"We believe that the virus is highly contagious. We based the mutation on viruses that are capable of airborne transmission."

"Through sneezing and coughing."

"Yes, but this virus can travel far more than a few meters. This one can adhere to the smallest aerosol particles."

"And float in the air. How far?"

"Kilometers. Wherever the wind takes it. And to wherever the rain deposits it."

Gavin stared at the scientist. "Why did you create this monster?"

"Our purpose was to examine its properties so that we could design a vaccine."

"And do we have a vaccine?"

Dr. Chen's eyes smiled. "We believe so."

Gavin sat back and stared at the heavens. It was the first piece of good news all day. And that explained why his chief scientist seemed so indifferent to the biosecurity breach.

"Do we know the effectiveness of the vaccine?"

"That has yet to be determined."

"Meaning?"

"It's too early. We haven't yet set up clinical trials."

Gavin was well aware that it took at least three months for a flu vaccine to pass clinical trials, so the vaccine couldn't help the city now. But knowing the genetics and epidemiology of a virus so early in the process gave his company a head start on any competition.

"Do we have adequate facilities to mass-produce the vaccine?"

"We can ramp up production on demand," Chen said.

That was excellent news. A vaccine was effectively a very simple concept. One either inactivated or weakened a virus before delivering it in the vaccine. That stimulated the patient's immune system to fight off future infections by the virus.

"And you're sure the virus is deadly," Gavin asked.

Dr. Chen shifted his weight uncomfortably. "We don't know for sure that the virus is deadly. We had incorporated lethal genes, but had only tested it on mice."

"And?"

"They died. But the tests are inconclusive. Mice aren't human."

"I know you can't experiment on people," Gavin said. "I just want to know what degree of certainty you have that the virus we released generates a high mortality rate."

"Well, General, we have a sample group now."

"You mean...?"

Dr. Chen nodded.

The lab technician and the rescue workers were a living test of the virulence of the disease.

Gavin calculated quickly. The victims had been exposed the day before he arrived. It had now been forty-eight hours since exposure. It normally took one to four days for influenza symptoms to appear.

Airborne viruses could hang around in the atmosphere for days, and anyone infected on the streets of Guangzhou might exhibit symptoms within the next two- to three-day timeframe.

"The good news," Dr. Chen said brightly, "is that we'll soon know the effectiveness of the vaccine."

Gavin blinked. "Were our workers vaccinated before the exposure?"

"One was."

The lab technician! She wouldn't have been allowed to handle the new strain unless she had been previously inoculated with the vaccine.

Gavin could barely assimilate all the information that Dr. Chen presented. It was both troubling and reassuring.

The lab had developed a more lethal form of H5N1 influenza, the earlier form already known to have killed hundreds of people in the past. Was the lab aware of how utterly irresponsible that was?

Even in the highest security labs at Fort Detrick within the U.S. Army Medical Research Institute of Infectious Diseases, it would take years to get such research approved.

And the National Institutes of Health, concerned about genetically modified viruses escaping from labs and the threat of people using the viruses for dastardly purposes, had halted all funding in the field.

Maybe that was why the company had been bought out by the Chinese.

On the business side of the ledger, however, there was opportunity. He could see bringing a highly profitable new product to market.

"Where is the lab technician?" he asked the scientist.

"She's downtown in an isolation ward."

At least the company and the city health authorities had done something right and put her in isolation. And with luck, the vaccine would have fended off the virus.

"I want to visit her."

"I can take you there this afternoon."

"And presumably the rescue workers are similarly quarantined."

"Not so."

That made no sense. "Where are they?"

"Here. Hard at work."

Gavin thought it through to its logical conclusion. Even if they showed no signs of the flu, they could spread it. Victims were most contagious the day before they came down with the first signs. And they could remain contagious for up to a week.

Those with the sledgehammers, axes, and saws, not to mention the welder with the acetylene torch, were walking time bombs…and human subjects for one of the deadliest forms of avian flu.

"Last question," Gavin said. "Which way was the wind blowing the day of the explosion?"

He remembered tales of the Soviet anthrax mishap in the closed city of Sverdlovsk. The leak of dried spores had luckily blown downwind of the city of 300,000 and only killed people in the hundreds, not the hundreds of thousands.

"The wind was strong," Dr. Chen said, "and there was a light mist blowing toward the city."

Gavin glared at him. "Did it blow over this building?"

To that, Dr. Chen gave a slight nod.

"Grab your surgical mask!" Gavin ordered.

He jumped up from behind his desk and hurried Dr. Chen out into the hallway.

"Get me a mask immediately," he added.

The two men sprinted along a carpeted hall of offices, and the chief scientist led him down an internal stairway.

The floor below had windows looking into laboratory facilities with white tabletops and cluttered counters. Researchers and technicians wore lab suits, but few had any form of protective mask.

Dr. Chen's office was across the hall from one such lab. He pulled two surgical masks out of a carton and handed one to Gavin, who put his on immediately. Even though respirators would provide better protection from inhaling the flu virus, for now Gavin had to go with what was available.

Which raised a question: how prepared was the facility for a mass casualty situation? With particles suspended in the air and able to be passed from person to person, everyone should be wearing protective gear.

"Do we have a public-address system?" Gavin asked through his mask.

"No," came the muffled reply.

That amounted to criminal negligence.

"Call around and have everyone from your scientists down to your secretaries put on surgical masks."

"That would create panic and stop business," Chen said.

Gavin could see everyone abandoning post and going AWOL.

"Fine," he relented. "Gather up the rescue workers who were first exposed to the outbreak."

"The facility manager has their names."

"I want them put in isolation at once."

"What isolation?"

Gavin was appalled. "Do you mean to tell me that this facility has no quarantine rooms?"

Dr. Chen shrugged as if it wasn't his responsibility.

"So where are our secure areas?"

"We have several buildings on site. The research, production and storage units are in separate buildings out back."

That could help with setting up an isolation ward. God, with all these deadly biological agents, here was a lab that had never performed a mass casualty exercise and had no decon team. And he was supposed to create an emergency response on the fly.

"Have the facilities manager gather the rescue workers and line them up outside in front of the quarantine rooms. You and I will arrange their new accommodations."

Dr. Chen made a terse call, frustrated by pushback on the other end.

Gavin spoke no Chinese, but he recognized the sound of resistance within a large bureaucracy.

"This way to the secure units."

Dr. Chen flew out the door and together they descended the staircase two more floors to ground level.

Their leather soles sliding on the highly reflective marble, they gained traction and sped for the rear of the building.

Outside, Gavin took in the outlying buildings in the complex. Concrete walkways crisscrossed the grass, leading up to single-story structures staggered in a pattern like white squares on a chessboard.

The only people visible were two laboratory workers pushing an incubator full of baby mice.

"Where should we set up?" Gavin said, breathing hard.

Dr. Chen came to a stop and reviewed the anonymous buildings with a strategic eye.

"In the back," he said. "More out of the way."

Gavin followed him through the maze of buildings. He noted with approval the HEPA-filtered air conditioning units attached to each building and the two sets of doors just to enter the buildings. There were no cracks in the siding, and the slightly slanted roofs efficiently funneled any rainwater through grates to an underground sewer system.

There were no windows on the buildings, and the only way to identify them was by the number over their front doors.

One structure stood out from the rest because of its blackened roof and the smell of charred plastic and melted metal.

Still at full trot, Gavin instinctively tightened the bands of his mask.

He noted the building's number. It was 13.

After passing a dozen more buildings, each roughly the size of two double-wide trailers, they came to Building 27. It sat at the end of the grass and up against a one-way road that appeared to circle the perimeter of the complex. Beyond that was a chain-link fence and the mountain rising immediately on the other side.

"We will make this our quarantine unit," Dr. Chen said.

"What's here now?"

"It was built as a lab, but we're using it for storage."

Gavin trotted behind the building to assure himself that it had the proper air conditioning and HEPA air filtration systems. It did.

"Does it have plumbing?" he asked.

"Running water and a single toilet."

That would have to do. This was no isolation ward as he knew it from Walter Reed or the Fort Detrick research facilities. And they were several feet from vine-covered trees with birds flying about, locusts singing in a deafening chorus, and who knew what other wildlife swinging from the branches.

But Building 27 would have to become their mini-hospital.

He and Dr. Chen were busily moving boxes to make room for beds when Gavin heard footsteps outside.

"Here come the subjects," Dr. Chen announced.

The brave souls who had attacked Building 13 to rescue the trapped lab technician were marching toward them.

Gavin quickly reviewed the signs to look for: sore throat, headache, fatigue, muscle ache, dry cough, watery eyes, runny nose.

All four were men, ranging in age and profession. The first was a robust, grease-covered mechanic in blue overalls. Behind him marched a white-haired welder with a bad case of hat hair. Next was a young office worker smartly dressed in a coat and tie. A young scientist in a sweat-soaked lab coat brought up the rear, perspiration dripping from his straight-up shock of hair.

To Dr. Chen, they were "subjects" of his latest experiment.

To Gavin, they were innocents unaware that they had entered prison with a potential life sentence.

"Take me to Nanfang Hospital," Matthew Justice told the driver who was waiting for him in the consulate parking lot.

They jumped into an official sedan and headed north, roughly in the direction of Orchid Mountain.

Matt wanted to visit the municipal hospital not only to check out the number of beds in its isolation unit, but also to see what lay inside. After all, he passed the hospital every day on his way to the local metro station.

As soon as he entered the hospital, he felt assured that the Chinese had medical care basically under control. The nurses looked prim and competent in their white outfits, the doctors seemed in charge, and the PA announcements were calm. The hospital looked as modern as any hospital in the States.

Matt showed the front desk his diplomatic credentials, and, with knit eyebrows, the receptionist placed a call and made an appointment with the head of the hospital.

Upstairs he met the hospital administrator, a young Chinese doctor named Liang. Tense and overworked, the man seemed slightly in over his head.

A bit of a salesman, Dr. Liang took a few minutes to give Matt background on the facility. Nanfang Hospital was one of the city's biggest hospitals and prided itself on being state-of-the-art. A former military hospital, the complex now had 1,500 beds and was connected to a medical school that, as Dr. Liang explained, took in many foreign students.

"Foreign?" Matt would be surprised if there were Western students there. "From where?"

"Burma, Nepal, Cambodia, Cuba."

Matt got the picture.

Dr. Liang finished his brief overview of the hospital, then picked up a phone that had been flashing at him for a full minute.

The phone call clearly agitated the doctor and seemed to send him in a new direction. When the doctor hung up, Matt asked if he could tour the isolation ward.

Still distracted, Dr. Liang assigned an orderly to give him a tour.

The ward was located on the quiet third floor of the otherwise busy hospital. Matt was happy simply to verify its existence.

Since the SARS epidemic, hospitals in China took disease outbreaks seriously, having handled dengue fever and similar threats to public health.

And, as the orderly opened the glass door into a quiet and antiseptic-smelling hallway, Matt was sure his report would be positive.

The quarantine unit consisted of individual rooms. Through observation windows, he saw that each had a single bed. In addition, on the wall of each room was a television and a window onto the outside world. Beside the hallway windows sat telephones much like what visitors to a U.S. prison might use. He checked that each door was locked from the outside.

The facility was far more advanced than the large bay with partitions between the beds than Matt would have expected in such a developing country.

The orderly, a young attendant with sideburns made from long hair that hung in front of his ears, was too busy to show him the entire floor. The guy was turning to leave when Matt heard a television playing loudly in one room.

He advanced on the sound, and saw an actual patient standing in green pajamas in the middle of her room swinging her arms in a bored fashion.

"Who's that?" Matt asked.

The orderly seemed surprised to see anyone there at all. "I don't know."

Matt performed a layman's cursory inspection of the patient. She had bandages on her face and bare arms and calves, but otherwise seemed in good health. "What does she have?"

Suddenly the friendly young man turned mum and signaled the hospital security guard who was posted by the elevators.

What followed was a string of new orders to the guard. From what Matt caught of the Chinese, the guard was supposed to prevent anyone, especially foreigners, from entering the ward in the future.

Matt seized the opportunity to pick up the telephone and chat with the woman behind the glass.

She shook her head and pointed to her ears.

Instead, she took off her company badge and held it up to the window.

Matt wrote down the name of the company: FutureGenetics.

How strange that a genetics firm had someone in isolation.

He'd have to research the company some more.

From her behavior, Matt could see no obvious signs of illness. "I'd like to know what she's suffering from and when she was admitted," Matt told the orderly.

"I am afraid we will have to leave now. That information is not available."

As they left the isolation ward, a group of policemen was running up the stairs to the scene.

Matt might well be the last foreigner ever to see a patient there again.

Gavin was freshly returned from the rear buildings where he and Dr. Chen had set up the makeshift quarantine for the exposed rescue workers. He was sitting in his new office before his unfamiliar desk when Billy stepped in.

"I forgot to inform you before you left your office, General. You have an interview with the local press."

"When?"

"Now."

Gavin cursed. He kept it under his breath so that those in the waiting room couldn't hear him. The last thing he needed was reporters snooping around.

A thin, young Chinese woman walked into the room. He couldn't tell from her stylish business suit whether she covered the medical beat or the social scene.

As she took her seat and brought out a digital recorder, he quickly reviewed all the possible topics she might cover.

Containment problems, quarantines, evacuation?

She smiled at him and cocked her head. "So, how do you like Guangzhou?"

The interview was for a fluff piece. Maybe there was no such thing as hard journalism in China.

But there certainly was in the rest of the world. And sooner or later the story would break.

Half an hour later, as he showed the cub reporter out of his office with a pleasant smile, his mind was already hard at work.

He was going to need a PR strategy, and fast.

He was proud of his company. They were on the cusp of something great. But dealing with something so world-changing also had its potential downsides.

Of course, there was the humanity involved. Many would die in the short term, and there was no guide to measuring the value of a person's life other than his own morality. Sometimes, morality required strength of logic rather than sentiment. It helped, in that respect, not to know China too well, otherwise people he knew personally would weigh more heavily on his decision.

Then, how long could he suppress information about his virus to the government? The WHO demanded notice within forty-eight hours of any new disease, and for good reason. Outbreaks, as he plainly saw, happened quickly.

But his first duty, as he saw it, was to minimize damage to his firm. With no FutureGenetics, there would be no luxury of deciding anything. The outbreak would simply kill the world.

He needed a backstop to deal with the business risks of the potential outbreak.

He would see the vaccinated lab technician in hospital that afternoon, treat her warmly and evaluate her condition.

He also needed to head off any crisis that the containment incident might set off within his company, both in Guangzhou and among investors in New York.

As a privately-held corporation, FutureGenetics had few stakeholders, mostly a handful of venture capitalists and anonymous Chinese entities, and it was vital to keep them all onboard.

Containing the spread of the virus and containing news of the event were two separate things. But they weren't his only responsibility. He had to minimize the financial damage to his company.

It was comforting to know that laboratory facilities were largely unaffected. For all practical purposes, the research could go on.

However, that could lead to a false sense of security. What happened when news of the biosecurity breach leaked out to the media, the investors, the stock market?

Now *there* was a containment problem.

Gavin picked up his phone and called Billy Liu.

"I want our chief financial officer to come to my office right away."

"I'll send Joe in at once," Billy said over the interoffice phone.

Five minutes later, a tall Chinese woman with high cheekbones walked briskly into his office.

Gavin was taken aback. "I expected a man."

She smiled in a way that instantly forgave him. "Don't let my name confuse you. It's spelled Z-H-O-U, but it's pronounced like the American name 'Joe.'"

"Well, I find that confusing. Take a seat, Joe."

She settled in the chair opposite him and took out a pen to take notes.

"Look, can you come up with a better nickname? Something more feminine."

She made a note on her pad.

"Okay. So here's the problem," he started in.

She took voluminous notes while he described the leak, the potential liability to the firm if deaths resulted, and the need for a public relations campaign to pre-empt a backlash in the media.

"What media?" she asked.

"Well, the Chinese press, initially."

She covered her mouth and tittered. "That doesn't require a public relations effort. All you need is a round of golf."

"I just saw a news article that golf courses are now illegal in China."

Zhou removed her hand from her mouth, but was still smiling. "Building new golf courses. That's illegal. The old ones are still open."

"So I won't be arrested?"

She shook her head.

Gavin contemplated the idea. How could he placate the local press with a round of golf?

"Who, exactly, do I play golf with?" He imagined newspaper bosses, several television station managers, bloggers…

"The party secretary, of course."

Gavin was growing tired of everyone saying "of course" to him, but he bit his tongue.

"Set that up for Saturday," he said.

"That's in two days."

"Find me golf clubs and sports clothes."

She made a note of it.

"Which party secretary do you recommend I play?" he asked, curious about his competition.

"I would say Pu Aiguo, the Communist Party Secretary of Guangdong."

"What's his last name?"

"He's Mr. Pu."

He wanted to say, "Okay, Joe, make it Mr. Pu."

Instead, he asked, "And how about New York?"

"Hmm," she said, her pen to her lips. "If all goes well, they'll never hear about this."

Fine. He'd have to play some terrific golf, though he wasn't used to losing on purpose.

"How about our liability?" he asked. "Don't you think we should take out an insurance policy?"

She made a note. This woman was all too efficient.

"Ah, what did you just write down?"

"I will inquire with Hank Ferris in New York about our risk exposure. But don't worry. I'll be discreet."

He raised his eyebrows and she rose to her feet and cradled her notepad.

He stood up and they looked at each other eye to eye. She had a straightforward expression, a darker shade of skin color than most Chinese he had seen so far, and a kind of wild, ethnic look. She was anything but a "Joe."

"Just work on a nickname," he said.

As he watched her swish out of sight, he began to rethink his original impression of his employees. Maybe Chinese business schools were more than fly-by-night operations.

Now for the business opportunities. He called Billy Liu to get Dr. Chen back into his office.

"Yes, General."

It didn't take long for Dr. Chen, freshly cleaned up and surgical mask disposed of, to climb the stairs to Gavin's office.

The first thing on Gavin's mind was his own employees. "Has a doctor evaluated the rescue workers yet?"

"I've got preliminary results," Chen said. "We're awaiting results of the blood work."

"And…?"

"We have seen the first signs of infection."

"Such as…?"

"Three of our four subjects have begun to show clinical signs consistent with influenza, specifically the H5N1 variety from exposure to our experimental form."

To most doctors, the fact that seventy-five percent of their patients were sick was bad news, but it seemed to make Dr. Chen glad.

"I'm just happy to learn that our new strain is so pathogenic," Dr. Chen said. "It passes the first test on humans, that the virus can be communicated to us."

That was in fact a breakthrough. There was no certainty that a synthesized avian virus, created by splicing genes that defied normal human immunity, would take up residence in a human subject.

That would be an exciting achievement under normal circumstances, but Gavin didn't consider this a simple experiment.

"I want you to document every stage of the illness," Gavin said. He could already begin drafting a notice to the World Health Organization's nearest Reference Laboratory. "What are the current symptoms?"

"Sore throat, high fever, coughing."

"Let's hope it stays within the normal H5N1 pattern."

"So far, it's the normal expression of the virus. But as you know, we didn't design this virus to stop there."

Gavin was well aware of Dr. Chen's designing the virus to easily invade human cells and quickly replicate there.

The mortality rate among humans would be significant information. And bring significant business opportunities. That was, if they still had a vaccine.

"So, about the vaccine," Gavin said. "Was it damaged in the explosion, or do we have some left?"

"The master viruses that we synthesized are stored in a different building that's highly secure."

Gavin would be the judge of that.

"And the vaccine?"

"Several weeks ago, we began a small production run. So far we have about five thousand doses. And, as you know, that number grows exponentially over time."

Gavin was beginning to regain confidence in his chief scientist.

There was a path forward to vaccinating a city, a country, a world from another deadly outbreak of bird flu.

"Speed up production," Gavin said, his voice gruff. "And I'll see you this afternoon."

Gavin had a medical degree, but was anxious about what he would find at the hospital. It could be a promising moment, or foretell a global disaster.

What if the inoculated lab technician was sick? It would mean the vaccine didn't work. It would mean the whole risky endeavor to wipe deadly influenza off the face of the Earth had failed. And it would mean the outbreak, already likely spreading across the city, would quickly infect the world.

From the consulate car, after visiting two additional hospitals where he had found a disturbing shortage of isolation units, Matthew Justice called Eve.

Since the consul general and Bart, Matt's boss, would be attending the American Chamber of Commerce Ball, he was left with a rare gap in his schedule.

"I miss you," he told her. "I've been away for two weeks and I can't wait to see you."

"I miss you, too," Eve said.

"When can we get together?"

"I don't know. I'm working until five."

"How about we do this up right. Let's meet at Shamian Island for dinner."

"That's very fancy," she said.

"That's because you're very fancy."

"That's too far away. How about if we meet at Mr. Woo's?"

"Mr. Woo's is perfect. I'll meet you there after work."

He hung up happy to know that he had a dinner date. If he could get out from under work.

They were just pulling onto the consulate grounds.

Matt called ahead to schedule a meeting with Patrick Kind.

"The consul general is available for the next ten minutes. Can you make it in time?"

"I'm on my way."

Matt avoided the elevator and dashed up the stairs and stood impatiently to get buzzed into the secure office.

He found Patrick Kind alone in his oversized office and working at this desk.

"What did you find out at the hospitals, young man?"

"Hit or miss. Nanfang Hospital had plenty of beds, two other hospitals are currently using their isolation wards for post-surgery, but could adapt them quickly if necessary. They'd just have to cancel all surgeries. Take your pick."

"I guess that's to be expected."

"Sir, I did see something I didn't expect. I saw a patient already in the isolation ward at Nanfang Hospital."

"What was the disease?"

"When I tried to find out, I suddenly got the cold shoulder. They wouldn't tell me and rushed me out of the hospital."

The consul general scratched his head, clearly unsure what to make of the news.

"However, I did get one piece of information out of the patient. She works for FutureGenetics."

"What's that?"

"I looked it up. It's a biotech firm here in Guangzhou. And guess who the president of FutureGenetics is?"

The consul general shook his head.

"General Gavin Peak. Our hero from the flight to China."

"Call him up. Let's find out what's going on."

When Dr. Chen cleared out of Gavin Peak's office making plans to increase the pace of production, Vincent Fong stuck his head in.

"Oh, Vincent," Gavin said. "I'm glad you're here. There's something I want to discuss."

Ever since Gavin had learned that there were signs of infection in the rescue workers, he knew that the company would need to create a news blackout on the issue.

"Vincent, we need to prevent the containment issue from leaking to the press. I want all inquiries directed straight to you. And you will deny any knowledge of the explosion or subsequent infections."

"We have infections?"

Gavin put a finger to his lips and shook his head. "I want you to create a news embargo on the subject, within the walls of this firm and beyond. Do I make myself clear?"

"Yes, General."

"Good. You handle this personally."

"I will."

"Now, why are you in my office?"

"General, tonight is the American Chamber of Commerce Ball," Vincent said.

A ball? Dancing and entertainment was the farthest thing from Gavin's mind at the moment.

He had floated among the business elite on the East Coast, but had skipped over the community of small business owners and mid-sized manufacturers with their unique economic challenges. In short, he had never attended an American Chamber of Commerce meeting in his life. In Guangzhou, he pictured a small cohort of sleazy Americans who shared highballs every Friday night and commiserated over their treatment at the hands of the Communist government.

"And there's a theme, General," Vincent said.

"Theme?"

"Yes, General. Tonight is their annual event. The theme is 'Yankee Doodle.'"

"What's that supposed to mean?"

"I researched the term and the history of the song. I think it has to do with livestock and pasta."

"What? People will ride up in ponies? Is it at some sort of Country & Western bar?"

"Oh, no. This will be held at the Grand Ballroom at the Garden Hotel. Over twelve hundred tickets have been sold."

Twelve hundred tickets? How could there be that many American businessmen in the city?

"Twelve hundred different firms?"

"No. These are factory managers, hotel managers, sales representatives, investors."

"So why do I have to go?"

"The American Consul General will be there."

Okay, so it was a big deal.

"What am I supposed to wear?"

"Don't worry. I have purchased a costume for you."

"Costume?"

"And General? You will need an escort."

"You mean bodyguards?"

Vincent tried to hide an embarrassed smile.

"So what do you mean?"

"A woman, General. You will need to come with a beautiful woman."

Stashing away sick people wasn't how Gavin wanted to spend his first day on the job. And calling up someone out of the blue to ask them to a ball that night was going to be socially awkward.

But he knew who he wanted.

With some trepidation, he reached into his trouser pocket and pulled out the business card.

Yvonne Yang perfectly matched the requirements of the American Chamber of Commerce Ball as Vincent set them out. Although she was short, easily flustered and not in her teens, he saw her as beautiful.

What worried him was that it might be easier to hire an escort for the evening than cloud things up with someone he took personal interest in.

He stared at his phone.

Should he ask Billy to set up an escort instead?

Almost immediately, he saw himself for what he was. Businesslike, impatient with social niceties, and intent on taking bold steps.

He reached for the phone and dialed his liaison at Orchid Mountain.

"Oh, Mr. Peak. Your beard is gone."

"Excuse me?" How could their conversation become so confused so quickly?

"I have drained your sink," she said. "We washed all the scum out and cleaned up the mess. You will be quite pleased."

He didn't want to date a housekeeper.

"Yvonne—"

"Eve."

"Eve, thank you. But I wasn't calling about my sink. I was calling about this evening. I know it's short notice, but would you kindly attend an American Chamber of Commerce event with me this evening?"

"Excuse me?"

Maybe it was a bad connection.

"I know it's short notice—"

"What's the event?"

"It's a Yankee Doodle ball."

"There are Yankees?"

"Ah. Basically."

"So the Yankees are playing ball this evening?"

"Ah. No." He wanted to use hand gestures, but they wouldn't convey over the phone. "Tonight is a ball, a dance party. I want you to join me."

She hesitated.

"I'm asking you on a date," he said.

"Um. Maybe tomorrow."

"No. I'm asking you on a date tonight."

"But what if I don't want to date you tonight?"

"But tonight is the ball, the dance party."

"The Yankee."

"Right. The Yankee Doodle ball."

"I see."

"And...?"

She came back with a small, almost hushed, voice. "Is this for business?"

"Yes," he said with relief. "Just for business."

"Then I am busy. That is not my job. I work for Orchid Mountain."

He considered for a moment that she might be confused about her job responsibilities and his personal request. There was only one way to resolve this.

"This is not for your business or for my business. I am asking you out on a date tonight."

"I know this is not my business. But I am busy tonight."

"I see."

"No Yankee Doodle."

She clicked off, and he hung up the phone reluctantly. He was experienced in dating women, but somehow, that conversation could have gone better.

Per the consul general's instructions, Matthew Justice tried to get through on the phone to Gavin Peak, the CEO of FutureGenetics.

"He's on the road," a switchboard operator at FutureGenetics said.

"Is there someone else that I can talk to about the patient in the isolation ward at Nanfang Hospital?"

He was put through to Vincent Fong, Chief Operating Officer.

Matt introduced himself as an officer at the American consulate general, then asked, "What can you tell me about your company's employee currently held in quarantine at Nanfang Hospital?"

"I'm sorry, sir. We have no information."

And the line went dead.

Matt dialed the consul general immediately.

"I'm being stonewalled at FutureGenetics. They say Gavin Peak is 'on the road' and their COO 'has no information' on the woman at Nanfang Hospital."

"Okay. Don't sweat it. I'll see Peak tonight."

Ah yes. The consul general would be attending the famed, and risqué, American Chamber of Commerce Ball.

That afternoon, FutureGenetics CEO Gavin Peak took his first trip into the heart of Guangzhou. He was on his way to a local hospital.

At least the city government had the presence of mind to quarantine the lab technician who had been exposed to an "unknown" virus. And just that morning, Gavin and Dr. Chen had successfully quarantined the rescue workers at FutureGenetics. But who knew where the other exposed victims were now? Hong Kong? Tokyo? New York?

Getting into Nanfang Hospital, a sprawling complex with a medical university attached, wasn't as hard as Gavin expected.

They walked past an ambulance unloading a patient on a gurney and headed straight into the emergency room, where patients lay waiting for treatment on more gurneys along the corridor wall.

Gavin tried to diagnose their conditions by quick visual inspection, but it was hard to tell because of the acquiescent looks on their faces. One young man in the corner was trying to fix his friend's dislocated shoulder by hand.

Nobody stopped Gavin and Dr. Chen from entering the elevator, and Chen confidently pushed the button for the third floor. Maybe it was the white laboratory coat he was wearing, but people made way for Chen.

"Are you a medical doctor?" Gavin asked, surprised to see his chief scientist get paid such deference.

"No," Chen said with a smile. "It's the attitude that counts."

The elevator door opened, and they stepped out onto the well-lit, but strangely quiet, third floor.

A policeman stood at the end of the corridor and stared menacingly at them.

With all the confidence in the world, Dr. Chen walked up to the policeman and showed him his FutureGenetics identification card.

The policeman looked at Gavin and said something to them, refusing entry.

Through the doors, Gavin could see a row of rooms with windows looking out onto the hallway, telephones set by each room.

It was the isolation ward.

Dr. Chen turned to Gavin. "I think the problem is you. No foreigners are allowed."

"What the heck?"

"Do you have some sort of badge?"

Gavin had yet to be issued a FutureGenetics ID, so he checked his wallet for something depicting a red cross or caduceus, the winged staff with two serpents on it.

He had left his CPR card at home, along with his medical diploma.

But he saw the young policeman looking at the greenbacks he was flashing in his wallet.

Dr. Chen plucked out a hundred dollar bill and handed it to the policeman, who shoved it into his pocket and looked away.

In an instant, Gavin and Chen were inside.

One of the rooms had its lights on. Through the large window, Gavin saw what looked like a normal hospital room, complete with a hospital bed, a reading chair, a table with magazines, and a television on the wall playing a Chinese soap opera.

All this was untouched by the woman standing in pajamas in the middle of the room. Judging from her appearance, it had to be his lab tech.

Talk about someone cut by a thousand knives. Medics must have extracted that many shards of glass from her face and limbs and torso. Any biohazard suit she might have been wearing at the time of the explosion must have been ripped to shreds.

But the real threat lay in the infectious disease that was once in those glass tubes. There was no smile on her face.

But why would there be?

Gavin was accustomed to employees at least acknowledging his presence with some form of deference, if not overt pleasure. This gangly young lab technician behind the bio-secure window nodded at Dr. Chen, but seemed to have no reason to smile at either of them.

Gavin gave her a confidence-inspiring thumbs up, but she only regarded him with round, skeptical eyes.

"Can she hear us through the glass?" he asked Dr. Chen.

"She can't hear a thing. She lost her hearing in the explosion."

Gavin remembered the blackened roof of Building 13 where rescue workers had blown up the lab trying to rescue her. The workers had saved her from suffocation, but exposed her to an explosion of at least 190 decibels that affected her hearing, perhaps for life.

"Does she know who I am?" Gavin asked.

Dr. Chen typed a text message into his phone, and the victim's smartphone flashed inside her quarantine room.

She read the message and looked up at Gavin, her eyes ever so slightly more curious.

Gavin was tired of thinking about her as a casualty. "What's her name?"

"Sunny."

The name didn't seem to fit her disposition, or her state of mind.

"Tell Sunny that we'll do our best to take care of her."

Dr. Chen typed the message and got a reply.

"I am not sick," she texted back.

That was terrific to hear. Especially after Dr. Chen's alarming description of the flu symptoms exhibited by three of her four rescuers.

Gavin's gaze returned to her bandaged arms, legs, forehead and cheeks. Clearly, she had been exposed to the virus. But either she had natural immunity, which was highly unlikely because it was a new strain of influenza, or the vaccine had done its job.

The results were encouraging, for her and for his company.

"Tell Sunny that she should be released by next week if she develops no symptoms."

Dr. Chen nodded, then typed.

"She asks, 'How are the others?'"

Gavin grumped. "Say we're watching them, too."

When they waved their good-byes, the skeptical look on Sunny's face remained.

On his way out of the isolation unit, Gavin checked if the other rooms were occupied. They weren't.

Wait a week, he thought.

To leave the former military hospital, they took the stairs down to ground level. There, they stepped out onto the quiet gardens that connected the dispersed hospital buildings.

They walked over a curved bridge that spanned a koi pond where several patients sat staring at the fish.

"What's this hospital's capacity in case of a widespread outbreak?" Gavin asked.

"I'm a scientist, not a medical doctor. I'm unfamiliar with this city's response capacity."

"Weren't you here during the SARS outbreak?" After all, reports of that deadly epidemic had first surfaced in Guangdong Province.

"I'm not so familiar with this city," Dr. Chen said. "I only moved here ten years ago."

"Where are you from?"

"Jinan."

Gavin shrugged. The name meant nothing to him.

"Tenth largest city in China?"

Still didn't ring a bell.

"Up north? In Shandong?"

Gavin gave him a "forget about it" look.

Dr. Chen gave up. "Then I studied in the States."

Gavin was aware of his chief scientist's PhD from Stanford.

"Then you worked in the States."

"Yes, at UrGen in Los Angeles trying to regenerate organs. We worked on programming pluripotent stem cells to produce tissue."

Gavin had heard of that startup, one of hundreds of promising new firms seeking to capitalize on advances in stem cell research.

"What kind of techniques did you use there?"

Dr. Chen laughed. "Same as here. Just lined up nucleotide bases into RNA that matched the genetic sequence we wanted. Then we used an enzyme to transcribe the DNA into the single-strand RNA genome."

"So you didn't need our CRISPR technology?" Gavin inquired, referring to the latest technique that their lab had adopted to improve the speed and accuracy of genetic engineering.

"Not for viruses. I went back to the basics of engineering nucleases. I couldn't be any happier."

Gavin was pleased that Dr. Chen hadn't been seduced by the wholly different approach to splicing genes. He had kept his eye on the science he needed to reach his goal, rather than experiment with what could be done.

"And why did you switch from stem cell research to vaccines?" Gavin asked.

Dr. Chen smiled. "I'm Chinese. I go where the money is."

They reached the corner of the complex, where they heard the ebb and flow of traffic.

"I'm encouraged that Sunny looks so healthy," Gavin said.

Dr. Chen seemed less sanguine. "It's a sample size of one."

Gavin stared at the hundreds of cars, buses, bicycles, and pedestrians crossing each other's paths at the busy intersection.

Maybe they should expand the number of subjects.

"How about we begin some inoculations right away," he suggested.

Dr. Chen looked puzzled. "We haven't started clinical trials yet."

Gavin could only think of the hundreds or even thousands of people already adversely affected by the containment breach.

"Can we afford to wait?"

Dr. Chen considered the question. "I could set up several live tests and run the test populations against the norm."

Gavin tried to imagine which demographic group to immunize first. "Cross-sectional analysis by age?"

"I was thinking geographically. I checked the direction of the wind the day of the containment breach. We could immunize small pockets of the city that were in the virus plume. That way we can draw broad conclusions about age, gender, general health, etc."

Chen's idea was bold, but fraught with difficulties. Foremost, it meant vaccinating entire neighborhoods, on a scale so large it would alert authorities to the problem. But then again, the reach of the new H5N1 strain could be on an epic scale. The second consideration was legality.

"What sort of medical ethics laws should we be considering?"

"General, this is a government that still harvests the organs of prisoners. And the privacy rights of patients? This place jails people as subversive for saying that human rights are universal. The China Food and Drug Administration and the China Center for Drug Evaluation have regulations for clinical trials, but they are designed to favor the state."

"Okay. That settles it. Design the experiment and send it to me. We can start it tomorrow."

"That soon?"

"Do we have any choice?"

Billy Liu was waiting beside their gray minivan.

"I have to change for the ball," Gavin said.

"That's okay," Dr. Chen said. "I'll take a taxi back to the office."

He raised a hand and a gold-colored cab pulled over at once.

"Enjoy the ball."

That evening dressed in a padded suit, a paunchy Benjamin Franklin wearing a wig with a bald spot and stringy hair rolled out of his car.

And an elegantly costumed Zhou, his chief financial officer, scooted out of the seat beside him.

In a powdered wig and low-cut bodice, she gracefully placed a hand on his proffered arm and the two strode toward the glitzy lights of the Garden Hotel, an elegant and prestigious structure with a revolving restaurant on the thirtieth floor.

"Have you come up with another nickname?" he whispered in Zhou's ear.

"Considering tonight, maybe I should have an old-fashioned name."

"Such as…"

"Fanny."

He didn't like it. He couldn't have a CFO named "Fanny." But he didn't want to disappoint her, either.

"For tonight, you're Fanny," he decided.

Through the lobby, he saw American Revolutionaries gather upstairs.

George Washington was chatting with Thomas Jefferson, highballs in their hands. Several Dolley Madisons nearly burst from their bodices and flitted about, looking authentic until Gavin saw the Asian faces beneath the curly blonde wigs.

There were pants turned under like breeches, with tube socks as knee socks. Several Chinese men, small and large, wore tri-cornered hats and powdered wigs. A brown-and-white patched pony stood patiently under a chandelier. Where had they found a pony in China?

Overall, it was a disorienting scene, but the bar was open, spirits were high, and it was an ideal setting to prowl around and introduce himself to those who owned or managed American concerns in South China.

The range of businesses was impressive. Many were in export industries such as shoes, clothing, electronics, and chemicals. But he met just as many hotel and resort managers. There were technical experts running labs that measured things and created flavors and smells and purified chemicals. One man simply made oxygen.

Then came the phalanx of lawyers and accountants who charged by the minute for their expertise. There was no end to the fascinating parade of players in the economic pageant. But as far as he could tell, there was no one there who manufactured killer viruses.

As the new man in town, he simply referred to his business as "biotech," which brought respectful nods from his semi-blitzed counterparts. And when he introduced Fanny to them, they didn't interrogate her, but rather gave her the appraising eye of those who also relied on escorts.

Rumor had spread that a celebrity had been invited, and speculation abounded. Some were hoping for an A-List celebrity, but most would settle for a local movie star.

There were plenty of Chinese nationals running American firms, as seemed natural to Gavin, but also a surprising number of Europeans.

He continued to question why he was even there, but began to recognize the value of the social ritual. In the end, the group relied on their numbers to influence Beijing and Washington.

There was a great stir of raised voices and hurrahs from the far end of the corridor, and Gavin saw a farmer with a feathered cap and straw at his wrists mounting the pony.

"That's our president," Gavin's latest acquaintance leaned over and told him.

Playing the part of a yokel, the gaunt American waved at the adoring crowd, fingered the feather in his cap, and shouted "Macaroni" left and right.

The double doors opened, the American Chamber of Commerce president ducked, and the pony plodded into the ballroom.

Fanny's eyes sparkled as they reflected the brightly lit stage. She tugged on his arm and led Gavin to their table near the center of the room.

On their way, they passed circular tables seating eight. Most appeared to be reserved by companies, with a male manager surrounded by his prettiest employees, dressed in silk ball gowns with American flags pinned to their chests. The white wig industry had profited from that night as snowballs outnumbered straight black Asian hair.

For her part, Fanny was dressed like a Chinese Dolly Parton, without the blue eyes, pale skin, short stature, or ample cleavage. In short, she looked like she was dressed for a school play. Yet, the music was loud, the colors were bright, booze was flowing and she seemed poised, elegant and in her element.

As Ben Franklin, Gavin was treated with the utmost respect, except for the occasional giggling woman who rubbed up against him and took a selfie with him.

The ladies were indeed beautiful and vivacious and Gavin wished to get a copy of some of those pictures.

They took their seats at a formally set table beside a man from Orlando who owned a golf resort on Hainan, wherever that was, and a Chinese woman who resided in Seattle and ran a real estate business.

Fanny leaned over to Gavin. "It's the largest commercial real estate business in China," she said.

Gavin eyed the lady with renewed respect.

Then the stage lights dimmed and a spotlight fell on none other than Tom Hanks. Or was it Tom's brother? Gavin vaguely remembered a movie in which Tom Hanks played a standup comedian. Now he was playing the real thing.

But he wasn't very good.

While the subtle jibes and obscure references didn't evoke the responses Hanks desired, his adoring fans clapped at anything he said, and roared with laughter when he affected a stumble on stage.

Just after the steak arrived at his table and Gavin had masticated it as best he could, considering that he was trying to converse intelligently with the Hainan resort guy while Tom Hanks introduced a loud video of some South Korean pop star, he felt a firm hand on his shoulder.

He looked up into a man's face. The man wore no costume, his glossy gray hair was real, and his eyes were sober.

"Hello, General," the man said.

Gavin stood up to shake the proffered hand. As he did so, Fanny whispered loudly in his ear, "It's the American consul general."

"Patrick Kind," the American diplomat introduced himself.

"Gavin Peak," he said, and returned the firm handshake with a muscular grip.

"I know Tim Beason well," the diplomat said.

Gavin knew when someone was pulling rank on him. And he was impressed. Major General Tim Beason had been the installation commander at Fort Detrick, while Gavin ran the U.S. Army Research Institute for Infectious Diseases. But despite the amicable greeting, Gavin caught the undertone of what Patrick Kind was saying. The U.S. diplomat knew who he was, who he worked for, and that he was new in town. Did he know about the leak?

The two men stood face to face, and Gavin was unsure of how to respond to all the implications packed in Patrick's few words.

But it was Patrick who relieved the uncertainty. "We're neighbors at Orchid Mountain," Patrick told him. "I'd like to have you over on Sunday for a small pool party."

"That would be...fine," Gavin said, taking the invitation for what it was: a social gesture. Of all the cheering buffoons in the madcap scene around him, he felt honored to be singled out, and took it as a compliment.

"Now," Patrick said, "I must take my leave before the bawdiness begins."

Patrick gave an offhand salute and the two parted company.

Bawdiness?

Gavin's question was answered moments later when Tom Hanks introduced dancers.

A shriek rose from the darkened room as a line of model-like Western women strode onstage.

"Russians," Fanny explained.

As if Gavin was supposed to know the significance of that. Were they from the Russian consulate? A visiting troupe? Prostitutes?

The music set the mood for one of the most sensuous and suggestive dance sequences Gavin had ever beheld. He even had to turn away at a certain point and cover his ears as the cries of men and women alike in the audience threatened to turn him deaf.

It was in that moment, bent over, his ears covered, and his eyes closed, that he realized he was happy not to have brought Eve. He doubted she would be shrieking along with the rest. And if she shrieked with the same sort of prurient joy, he didn't want to hear it.

And then, his ears still clasped, in the shifting undercurrent of muffled music and voices, he imagined someone turned deaf to all sounds. He thought of Sunny, caged in her quarantine cell, deaf to the world, her body a battleground of virus and vaccine locked in a war that might be replayed at any moment on the streets of Canton.

Matthew Justice battled the crowds to get onto the metro heading away from the Jujiang New Town district of Guangzhou. It was already nighttime and the street was busy, so taking the subway made a practical, if uncomfortable, alternative.

"When do you say 'smart' and not 'astute?'" a young man with a briefcase and a sheave of papers asked as he ran onto the brightly lit subway car and bumped into Matt.

Matt was accustomed to being asked random English language questions by strangers. After all, most of the English teachers in China were young Westerners like himself and it was natural to assume that Matt was also a teacher.

The two became locked in an intense conversation over grammar. Nearly missing his stop, Matt wished the guy good luck and squeezed out through the well-dressed crowd of commuters.

Taigu Hui was the city's latest shopping mall, hotel, and office and residential complex. It was home to flagship stores and the priciest food in the city.

So Matt avoided the escalators and squeaky clean floors and dipped into a stairwell that led down from the sidewalk.

Mr. Woo's was where style and posing ended and people got down to the serious business of eating.

Eve was already waiting for him, one foot wedged in the front door to keep her place in line. Her only concession to the chic nightlife was that she had let her chestnut brown hair down, and it splayed over her shoulders.

"Matt!" she cried, and waved for him to jump the line.

He asked to be excused, politely but with firm authority. Then he slid around the line of couples, children, and groups to reach the door.

In the United States, Matt would have given Eve a brief, but loving kiss on the lips when he finally got to her. But this was a different culture, and a friendly squeeze of her shoulders had to suffice.

Mr. Woo's was the kind of busy restaurant where one could get run over by a waiter if not careful. So Matt gave Eve a quick pat to get moving and they plunged in.

Tables were set so close together that it was hard to pull out a chair for Eve to sit down. The noise of people talking was at the highest decibel range of human tolerance. Warm yellow lighting reflected off the bright murals and glass-topped displays of toy buses, a nostalgic take on old Hong Kong.

But the harsh environment dulled after half a glass of Pearl River lager.

Matt studied the waitress, a high school-aged girl who hovered over Eve the minute she sat down.

Fortunately, Eve didn't need a menu. She, like most Chinese, went to a restaurant with an exact order already in mind. The waitress jotted down the endless list that Eve gave her, then threw two pairs of wrapped chopsticks onto the table and left without a word.

Finally, Eve's dark brown eyes landed on him. "I ordered for you," she said, unnecessarily, but for politeness sake.

Matt understood. The two had eaten there many times over the eight months they had been dating, and she knew his tastes to perfection.

He fingered his large, cold 600ml bottle of beer and offered the rest to her.

"I ordered tea," she said.

And just at that moment, the waitress slapped down a pot of tea that rattled their plates.

So Matt poured the ginseng tea for her.

He took in her innate beauty as she sipped the cup with two hands, her fingers gingerly poised on the edges of the cup to keep from burning them.

Eve didn't have any single facial feature that stood out or was emphasized by makeup. She didn't have a broad forehead, stylish haircut, large eyes, painted eyebrows, a particularly flattering nose, or a pointed chin.

Instead, she had the defined, but softer features of a race of people that had mingled over the millennia with others in Southeast Asia.

To Matt's discerning eye, she even had a touch of Western features about her eyes. To a Chinese mother, she might not qualify as a beauty and, if it weren't for her good education, might be hard to marry off.

Which raised a question in Matt's mind. "Has your family ever tried to arrange a marriage for you?"

She gave him a level look that meant he was treading on highly personal ground.

"Is this some sort of family secret?" he asked.

"Matthew that is a no-no."

He nodded as a plate of brilliant green beans landed on the table.

He had had difficult conversations with American girlfriends in college, when they guarded their past lives jealously. It was as if their hearts were locked repositories of emotional memories. It appeared that arranged marriage proposals also fell into that category.

So they had never discussed her early infatuations and relationships, if there ever were any.

He tore the plastic off his chopsticks, broke them apart, and was just reaching for the beans when two bowls of white rice landed in front of them.

Eve began eating at once, and for a full minute, all Matt saw was the zig-zag part on the top of her head.

He made a stab at the sesame-coated walnuts, but only managed to flip a couple onto the glass tabletop before reaching for them with his hands.

A steaming plate of spring rolls almost landed on his fingers.

"Yum. Spring rolls," he said, and dropped the nuts into his mouth.

A quick, darting pair of chopsticks snatched one of the spring rolls before he could make a move for them.

He rearranged the bowls to get to his beer. The little, round table was already reaching capacity.

He refilled his glass, took a swig, and contemplated his dinner companion with the detachment that only alcohol could provide.

The two had dated each other exclusively since the day they met. She had been happy to join him on his trips to the ancient temple and kiln at the neighboring city of Foshan.

They had enjoyed the springtime flower festival where markets sprouted up across the city. Street markets competed against each other for color, noise, varieties of flowers, quality of decorations, and size of the crowds. The city of flowers thrived year-round in that climate. He remembered her purchasing some pussy willows holding them gently against a cheek.

They had taken the train over the paddies and fishponds that were scattered across the Pearl River Delta on trips to Shenzhen and Hong Kong.

They had hiked in the mountains north of Guangzhou and taken forays further afield, most notably a five-day trip to Guilin on the Li River.

Then came the stir fry, sizzling hot. He would let it sit, but Eve dug her sticks into it immediately.

Maybe he would try the stir fry, but a plate of *mantou*, deep fried bread to be dipped in sweetened condensed milk, hit the table before he could reach it.

He was forced to retreat and grab plates before they fell off the table.

Long conversations on park benches, her sleeping against his shoulder during taxi rides, and shared hotel rooms in old cities all contributed to a comfortable familiarity between them.

She looked up. "Why aren't you eating?"

"I was just getting to it."

"I ordered this food for you."

Then she buried her face in her bowl, her chopsticks rapidly shoveling the mixture of ingredients from the bed of rice into her mouth.

Matt had just taken a bite of the stir fry when the steamed dumplings arrived.

Plates had to be consolidated and stacked.

Matt took over for the waitress, who seemed too busy to make the small table work for them.

Then the chili peppers in the stir fry hit him. First, sweat dripped from the back of his ears and he used his paper napkin to soak it up. Then his forehead beaded up with rows of droplets, followed by both his chest and back growing damp. He was rapidly turning into a sprinkler system.

"What happened?" Eve asked.

"I was just thinking about our hotel in Guilin," he said, and stuck out a hand for the round, yellow bun of bread.

"I made prints while you were away." She reached into her handbag and gave him an envelope from a camera store.

He never got to the bread.

"Nice," he said, as he wiped his forehead with the back of one hand and admired the shots with the other.

But the store hadn't bothered to compensate for the high contrast, and in most of the pictures Eve's and his faces were in deep shadow.

Nevertheless, the pictures were like tangible treasures for the photo album of their life.

"I like the Elephant Trunk Hill," he said, and held up the image of the cliff opening that looked like an elephant drinking water.

"Eat," she said.

The waitress was already eyeing him overtly whenever she slid by their table.

It was time to get serious with the food. So he picked up his chopsticks, lined them up evenly, balanced them so that they weren't too long, and his milk shake arrived.

He liked the red bean drink with the beans floating in the bottom, but only for dessert. So he scooted the strong, sweet smell away from him so he could concentrate on the savory.

He had to pick the peppers out of the stir fry before taking his first mouthful.

But the ends of his sticks sent his beer bottle teetering. He decided to finish the bottle off to make more room, and poured the rest into his glass.

The waitress swept by and took the bottle out of his hand and set a plate of mango tarts down in its place.

At that point, he gave up all attempts at conversation and bore down on the task at hand, which was, after all, why everyone was there.

Eve sat back with barely concealed impatience and waited for him to polish off the heaping mounds of food as quickly and as best he could.

Unfortunately, both mango tarts and two of the three red been dumplings were gone before he got around to them.

"Drink your shake," she said.

He smiled at her efficiency. To her mind, he wasn't enjoying his dinner unless he was eating.

So, to demonstrate his enjoyment, he kept his mouth full while she checked her phone for messages and drank cup after cup of tea.

"I have a busy week coming up," Matt said between mouthfuls.

She nodded, a pleased look on her face.

That threw him. A busy week was their code for his not being able to see her.

"Why does that make you happy?"

"If you are busy, that means you have a good job."

It occurred to him for the first time, that she didn't understand his job. The State Department required steady work over many years, whereas she was still living on a week-to-week basis.

"But the Marine Birthday Ball is next Friday," he said. "Do you have a dress yet?"

She nodded with a shy smile. He couldn't underestimate how big a deal the ball would be for a working girl living on the fringes of the big city. Just eating dinner in the exclusive company of the rich and famous of Canton was stretching her social standing.

But she deserved an elegant evening out. Beauty and position in society might be a function of birthright, he felt. But there was no way to inherit the inner tenderness that allowed her to understand others and know what was right.

He wasn't getting much of that tenderness, though, as she shoved the final dish of watermelon pieces onto his plate.

Maybe she was looking forward to one of their long walks. But he'd be lucky if he could stagger up the steps and out of the restaurant.

At last they were free of the noisy place and found themselves on the cooling sidewalks of downtown Guangzhou.

A young woman skidded by in a kimono, square backpack, and white socks. A turbaned man and a woman in a sari stepped out of a black limousine. An African trader hustled past with a heavy travel bag over one shoulder. Neon lights caught the varied colors of their faces.

The Chinese women were tall and thin in that part of town. Their high heels and cocktail dresses emphasized their slender proportions and expensive tastes.

Matt leaned his angular frame over Eve and held her protectively by the shoulders. He expected to live in many countries in his career, most of which weren't so affluent.

Could Eve thrash through jungles or snowshoe across the tundra?

"Where would you most like to live?" he asked her.

She wore heels, too, and they clopped shakily on the sidewalk, so she took his arm and leaned against him as they walked.

"I always wanted to live in Russia," she said. "Like in *Doctor Zhivago*."

Now there was an adventurous spirit.

"How about Australia?"

It didn't take long for her to react. "Yes. The Outback."

"South America?" he asked.

That one took some consideration. "I took a course in Spanish," she said, thoughtfully.

"No."

"*Si!*"

She was a constant surprise to him.

Straight and lonely trees lined the swarming street, but provided them with a wide, safe space to walk.

They had often veered into discussions of the future, but only in vague terms. She had spoken of her closeness to her family, her career aspirations, her interest in what he did for work, and how much longer he had left in Southern China.

Now he was talking dreams that might soon become a reality. He would have to bid on his next post within the coming months. And that afternoon, he had been studying the latest cable of vacancy announcements.

She looked up at him with round, interested eyes. "Did they tell you where you're going next?"

He smiled. "In the United States, you're not told. You negotiate."

"But the government is your boss."

"Yes, even the government gives you choices."

She held his arm tighter and leaned against him, but seemed lost in thought.

Freedom might be an alien concept to her, but it might also be frightening, especially when he might end up anywhere in the world.

"But don't worry," he told her. "We can talk about where we go next."

She stopped dead in her tracks.

"*We?*"

He thought that that had been understood.

"You can take *me?*"

What did she not understand about that?

Then he finally got it through his thick skull. Uprooting her meant much more of a commitment than buying a plane ticket. And she had never seriously considered permanently transplanting herself. Even with him.

But the way he had put it, they were a couple. And she grew silent for the rest of their walk.

He didn't mind the quiet, but wondered what storm of emotions roiled within her.

Eventually, he spotted a taxi coming their way.

"Can I take you home?" he asked.

She nodded.

By the time she stumbled off the sidewalk and into the cab, she looked like an emotional wreck.

And as the taxi took them north to the outskirts of the city, her head fell heavily against his shoulder.

With so few words and such heavy meaning, he had managed to thoroughly exhaust her.

But such thoughts, he assured himself, meant that she was seriously contemplating their future.

CHAPTER 2

Outbreak

No longer wearing his Benjamin Franklin wig, Gavin woke up in his new bedroom that Friday morning.

Still suffering from jet lag, he knew it was too early to get ready for work.

So he spent some time looking around his bedroom. He was already growing used to the generous floor space, the chandelier, the gold-framed reproductions of post-modern masters on his walls.

It helped to sleep alone. He was among that special breed of men too preoccupied with work to settle down with a life partner. He had been raised in a liberal household with a working mother and father, and didn't need the constant companionship that many did.

He did, on occasion, miss the feel of soft skin against his. And, due to his impatience, he had tended to rush relationships too quickly in his past. But he had few expectations of life. His business was his life. And this endeavor had taken him to a strange place indeed.

Figuring he had an hour before Billy arrived, he shrugged into a white bathrobe and padded downstairs through the air-conditioned house to the garden.

That morning, the sun was already burning through some of the overcast sky and warmed his face.

He held up a hand to cast a shadow over his eyes so that he could judge the angle of the sun. That close to the equator, the sun would pass directly overhead.

He sat on a pool chair and looked out at the valley and the distant city. The slight breeze changed direction to the north, and the horizon took on a green tinge among the light gray clouds.

Wind rippled in patterns across the pool. A large flock of seagulls flew back and forth, practicing aerial maneuvers over the valley.

A dry leaf scampered across the patio.

There was a definite coolness in the air.

A moment later, the horizon was obscured in a haze of mist. Soon the ground would be damp.

How much of the city was being drenched by the new H5N1 virus? Was he at risk?

It was time to step back inside.

Upstairs in the kitchen, a housekeeper had left the coffee maker prepared. So he pushed the button and listened to steam build inside the machine until the acidic grounds brewed into a smooth, roasted aroma.

He stood by the railing that overlooked the living room and observed the first drops of rainfall as he sipped from his cup.

His life had rapidly taken on an orderliness since he had arrived two days before. Yet, he could still feel excitement from his new environment.

He wondered how long the tingle of newness would last before the sameness became stifling and he would want to move on.

As part of his mission in life, he wanted to leave a place better than when he arrived. And he saw real possibilities in China.

For one thing, his company was sitting on a gold mine. Dr. Chen had proven to be a real asset to the firm, and Gavin could see money rolling in for the next four quarters.

In addition, Gavin's retirement plan consisted of a profit-sharing scheme that included a golden parachute that would deploy if the company enjoyed an extraordinary increase in revenues. If sales of the new vaccine went global, as he considered highly possible, he could count on a nine-figure retirement bonus.

From a medical perspective, FutureGenetics was on the brink of creating a sea change in public health. Having engineered the worst of all possible influenza viruses, they had also developed a matching vaccine.

That day, Dr. Chen's scientists would fan out to different neighborhoods across Guangzhou and begin giving test inoculations. To experiment on unsuspecting populations was a method no reputable scientist would condone, but time was of the essence. And history would prove his decisions correct, if not heroic.

He liked bold steps and he began to contemplate the next big thing down the road. Would he tackle antibiotic resistance? Neglected tropical diseases?

The world awaited his next move.

But, lest he get too far ahead of himself, he had a potential pandemic to avert. Somewhere out there in the rain, scientists from FutureGenetics were laying the foundation for the city's survival.

He surveyed the villas of Orchid Mountain below. Would all his neighbors die? Would he? Would Eve?

He shuddered and resolved to have Dr. Chen add Orchid Mountain residents and staff to his inoculations.

A few minutes later, he was shaving with satisfaction, knowing that his sink would drain properly. Eve had done her job well.

As he glanced at that robust, handsome man in the mirror, he observed that his brush cut of graying hair was good for another week. His thick eyebrows compensated for the aging of his hair and complimented his taut facial muscles.

Fortunately, for an aging man, his physique held together well. He had never met a man he couldn't wrestle to the ground, and as far as he knew, that was still true.

A few minutes later, as he stood in the shower, he noticed the previous morning's water still standing in the drain. He ran a brief burst of water from the rainforest nozzle, and water started filling the glass-enclosed stall.

He completed his shower quickly and sloshed out of the flood onto a dry towel.

He'd have to give Eve another call.

Gavin Peak sped south along the rain-soaked highway until his minivan reached a long line of red brake lights.

Billy Liu came to a halt, threw the engine into neutral and yanked on the hand brake to wait for the next forward lurch in traffic.

Gavin reached for his phone and placed a call. "Chen? Have you started the vaccine program?"

Rainfall on the other end of the line nearly drowned out his chief scientist's reply.

"Going well," Dr. Chen said. "We're in the Tianhe District now. Focusing on a city block."

"How long will that take?"

"A thousand shots, ten nurses, the whole day."

"Chen, I want you to vaccinate Orchid Mountain this afternoon. The whole staff."

"How about the occupants?"

Gavin liked the idea. "We can inoculate a more diverse population that way."

"Okay. Our truck is passing that way right now. We can drop off a batch."

Gavin briefly wondered if he should be part of the experiment, too.

"How's our patient Sunny doing?" he asked.

"So far no symptoms."

"Great. She should be out in a week. And our other patients?"

"Not so good. High fever in three out of the four. We're trying to bring their temperatures down, but the fevers are raging."

"And the fourth?"

"So far nothing."

Gavin didn't know if that was good news or bad. Had they really hit upon the deadliest virus possible? Spanish Flu had knocked off somewhere between ten and twenty percent of those infected. His new flu had a seventy-five percent infection rate. But mortality had yet to be determined.

He hung up on his scientist and turned to his laptop, where he began to draw up a report.

After half an hour in the torturously slow traffic, he punched in Eve's number.

"*Bonjour*," he said when she picked up.

"*Wei?*"

"Hi. It's me."

"Good morning, Mr. Peak. How may I help you?"

So much for the niceties. She was all business.

"I missed you last night," he said.

"How was Yankee Doodle?"

"Interesting. Now I have another problem."

"You need another date?"

"No. And that wouldn't be a problem."

He bit his tongue. That didn't come out right.

"My bathroom sink works fine."

"I'm glad."

"But my shower is clogged."

"I'm sorry. I will fix it right away. Anything else?"

She sounded impatient, and he didn't want to detain her. But what was so important?

"Are you busy?"

"Yes. I have to arrange flu shots for Orchid Mountain's staff and tenants."

Gavin smiled.

Perfect. Everything was going according to plan. And the real benefit was that Eve would get her vaccine.

"Good luck with that."

He wondered if she even knew it was his company that was protecting her.

"I have to go now," he said, eager to be the first to end the conversation.

The van picked up speed as they pulled onto the shoulder to get to the next exit.

Later that morning in the econ section, Matt received an email from Orchid Mountain.

It read: "We want to notice you that American flu shots will be given between 4:00 and 6:00 p.m. this afternoon curiosity of Orchid Mountain!"

Someone's spellchecker had gone haywire over there.

Since he and the consul general were the only American diplomats living at Orchid Mountain, Matt decided to call Patrick Kind to see if he and his wife were going in for their shots.

The consul general was surprised to hear the news. "The consulate hasn't even received our batch from the States yet."

"I'd feel bad about getting the vaccine before the others," Matt said.

"Are you kidding? A flu shot is a flu shot. This is flu season, and we're at Ground Zero of the influenza world. I'm going to head home early and round up my wife and staff to get ours as soon as possible."

"Fine," Matt said. "You talked me into it."

"And while we're on the subject," the consul general said, "I saw your cable on the shortage of quarantine beds. Frightening. Now I'd like you to find out how prepared the city and province are with vaccines for this flu season."

"I'll get right on it."

Matt hung up and considered his approach to the problem. First, he would find out how the vaccine was being distributed.

He jumped on the phone and called Orchid Mountain. It took a minute to get the nurse from the compound's medical office.

"I'm glad that you're vaccinating people," he began, "but who gave you the vaccine?"

"I don't know the company name," the nurse replied. "It's an American company."

"I see. Are these leftover vaccines that the company didn't need, or do you mean they were made by the company?"

"I don't know for sure. All I know is that these were donated by an American company."

"Does your management know where the vaccines came from?"

"No," Orchid Mountain's nurse said. "They aren't involved in the medical office here. I received the case this morning and I don't have a refrigeration unit, so I have to act fast to administer the doses."

"Is there a company name on the case?"

"No name. Just a box and the fact that they are flu vaccines that have to be given today."

"How do you know it's from an American firm?"

"All the labels are in English."

That didn't give him much to go on, but he thanked her anyway and hung up. He loved how business was transacted so unofficially in China.

He wanted to find out how an American company could be so far ahead of the U.S. Consulate in receiving the vaccine.

It was just before bedtime in Atlanta, Georgia, where the State Department's main contact, Gina Woods, worked at the CDC.

"Sorry to bother you at home," Matt apologized over the phone. "But does the CDC have the flu vaccine yet?"

"I know. I know. Our companies are late getting the vaccines out this year. It took longer to get through trials. But we'll be shipping it out in a week."

"So nobody has it yet?"

"Nobody."

"How about China?" Matt said, confused. "I'm getting my flu shot today."

"Okay, well, every country is different. I know that several Chinese companies are in the vaccine business. But their vaccines are likely different from ours. After all, each country chooses what candidate viruses to include in their seasonal flu vaccines."

"But they said this vaccine was from an American company."

"I...have no idea where it came from."

"So who the hell's in charge of flu vaccines?"

Gina hesitated. "Do you want a rundown?"

"I have time." Matt leaned back and rested his long legs on his desk.

"Okay. It's a worldwide effort, but countries make their own decisions. Hundreds of labs around the world monitor new strains of flu viruses. These thousands of strains are sent to the World Health Organization. Twice a year the WHO convenes scientists to determine the results and make recommendations about specific viruses to include in vaccines. But each pharmaceutical company and each country makes its own choices."

"So if this is a Chinese vaccine, who knows what's in it?"

"Ask the company."

"I don't know the company that made it."

"One sneaky way to learn what's in Chinese vaccines is to ask the World Health Organization. If the Chinese want their vaccines bought by UN agencies, they must submit their vaccines for approval. You might check with the WHO in Beijing."

"Thanks. I will."

"Stay safe out there, Matt."

Matt got the WHO's number in Beijing and called it.

A pleasant female voice answered. "This is Yukiko Eto."

Matt introduced himself, then began by asking, "Has China released a flu vaccine yet?"

"Not that I know of. We have not received any submissions from Chinese companies this year."

"Do you have a list of those companies and their contact information?"

"For that, you might call Dr. Nils Andersson at the WHO in Geneva. They keep an overall list."

Matt took down Nils' number. "So a Chinese company might be marketing a vaccine here, but not internationally?"

"That's always a possibility," she said.

"Then you wouldn't know what's in the vaccine?"

"That's correct. You know, there have been several criminal cases of improperly refrigerated or expired vaccines sold in China. It's a million-dollar industry selling old vaccines. If you're really worried, you might want to alert the Chinese version of the FDA, called the SFDA. You do have to be careful."

On that cautionary note, he hung up and checked his watch. It was too early to call the WHO contact in Switzerland to learn what vaccine-creating companies operated in China. He'd have to call later in the day.

He leaned forward over his desk pondering the question: how did Orchid Mountain get hold of that vaccine?

He picked up the phone and dialed the consulate's medical unit.

Betty Baker was a physician's assistant temporarily on loan from the consulate in Hong Kong. She confirmed that the seasonal flu vaccine had yet to arrive at the medical unit.

Furthermore, she didn't know anything about the vaccine available at Orchid Mountain, but volunteered to call the Regional Medical Officer in Beijing for guidance. The RMO had contacts with China's FDA and could confirm the validity of the vaccine being offered at Orchid Mountain.

Matt thanked Betty and gave her his cell number. He anticipated hearing back from her while on the road.

His last call was to the consul general.

"According to the CDC, there's no seasonal flu vaccine available from the States yet."

"That's strange," the consul general said. "So what's the nurse at Orchid Mountain about to stick into my arm?"

Matt, for one, wasn't about to have an unmarked, unknown substance injected into him. "I'm still looking into it, sir."

Gavin Peak spent the rest of the morning reviewing reports behind the rain-streaked windows of his corporate office.

After scrutinizing the normal financial reports, he turned to Dr. Chen's experimental design for testing the vaccine's effectiveness.

The plan was to inoculate a thousand citizens and take their names and cell phone numbers. A quarter of the injections were placebos for control. Every other day, Chen's nurses would call the subjects for a verbal report on their health.

Like most flu vaccines, it would take two weeks after vaccination for a sufficient number of antibodies to develop in the subjects to protect against infection from the new strain. Chen would record cases during and after that two-week period to determine the effectiveness of the vaccine for infants, children, and adults.

Gavin approved, dated the report retroactively, and signed off on the study.

He briefly reviewed his company's cash on hand. The next day, he'd play golf with the Party chief and might have to hand over cash. After all, he needed to reveal to the chief the leak and the potential dangers it posed in order to muzzle the press for a couple of weeks until the new vaccine was proven effective.

Of course, he was aware of the restrictions on bribery placed on American firms by the U.S. Foreign Corrupt Practices Act. But being majority Chinese-owned exempted them from the law. All he needed now was for the weather to improve.

Dr. Chen returned to headquarters shortly after noon and appeared, dripping wet, at Gavin's office.

"I can report that the inoculations are going well. The vaccine is the injectable form, so that takes slightly longer to administer than the nasal spray version. But given time, we can create either form."

"Time is not our friend. Which is faster to produce?"

"We have the inactivated virus on hand for injection only. It would take longer to develop and test the live, attenuated form for the nasal spray."

"Fine. Go with the injected form as we ramp up production. But I *would* like to tour our facilities."

"How about now?" Chen asked.

Gavin grabbed an umbrella in preparation for going outside. "Take me to the lab."

A minute later, they left the air-conditioned headquarters for the warren of buildings outside.

Dr. Chen took him around the campus, pointing out two cellular level laboratories, two animal laboratories, and an anatomy room.

The two cellular level laboratories, Dr. Chen explained, were outfitted with the latest in pressurized suits, complete with their own air supply.

Gavin stared at the cluster of buildings dripping in the rain. He was pleased to hear that his company had gone beyond the normal requirements for bio lab security.

In addition to immunizing key laboratory personnel, the double sets of doors, the tiled floors, sealed windows, and filtered air were elements of Biosecurity Level Four labs, the most stringent security level in the industry.

Among the research facilities was a full complement of laboratories for creating new viruses and testing vaccines.

"Would you like to inspect one of the labs?"

"Of course. Show me where the virus was first created."

Dr. Chen led him to Building 5, where he keyed in a security code. Soon they were out of the humidity and standing in the cool entryway of the lab.

"Do you have time to suit up?" Chen asked.

"I want the complete moon suit tour."

So Chen led him to the changing room.

The two got into scrubs and nitrile gloves, then duct taped their socks and gloves to the scrubs. After that, they donned a second pair of gloves to fit over the first pair.

Then they entered the room that had the space suits.

Several orange suits and glass helmets were lined up on the wall. Gavin chose the largest suit available and stepped into it. Dr. Chen helped him zip up and attach the helmet, and, per ritual, Gavin made sure Dr. Chen's zipper was completely closed and helped him with his helmet. Then the two connected their suits to the breathing-air line.

Dr. Chen pointed to the next room, and they entered a short corridor where they took a disinfectant chemical shower that pattered against the outside of Gavin's suit and glass visor.

The two men grabbed long-handled brushes, and for a full minute scrubbed down their suits and suit boots. Then the water cycle rinsed away all the detergent and disinfectant.

Rather than toweling off, they walked into a vacuum room. Gavin instinctively held his breath as the machine sucked the water droplets and microbes off the exterior of the suit.

In each room, they had to carefully detach and reattach their suits to the breathing-air line and ensure that they had air to breathe in the space-like low pressure rooms.

The whole process took over half an hour, and he remembered the tedium of his research days at Fort Detrick.

When they finally entered the lab, Gavin felt the final suck of air as they stepped into the low-pressure environment, designed to keep air inside the laboratory.

Normal work with flu viruses didn't require such precautions, but

FutureGenetics wasn't dealing with normal viruses. Their genetic engineers were creating new, experimental viruses on a daily basis.

He nodded to himself. The heavy cost of upgrading the BSL-3 laboratory to higher level precautions was well justified.

If only the rescue crew hadn't blown apart their virus production lab.

Gavin took a moment to appreciate the birthplace of the new strain of H5N1 virus, the most virulent that man could create. He studied with proprietary pride the thermal cyclers, microscopes, centrifuges, and gene guns, all in Class II and III biosafety cabinets with filtered air.

Three workers slogged around in orange suits, reaching into glove boxes and peering into the airtight cabinets where the world's newest technology was creating the world's smallest creatures.

Using gene splicing techniques, the old virus RNA was being edited to insert genes from other viruses.

If they didn't look like spacemen, these researchers would appear to be mad scientists tinkering with the building blocks of life, and death.

An electron microscope displayed an image on the wall. The fuzzy object looked like a golf ball with hundreds of long nails and pins protruding from the surface.

"Which virus is that?" Gavin said through his speaker, and gestured toward the wall.

"That's our baby," Dr. Chen said proudly. "That's our H5N1 virion. I think it needs a name."

Gavin thought about it. The WHO promulgated guidance on how to name new diseases, generally eschewing the use of the name of the place where it was discovered. Talk about forever ruining an area's tourist potential. But still, it was the privilege of the scientist who discovered a disease to name it.

"Any ideas for a name?" Gavin asked.

Dr. Chen stood like a statue in his suit. "I was thinking 'Whampoa virus.' That's the name of this district of the city."

In the end, it didn't matter much to Gavin. "It's up to you."

Gavin took one last, appreciative look at the researchers at their instruments. This was his company's brain trust at work.

"Do you want to visit the virus production rooms?" Dr. Chen inquired.

Gavin was naturally intrigued, but then considered the route there. They would have to pass back to the suiting room, choose a new suit, and go through the same disinfecting procedure all over again.

As it was, this single experimental zone tour would already consume more than an hour of their time.

Gavin shook his head and pointed to the exit.

He'd had enough.

As they lumbered back through the disinfection process, Dr. Chen explained that most of the buildings were virus storage and vaccine production units.

Virus production was Gavin's company's equivalent of the factory floor.

"Do we grow the virus in a medium such as eggs, or do we engineer each virus?"

"We've found that culturing them in animal cells is the quickest process," Dr. Chen said. "It was one of those labs that blew up. Fortunately, we have four other labs working steadily to produce the virus, so we weren't slowed down much."

"I've seen photographs of the production labs. We're going to keep them very busy."

Dr. Chen nodded as he hung up his helmet on the wall. "The back of our lot is the vaccine storage area. At least we can see that."

Gavin consented. By that stage in the production process, the virus was killed and, presumably, stored in vials for dissemination to health clinics. There was little need for extensive safety precautions.

Outside, rain clouds had been dispersed by a hot noonday sun, and steam rose off the wet concrete pathways. But after the chilly lab, the warmth felt wonderful. They walked to the units that backed onto the perimeter road where trucks could load up on product. Then they stepped through another set of self-opening doors.

"Vaccine storage facility," Dr. Chen announced.

Gavin was knocked off balance by the blast of cold air.

"We keep the temperature a constant forty degrees Fahrenheit," Dr. Chen explained.

Gavin remembered the disaster in Building 13. "What if the power goes out?"

"Ah. We have installed portable backup generators now."

Gavin struggled into a heavy jacket. Then he donned a gown, which he expertly tied behind his back. Caps and booties made the two men's ensemble complete.

Light was low in the frigid warehouse. Gavin made out shelves of boxed vaccines ready to ship.

Near the back of the room, workers wearing gloves and winter jackets were placing vials into sealed packets and assembling them in groups to be placed in plastic containers for cold storage, packaging, and transportation out of the facility.

The room had all the charm of a morgue on a slow day.

The only thrill he got from the sight was the thought of how each vial represented another human life saved by FutureGenetics' wonder vaccine.

He couldn't put a value to each vial, but he could estimate the value of the contracts signed by national governments around the world. The Americans would want a hundred million units minimum, in addition to their Strategic National Stockpile. China, even more.

They had to plan for a billion doses within a year.

"We'll need to greatly expand our facilities," he said.

Dr. Chen smiled. "I believe we will. Every day, the viruses double in quantity several times over."

"I don't want our headquarters to become a warehouse. I'll have Vincent Fong start renting space for more storage."

So far, the poor woman who had lost her hearing in the lab explosion had proven the vaccine successful. In two weeks, Dr. Chen would have definitive results on the population study in the neighborhoods of Guangzhou.

Was it worth the two-week wait, or should Gavin announce the new product sooner?

"I want to get these on the street as quickly as possible."

Dr. Chen removed a vial from one of the plastic bins.

"How would you like to start things off?" he said.

Gavin's first reaction was to refuse to be covered before the rest of his employees were vaccinated.

"How many employees do we have on site?"

"There's a professional staff of two hundred and a clerical staff of double that number. Then we have maintenance staff and drivers and facility workers.

Gavin looked over the trays of vaccines ready to administer. There was enough to cover the entire company many times over.

He rolled up his left sleeve reluctantly. "Okay, but only if we vaccinate the rest of the company right away."

Dr. Chen wiped the shoulder clean and jabbed him. Then he said in a low tone, "Are you sure you want to raise suspicions?"

Damn the rumor mill. "Let's just say this is standard policy."

"You know, the staff is talking about the four missing workers." Dr. Chen gestured toward the back of the campus.

"How much do they know?" Gavin asked, suddenly alarmed.

"Not much. Just speculation. It's getting hard to hold off the family members."

"Jesus. What are you saying?"

"That the employees are all here and all are well. They just volunteered for an experiment and we have to keep them under strict observation."

"And has that worked?"

"So far."

Dr. Chen applied a Band-Aid to Gavin's arm with a flourish.

Gavin rolled down his sleeve and buttoned the cuff.

He knew it might be too late and might tip the public off, but he was damned if the captain was more protected than his crew. "Vaccinate the rest of our staff," he growled.

"I'll set that up immediately. Now, would you like to pay a visit to our subjects?"

The fun never ended. "Sure. Love to."

To visit their sample group, Gavin and Dr. Chen had to step outside.

From his visit downtown to Sunny, Gavin could tell that the city government was doing nothing to quarantine the policemen who had been exposed to the liquid and aerosol vectors of the virus while working to free the lab technician.

But he had taken immediate action to quarantine those members of his firm who were exposed.

His company had sealed off a BSL-3 laboratory with its own HVAC system and put the rescue workers inside.

Gavin stood with Chen on one side of the locked and sealed door and peered through the window.

The lab had become a mess of scattered beds, wadded up clothes, and trays of unfinished food. Gavin was thankful for his mask, otherwise the air might be too foul to breathe.

The mechanic lay immobile on one of the beds. He didn't bother, or was too weak, to respond to the visitors.

The youngest, the scientist with a wild shock of hair, sat hacking over a bucket.

Only the white-haired welder and the office worker stripped to his T-shirt had the strength to stand up and approach the window.

Speaking loudly through his respirator, Gavin greeted the men. They nodded respectfully, but hostility was apparent in their eyes.

From Chen's interpretation of their demands, all they wanted was to get out.

As for giving them comfort, Gavin could provide ventilators and antibiotics for secondary infections such as pneumonia. But there was more to be gained by studying the progression of their disease.

He thought back to his final days in medical school and swearing to the Hippocratic Oath at graduation. He had raised his right hand and sworn to "apply, for the benefit of the sick, all measures that are required." But moments later, in the same oath, he had sworn to "prevent disease whenever he could, for prevention is preferable to cure."

It was tough for an MD not to reach for his medical bag when he saw a patient suffering. But in the end, he believed that every person also owed a duty to society. In that sense, he had to sacrifice the few to save the many. He and the victims were doing what was best for mankind. They were all heroes, testing a new virus and creating a vaccine that could save the world.

As to their chances of recovery, he was a realist. There was nothing to say other than this: the firm would make their stay as comfortable as possible. Aside from that, he informed them that no family members were allowed to visit the company or know what had befallen them.

That sector of the complex was under total lockdown.

He was looking at the walking dead.

And judging from their downcast expressions, they knew their days were numbered.

But from his standpoint, he could rest assured that they would not spread any contagion to their loved ones, or the rest of the city.

When he stepped outside, he felt a faint breeze. He could only imagine how much of the virus still swirled around up there.

It was just past three o'clock in the afternoon, and Matthew Justice still wanted to know who was making the vaccine that was being administered at Orchid Mountain.

He reached for his desk phone and dialed the physician's assistant in the consulate's medical unit. Betty Baker was still waiting to hear back from the RMO in Beijing and she promised to call back that afternoon.

He looked for the Geneva number given him by Yukiko Eto at the World Health Organization's office in Beijing. Was it still too early to reach Dr. Nils Andersson in Switzerland?

He pulled up Google and typed: "time in geneva"

The answer came back: "8:14 AM"

That was good enough.

He dialed the number of Dr. Nils Andersson at WHO headquarters in Geneva.

To his surprise, it was a direct number and Nils was in, answering the phone with a clear Scandinavian accent. "GISRS."

"Sorry," Matt said. "What is GISRS?"

"Global Influenza Surveillance and Response System."

That sounded close enough to Matt. He identified himself and gave his job title and workplace at the U.S. Consulate General in Guangzhou, then immediately launched in with his question.

"Are you aware of any companies shipping flu vaccines yet this year?"

"Northern Hemisphere?"

Matt had to remember that he was talking with an international body. "Specifically here in China."

"*Ja*, it's still early," Nils said. "Even the American companies are running late. It has been an unpredictable season."

"Well, I'm here to tell you the Chinese are vaccinating people as we speak."

"I wonder what the problem is."

"The problem is I can't figure out who's distributing the vaccines."

"For me," Nils said, "the problem is why the vaccines are being distributed so early."

"Why? Do you expect an epidemic?"

"Tell me this," Nils said. "Have you seen any signs of flu season striking in China?"

"I've seen the normal number of protective facemasks here in Guangzhou. Maybe a few more than usual. It's hard to say if that's a preventative measure or because people are already sick."

"Nothing reported in the media?"

Matt chuckled. "Since when would the Chinese report on their own diseases?"

"I see your point," Nils said. "You need to do some investigative work then."

"I thought that's what *you* guys do."

"Only if we're invited to a country to study the situation."

"Well, I have been to several hospitals," Matt admitted. "I was investigating the city's preparedness for a possible epidemic, and I saw only one sick person in isolation."

"That's positive news Just out of curiosity, why was the patient there?"

"Unclear. She didn't look sick to me."

"Well, one person is not an epidemic."

"Funny thing is, she works for a biotech firm here in Guangzhou. You'd think she would be the last person to show up at the local hospital."

"Which biotech firm?"

Nils had all the instincts of an inquisitive police detective.

Matt remembered the patient showing him her company ID and his calling the company, only to get the brush off. "It's called FutureGenetics. I have no idea what they make, or if she even caught something there. It is a strange coincidence, though."

"We deal in strange coincidences all the time. In fact, that's what we look for. Were her blood samples sent to a WHO reference laboratory?"

"I have no idea what you're talking about," Matt said.

"A reference laboratory?" Nils said.

Granted, Matt was relatively new to his job. He was willing to sit still for a lecture on something he probably should already know. "Yeah. What is a reference laboratory?"

"The WHO has five reference laboratories around the world. Hospitals send samples of new diseases every day, and we keep reports on the symptoms and locations and sequence the genomes if necessary. As cases arise, the WHO can check their reference laboratories for a match."

Matt thought about it. "I'm not even sure China has a reference laboratory."

"It sure does. It's in Beijing and it's called the National Institute for Viral Disease Control and Prevention."

"Then you'll check with them on whether they received the woman's blood sample from Nanfang Hospital in Guangzhou?"

"*Ja*. I will," Nils said.

Matt felt confident that Nils would follow through.

"So, should I get my flu shot?" Matt asked.

"You should always get your flu shot."

Matt hung up unsure whether Nils was giving WHO's standard line, or whether he deemed Matt overly concerned.

After all, maybe Matt was being childish trying to avoid the needle. It was time to suck it up and get his flu shot.

Trained as a medical doctor in Stockholm's prestigious Karolinska Institutet, Nils Andersson had traveled to Zaire in 1995 to help investigate an Ebola outbreak in the countryside on the edge of the forests in Eastern Congo. From then on, he was hooked on solving public health mysteries. To his mind, he had to cure more than one patient at a time. There were thousands who could be saved every day.

He had spent the following two years of residency training with the CDC's Epidemic Intelligence Service on disease surveillance from a data perspective. And in the intervening years, he had become known as the WHO's premier data investigator.

And from what Matthew Justice was telling him, this one smelled like trouble.

Born short and trim, the years had piled up on Nils. He had that pot belly that nature bestowed upon men of a certain age. His bristly hair and beard still stood on end, but the blond color had turned a mottled gray. In general he preferred the office, but was fit and ready to deploy anywhere in the world at a moment's notice.

The fact that only a single person was in isolation shouldn't have been sufficient evidence to begin an investigation. But the fact that the patient worked for a biotech firm raised a red flag.

If anything had appeared abnormal in the patient's clinical signs, the hospital would have sent a sample of her blood to the reference laboratory in Beijing.

No blood sample would either mean they were negligent or she had no symptoms.

Given China's difficult past with Hong Kong Flu and SARS and their participation in the WHO Reference Laboratory Network, he was sure that negligence was no longer a problem. And if there was a blood sample, he wanted the details right away.

So, he got on the phone and dialed his contact, Yukiko Eto in Beijing.

"Hi Nils," she responded upon hearing his voice. "I just referred a young man from the American consulate general in Guangzhou to you."

"I just handled his call. He's concerned about the distribution of vaccines that has already begun in Guangzhou. Are vaccines already available in Beijing?"

"No vaccines here yet. It's too early."

"No signs on the street of the flu?"

"Nothing. What have you learned?" she asked. "Find anything on social media?"

Over the years, Nils had developed tools to track social media. The sites kept changing and varied from country to country. But he was able to conduct social media surveillance on Twitter, Facebook, and Snapchat, as well as their Chinese government-approved equivalents Weibo, Renren, and WeChat. He could scan for terms such as "flu," "sick," and "fever." Now, Nils was in charge of monitoring the resulting maps and databases.

"Nothing abnormal has shown up on the computer monitors, but I'll keep a close eye on it."

But something else that he had discussed with Matthew bothered him more than the vaccines.

"Matthew told me that there was a female patient in the isolation ward in his local hospital."

"Lucky that he can get into an isolation ward," Yukiko said. "Access to the wards here is severely restricted."

"I'd like you to check if a sample of the patient's blood arrived at our reference laboratory in Beijing."

"I will do that. But what arouses your interest in that case?"

"It was a combination of factors. Number one is they are already distributing flu vaccines in the city, and number two is that she is an employee of a biotech firm in Guangzhou. I don't like how that adds up."

Yukiko agreed to follow up, and Nils put himself to work looking over recently reported cases from China while he waited for her return call.

The call came an hour later.

"I checked all new samples from the south of China," Yukiko said. "There was nothing from a hospital in Guangzhou."

"Well, I guess there was nothing unusual for the hospital to report," Nils said, and thanked the dedicated employee for her help.

He hung up wondering if he was jumping the gun on the Northern Hemisphere's flu season.

Still, why were his spidey senses still tingling?

He turned to his computer programs that monitored key words in the internet traffic flowing around China.

As soon as something happened there, he'd know.

Later that afternoon, Matthew Justice sat in the clubhouse at the base of Orchid Mountain. From behind a magazine he wasn't reading, he watched Eve organize patients for their flu shots. By the way she calmly answered questions and kept everyone in good spirits, she reminded him of a Chinese Florence Nightingale.

"Next."

It was his turn. Giving the shots was Orchid Mountain's own resident nurse.

He took a seat on the examination table and said in a casual tone of voice, "Tell me. How did you get the vaccine so fast? Who gave it to you?"

But the nurse was all business and had no time to chat.

She handed him a sheet of paper explaining the side effects and warning signs if things went wrong.

Then she asked him *pro forma* questions about previous reactions, egg allergies, etc.

"Okay. Roll up your sleeve."

"No nasal spray?" He preferred the kid's favorite alternative to getting stuck by a needle.

"No spray. We only have injections."

Being right-handed, he decided to unbutton the cuff and rolled up the sleeve of his left arm.

He felt the cool swab of an alcohol wipe and the firm pressure of the nurse's hand. He preferred not to watch the rest of the procedure.

Then *jab*, like a dull punch, the needle quickly went in.

A moment later, the nurse stepped back and told him he could go.

"No Band-Aid?" he said, once again feeling like a kid.

"If it would make you feel better."

"No. That's okay."

He guessed there was no medical need for a Band-Aid.

"Who gave Orchid Mountain the vaccines?" he asked again, as he hopped off the table.

"I don't know. Next?"

The nurse had a long line of patients before quitting time.

Rolling down his sleeve, Matt took a seat in the waiting area.

"Aren't you going home?" Eve asked.

Matt had planned to wait for General Peak and ask him about the patient in the isolation ward. "I'll just hang around and see who comes and goes."

"I don't want you staring at me."

"Okay. I'll avert my gaze."

He grabbed a *That's Guangzhou* magazine and flipped through it, looking at the pictures of expatriate celebrities and reading local gossip.

Patrick Kind and his wife arrived to get their shots.

"I feel like we're jumping the line," Matt said.

"Don't. I presume other housing areas are also getting their doses."

An influx of employees arrived at five o'clock, quitting time across Guangzhou, and Eve was extra busy keeping them in line.

"You are not averting," she said.

Matt shifted his attention back to the magazine.

The last few arrivals were foreigners coming straight from work. Matt was disappointed that General Peak wasn't among them.

Eve checked her list. "That's all," she said.

Even though the final foreigners had left, Matt remained.

"May I walk you home?" he said, now that they were finally alone.

"I have my bicycle."

"Then I'll walk quickly."

Just then, Matt's phone rang.

He excused himself to answer it.

"Matt? This is Betty from the Medical Unit. I hope it's not too late."

"For what?"

"The advice from our doctor in Beijing is to definitely *not* get the shot. Under any circumstances."

It was Saturday, golf day. But Gavin Peak needed to wake up early. He had scheduled a call to overlap with the end of New York's workday.

That morning, he would hold his bi-monthly shareholders conference by phone.

He splashed water on his face to clear his mind.

While his New York and San Jose investors would be eager to hear his quarterly numbers, Chinese investors would look for long-term stability.

He knew most of the New York money men who were underwriting the speculative venture, but the anonymous Chinese investors, who held a majority of the shares, were a cipher.

He picked up the phone and the teleconference began.

On the line were Mr. X, Mr. Y, and Mr. Z, none of whom spoke a word throughout the conversation.

The major point he wanted to make, after requesting complete confidentiality, was that earnings would greatly exceed expectations for the quarter. "We have a product in the pipeline that will finally produce income."

He knew it sounded vague, but his investors wanted it that way so as not to reveal trade secrets.

New York wanted to know if this would be the company's first profitable quarter, and Gavin assured him that it would be the first profitable *year*.

San Jose had a question about competitors replicating the product, and Gavin assured him it wouldn't be possible.

He gave his Chinese investors a chance to speak, but none did. It was a shame they didn't want to celebrate the good news.

His last question came from the New Yorker. "So, how do you like Kwangchou?"

Gavin wanted to correct him on his pronunciation of the city's name until he realized that the mistake was intentional. Most of the world had never heard of Guangzhou, and therefore considered it a backwater.

"I just got here. I'll let you know after my golf game."

With the phone call concluded, he padded in his slippers across the house to turn on his coffee maker.

In the dark, he reached for the switch to turn on the lights.

Nothing happened.

He looked at the microwave panel. It was dark.

To his dismay, there was no electricity in the entire kitchen.

He grumped about playing golf without his coffee.

It was irritating that things broke so easily in the house. Was that indicative of the rest of China?

Then he was aroused by a curious thought. Maybe Eve had planted his plumbing and power inconveniences to get his attention.

Through the dark windows, he saw daylight breaking over the near ridge.

He went back to his bedroom and stepped onto the balcony to gauge the weather. Could he play golf today?

Storm clouds raced westward, leaving hot and muggy conditions. And the morning rain hadn't cleared the smog.

Only then did he notice his view of his neighbor's back yard. Their villas stood side-by-side on similar lots. But whereas Gavin's swimming pool was at the end of his property, theirs was closer in, just behind a row of blossoming plumeria trees.

And what he saw in that pool made his heart skip a beat. The woman's arms and legs barely rippled the surface. Like an otter, she kept her head elevated as she performed her breaststroke, keeping her blonde hair dry and her heart-shaped face exposed to the morning light.

He withdrew from view and stared hard at the sky, taking deep breaths to restore his normal heartrate.

Now that he looked for it, he did see occasional patches of blue peeking through the cloud cover.

It would be a good day for golf.

Saturday morning was when Matthew Justice put on his Brooks running shoes and played weekend warrior in the mountain range that spanned the horizon behind Orchid Mountain.

Getting there wasn't easy, as the compound had walled itself off from the outside world. So the young diplomat had to step out the front gate and jog through town to get to his workout area.

Jogging uphill, Matt soon encountered fenced-in, single-family dwellings. Just before the forest, he passed a vacant field full of rubbish where a rooster was raising a racket.

Then he mounted concrete steps with a suspicious-looking liquid seeping down the middle.

That led him to an entirely different world too steep for the city to reach.

Straight, slender trees covered the mountainside, creating a continuous canopy. And between trunks floated wisps of fog.

Matt stretched his long legs in the woods and picked up speed, but he wasn't alone. In the next hour on remote paths, he encountered couples, singles, old people, and families hiking the mountain paths.

Many carried empty water bottles, some on poles, to fill at the spring at the top. Others came for exercise, including a middle-aged woman, pudgy but fit, with her slight husband struggling to keep up while holding a transistor radio for her to hear.

Young children walked in single file between their parents, with a grim "forced march" look on their faces.

The grade was steep and the fog constantly threatened to form into rain.

People wore floppy cloth hats, perhaps to soak up sweat or ward off bugs.

Colorful butterflies, red, white, and blue varieties, fluttered around looking for a home. Cicadas chanted in great choirs, having invaded an entire tree here and there. He heard the occasional deep-throated ribbit of a frog or toad. Something was draped over the top of a shrub. It was the molted skin of a meter-long snake. Snails and plump slugs slimed out from under leaves and left a trail on the stone path.

Running full tilt along the irregular spine of the mountain range, Matt quickly lost direction. Sometimes he was unsure if he was heading north, east, or doubling back. He could see far ahead under the trees, but not outward until he reached the occasional pagoda or cliff.

Even then, there was no real view. Whatever buildings were in the distance were lost in the smog that hung suspended and unmoving from the eternally overcast sky. Rain might rinse the air in one neighborhood or another, and he could see a nearby cluster of apartment buildings or a snaking highway, but it was a large city and it was rare to see it all at once.

He could call that morning's run part of his job. He even began to sketch out a cable on the urban environment, deforestation, despeciation, etc.

But naw. He was out there for the exercise.

Not that the lousy air did his lungs any good. He was conscious that every labored breath brought in all the toxins and large particle pollutants spewed out of the factories and traffic that extended from there to Hong Kong, not to mention the steady mass of pollution-laden clouds from the surrounding industrial provinces.

Sometimes, he just had to stop thinking, and concentrate on his breathing for breathing's sake. At least the woods had a nice, earthy smell.

Despite losing his orientation several times, he eventually found his way back down the mountain the way he had come up.

Ahead, several women in colorful T-shirts were dancing in formation to a tape player.

Under the pagoda, men sat in tank tops drinking tea.

And a young woman led children on bare feet across a pathway of pebbles set in concrete.

Matt came to a stop and wiped the sweat from his eyes.

It was Eve.

He leaned over breathing hard, hands on his knees, and watched the fun parade.

She moved with ease across what would have caused him to howl in pain. The children stepped gingerly and struggled for balance on the sharp stones.

When she reached the end of the path, Eve looked up and saw him.

As they often met there on weekends, no surprise registered on her face. Rather, she seemed repulsed by his sweaty, and probably reeking, body.

"How long were you running?" she asked, and put a hand over her nose.

"An hour or so."

She dropped her hand and shook her head. "You smell like a farmer."

"Hey, nice shirt," he said.

She was wearing a pink T-shirt with the words "Dumb Ass" on the front.

"Do you know what that means?" he asked.

"Of course I know what it means, dumb ass," she said.

Did she just call him a dumb ass?

"You donkey," she said.

Ah, that was better.

He took a swipe at the sweat that dripped off the end of his nose.

"May I walk you home?"

She gave a wry smile. This already was her back yard.

"I must do my reflexology," she said. "It's good for my pancreas."

"How will that help your pancreas?" he asked, unsure if he even knew what a pancreas was.

Balanced on one foot, she lifted the other foot and showed him the dirty sole. She bent slightly and pointed to the area at the bottom of the foot where walking on rocks helped the pancreas.

It was right next to the spot that helped the bladder and the lungs, she explained.

"Okay, fine," he said. "Enjoy fixing your pancreas."

"I'll call you for dinner, dumb ass," she said.

He took it as a mixed message. As he turned to head downhill, he saw the line of children wobbling behind Eve as they stood on one foot and pointed at their soles.

The Luhu Golf Club was an eighteen-hole golf course right in the middle of the city.

Gavin Peak was driven by Billy Liu past a modern-looking art museum onto a forested road where city dwellers walked and jogged around a lake for their weekend exercise.

To Gavin's eye, the peaceful lake and trees presented him with the quintessential image he had of China, and he began to relax.

By the time they reached the far end of the lake, Gavin was feeling in a Buddha-like state. Then the road curved uphill toward a clubhouse.

"Here is Mr. Pu," Billy announced, and pointed at a man in a green polo shirt. He stood under the white marble portico like he owned the place. The Communist Party Secretary of Guangdong was of medium height, round torso, and bushy black eyebrows. Oversized horn-rimmed glasses sat plastered against his face, barely held there by a small, flat nose.

"Piece of cake," Gavin muttered to himself. The fellow wouldn't be much competition.

He slipped out of his suit jacket so as to fit the informality of the day, then eased out of the car.

Mr. Pu greeted Gavin with a deferential bow, revealing a shiny bald spot that reached from his forehead all the way past the crown of his head.

Gavin wasn't fooled by the kowtowing. After all, the guy ran the richest and most populous province in China, of which the city of Guangzhou was a small part.

Gavin only ran a company.

Nevertheless, Mr. Pu seemed excited to meet him. "I look forward to playing golf with you," he said in crudely formed English, but with much glee.

Gavin took this to mean that Mr. Pu was a golf enthusiast, and wasn't particularly there for business.

That was fair enough. Gavin would have to go easy on the guy and allow the man his fun.

As Mr. Pu was a member of the club, or possibly owned it, all fees were waived for Gavin.

Billy unloaded FutureGenetics' fresh set of Callaway clubs from the trunk and lugged them over to Gavin on the stairs.

"Off we go," Mr. Pu said.

The man's metal spiked shoes clicked and clacked on the marble as he led Gavin across the clubhouse lobby. Either the Luhu Golf Club wasn't a "soft-spike only" club, or the management allowed Mr. Pu to wear whatever he wanted.

The golf range and links were surprisingly wild and hilly. The forest and terrain gave a sense of natural beauty to the land that had been gobbled up over the centuries by the sprawling city.

Mr. Pu's caddie was lugging an impressive set of Japanese-made Honma Five Star golf clubs, but that didn't translate into success for Mr. Pu.

By the third tee, Gavin was ahead by four strokes and had to start reigning himself in. It was tedious to watch Mr. Pu's caddie hunt in vain for errant shots. Gavin wasn't ready to harm his swing by shanking the ball, so he decided to mess up on the greens instead.

There, Mr. Pu was more proficient and by the fifth hole, the guy one-putted from twenty feet to bring the two players to a tie.

"I am a very determined player," Mr. Pu explained.

Apparently, self-deprecation was expected in China.

Gavin smiled at the man and tipped his visor. "You are very talented."

The intensity of the game was broken by their camaraderie and the evenness of the score.

Mr. Pu jotted down his eight on the par-four hole and suggested,

"Let's rest for a moment."

They waved the next party through and sat on a bench in the generous, scented shade of a magnolia tree.

The two caddies wandered out of earshot.

It was time to talk business.

Gavin looked over the wide, perfectly manicured fairway at the downward slope of the city. It faced west where, somewhere in the smoggy haze, the Pearl River flowed toward Hong Kong. It was amazing to think that the Party apparatchik seated beside him was the ruler of all the land before them.

"What gives me the great honor of meeting you here today?" Mr. Pu asked.

This was the moment of truth. It was the first time Gavin would reveal his company's dirty little secret. With luck, he could extract a pledge from Mr. Pu without having to spell out the larger danger to the public.

"I have a simple request," Gavin said. "My company needs time to develop certain therapies that will greatly benefit the people of China. But to do that, we need the cooperation of your government."

"You are a Chinese firm. We are all friends."

"Specifically, we need room to operate, a certain freedom to experiment and make mistakes before we reach our lofty goals."

God, he was beginning to sound like a poorly translated Chinese poem.

"And the goal is what?"

"Eliminate influenza forever."

Mr. Pu gave him a thick-lidded look. The man was right to be skeptical. After all, he operated in the world's largest cauldron of monster soup and knew his diseases.

"How are you developing these therapies?"

"We use old gene editing technology…" Gavin began.

"Not CRISPR? Many Chinese labs are going great guns with that. China is the first to use CRISPR to edit genes in a monkey and a human embryo."

Gavin knew about those dangerous experiments with Mother Nature, and was surprised that Mr. Pu knew so much about the subject. Maybe he, like Gavin, had read headlines in *People's Daily* that hyped the promise of the new technology.

"Well, I hope to make China proud," Gavin said. "Our company is leading the charge on a super vaccine for avian flu."

Mr. Pu sat back and squinted thoughtfully.

"You need freedom to experiment. How?"

"Live subjects from a large population."

"Use clinical trials. China has rules and procedures."

"Flu season is upon us," Gavin said. "I'm afraid a deadly strain is out here among us. We need to act quickly."

Mr. Pu nodded. "So what do you require of me?"

"I need a news blackout on the current outbreak until we have a vaccine ready."

"What outbreak?"

"Should there be one," Gavin tried to recover himself.

Mr. Pu's eyes shifted from Gavin to the horizon and back. There was a deliberate attempt to hide emotion. But there it was. The truth was out, and Mr. Pu grasped it.

Gavin reached inside his golf bag. He was about to whip out the wad of cash.

Mr. Pu turned his attention to adjusting the Velcro straps on his golf gloves. "You know that we have the Canton Fair starting this Thursday and the Boao Forum the next week."

Gavin had read about those upcoming events, but was unclear about their importance on the world stage. "What, exactly, *is* the Boao Forum?"

Mr. Pu's eyes flashed, as if Gavin had wounded him personally.

Mr. Pu looked at him significantly. "You know the Davos Forum in Switzerland?"

Gavin nodded. Who didn't? It was the largest get-together of international business and political leaders, which met every winter in a tiny town in the Alps to discuss the most pressing economic issues of the day.

"Well, the Boao Forum is the Asian equivalent. There are many big fish from around the world. Our president will speak there."

"…and you don't want an avian flu outbreak to disrupt the forum."

Mr. Pu nodded. "Nothing will disrupt the forum."

"Where is it held?"

Mr. Pu pointed with his chin downriver. "On the island of Hainan. There will be no outbreaks."

Gavin silently withdrew his hand from the golf bag.

If Mr. Pu was worried about the outbreak canceling the Canton

Fair and the Boao Forum, there was no need for a bribe.

If anything, Gavin had leverage over the good party secretary: going public with news about the outbreak could seriously harm Mr. Pu's standing.

Mr. Pu got to his feet and swung his arms back and forth, filling his lungs with air.

Before he got back to throwing his game, Gavin wanted to make sure there was no misunderstanding. "So can I assume there will be a news blackout on this subject, including newspapers and television?"

Mr. Pu paused his vigorous arm movements. Despite the exercise, he looked pale. "It is in everyone's interest."

Then he signaled the caddies.

That sealed the deal as far as Gavin was concerned. There would be no bribes, no press, and officially no outbreak.

Several hours later, after discussing Mr. Pu's children who were studying in England and Scotland and after flubbing numerous putts, Gavin was happy to drop the party secretary off at the club restaurant.

Business complete, Gavin jumped into his car, happy to be rid of the duffer.

He had to thank Zhou for suggesting the event, not for the golf, but for the results it had produced. For the price of one set of golf clubs, FutureGenetics had won the right to pursue their risky but lucrative vaccine without government interference.

And the world might avoid a pandemic.

Billy steered around the pretty lake into herky-jerky traffic.

"Let's head for home," Gavin said.

As he mapped out the rest of his day, he remembered the power problem in his kitchen.

He reached for his phone and dialed Eve.

"Hello, Mr. Peak. How may I help you?"

She had to end all that formal crap. She was the one he felt most strongly about in China, and she had to understand what she meant to him.

Still, there was that problem with the electricity. He could ask her to send the engineers over.

But he didn't. He wanted more from her. But what?

He was about to hang up with the feeling that their relationship was losing traction. What else did they have in common?

"Oh," he said. "Did you take the vaccine?"

"No."

That stopped him cold.

"Why not?"

"I have a theory," she said.

He sunk his head in his hands. Not another vaccine-denier. Not another mercury poisoning freak.

"I believe that since I am a single person, others need the vaccine more than me."

That was a new one. And totally ridiculous.

"Take the vaccine," he ordered.

"It's too late," she said. "We used up all the injections."

That was not good. He'd stop by the office and pick up a needle and inoculate her personally.

"You don't understand how dangerous this is," he said. "Are you in the office today?"

"No. I'm at home."

"What's your address? I'll stop by this afternoon."

It turned out that she had no simple street address. It took ten minutes to describe the route on foot from Orchid Mountain to her family's place on a hillside in the neighboring village. He sketched a map as best he could per her instructions.

Then he hung up and tapped Billy on the shoulder.

"Change of plans. We'll swing by the office on the way home."

He had a fresh needle and vaccine to pick up.

Dropped off at home an hour later, Gavin cleaned up from his morning of golf and prepared to walk to Eve's place.

To make a good impression, he put on his suit jacket. Then, armed with his hand-drawn map and with the vaccine needle in his pocket, he headed downhill to see her.

He stepped out of the compound just as a couple, sandwiched together with three children clinging to them, zoomed by on a motor scooter. None of them wore a helmet, but all five looked at him from behind white facemasks.

Orchid Mountain was on the outskirts of Guangzhou. It seemed to exist on the very fringe of civilization.

The area was so far removed from the center of the city that few buses came that far.

He knew that there was a metro station a mile away, but that was too far for most people to walk, even if it were a cool, dry day. The pace of life was too hectic to waste time walking.

A bus came by, dropped off most, if not all, passengers, and continued up the green valley.

Where that bus went, and what was up that valley, he might never know.

Meanwhile, a container truck with the misspelled logo "Excenllent Quality" rumbled by, decided it had made a wrong turn, and blocked traffic as it turned around.

Where was it headed? He could only assume that there were factories up there.

As he followed his map along the main road, he walked on a broken tile sidewalk past ditches of pipes being laid. He skirted dust-coated trees whose trunks were painted white, inches from whizzing traffic.

His neighborhood consisted of narrow workshops with open fronts. There was a block for car mechanics with a line of disabled cars next to a block for recycling followed by a block for home improvements where welding equipment sparked in the darkness.

After a quarter of a mile, the fumes of traffic and the heat of the day got to him and he shed his jacket. He stuffed it under one arm and continued puffing along.

Finally, he reached a car wash that he had marked on his map. The operation was makeshift. It consisted of a guy standing on the corner with a hose and a rag cleaning cars that lined up for him.

Gavin swung wide, careful to avoid getting creamed by traffic.

There he turned and entered what looked like a shopping street that sloped into the valley and up the other side.

Storefronts lined the road. Stacked above them were apartments, each with balconies that were randomly enclosed. If he had been hoping for a Romeo and Juliet-type setting, he quickly put the idea aside.

He had trouble imagining Eve living there.

To figure out who she lived among, he studied people's dress. Those in white shirts and black pants might be office workers. Those in service uniforms and high heels might be waitresses or shop girls.

Old men sat around in shorts and sandals and loose, sleeveless T-shirts. At-home women threw on whatever flower pattern or striped dress was handy.

The young wore T-shirts. Every T-shirt needed text on it, preferably in English, no meaning required.

One young woman's shirt read, "CRAZY NOISY FART."

A little boy wore "DIE CHILDREN FIGHTER."

There seemed to be no order to the buildings, zoning, or ethnic base to the community. People just seemed happy to find cheap accommodations and low priced goods, with a direct bus line downtown, Gavin guessed these were either families and couples on the make or workers who performed the low-cost services usually relegated to the fringes of huge cities.

It was Saturday, but students with backpacks were skipping home from school. For the first time, Gavin wondered if his company should also work weekends. The more he thought about it, the more he liked the idea.

Descending the street, he passed shops selling shoes, cakes, custard pies, and anything else a consumer might need or want.

At a noodle stand, a female cook wore a facemask as she served her customers. Was that just out of curtesy?

He walked past a wet market with vegetables, fruit, spices, live chickens, meat slabs, and fish on ice. Workers wore masks there, too.

Then he walked through a warm cloud emanating from a stack of bamboo baskets that contained steamed buns. His appetite was growing.

A car tried to navigate the stream of people walking up and down the street. Pedestrians stood back at the last minute to let it pass.

The road crossed a stream that trickled down from the mountains toward the city. Only a foot deep, the water was dirty and barely moved. Steep concrete embankments ensured that it would never rise to street level.

The map had him turn down a side street. The alley was full of cheap restaurants, plastic tables under canopies where food was served.

Fresh-faced youths tried out their English on him. Grandparents watched younger children, who were bouncing balls and bathing in tubs.

Everybody was busy. Even the lone woman eating a late lunch was texting on her phone.

Huge high-voltage transmission lines ran down the valley from the mountains straight over the restaurants, with giant, steel lattice towers sprouting out of shopfronts and straddling the alley.

Gavin was supposed to turn at the bus stop.

He came upon a group of the smaller types of city buses that made a circuit through the area up to the opposing ridge and back. They were parked at a wide Y in the road where the drivers could eat a meal and have their bus scrubbed down. There was a dry gravel smell to the area that turned to wet dust under the bus washer's hose.

Gavin wasn't sure it qualified as a real bus stop, but he followed instructions and made the turn.

As he climbed up the other side of the valley, he passed recycling shops. Every item of metal, paper, or Styrofoam was precious. One family worked on taking apart a small engine. Newspapers were neatly stacked and tied off in bundles. Cardboard was piled high on the back of motorcycles. Fenders and iron posts lay in the dust ready to be bargained over with metal collectors.

These open warehouses gave way to laundry lines, and vegetables were planted along the upward curving road.

He stopped, sweating, at another crook in the road with the sounds of the city behind him. There, under a metal awning sat a pool table with a pair of young children dancing on top in bare feet.

He avoided the urine-soaked corner of a dark alley that led between major apartment buildings. He was happy Eve didn't live down there.

Instead, he continued uphill.

Flattened jasmine petals lay underfoot. He rescued a handful, sniffed their clean scent, and decided he would present them to Eve.

He passed an elementary school built into the side of the hill. There was an apartment building with a nice view and a Mercedes under the awning. Then he walked past numerous elaborate gold-festooned gates that hid small compounds. With only a forested hillside ahead of him and the entire city behind, he was running out of buildings.

He looked across the narrow street and saw house number 84. He couldn't believe it. He had found Eve's place.

He stood at the solid metal gate and rang the doorbell.

Someone opened the door inside. There were sounds of people moving around. Then the latch to the metal gate slid open with a violent jerk.

He was met by Eve's angelic face as she peered through the opening in the gate.

"Welcome, sir," she said with a slight bow.

"Gavin," he reminded her, and handed her the jasmine petals.

She gave the delicate white flowers a sniff, and smiled. "Please come in."

He patted his jacket pocket and heard the crinkle of a wrapper inside. The needle was still in there somewhere.

Then he took a deep breath to appreciate the moment and stepped through the gate and onto Eve's family compound.

A rooster crowed to announce his arrival and a group of hens and wild birds fluttered away.

There was bird poop everywhere. It was the perfect laboratory for viruses jumping species. But the stone path to the one-story place was clean enough.

Just inside the house, a man and woman acted as doorposts through which he passed. They were short and bandy-legged, perhaps from rickets, and their hair was gray. Surprisingly, they had a pleasant, welcoming look.

They bowed wordlessly all around, and the old woman took his jacket.

There weren't many lights in the place, but sunlight came straight down on plants in the windows.

Standing behind a coffee table was another male-female pair, these with darker hair.

"My parents," Eve said.

Gavin reached out to shake the man's hand and got a firm, if not stiff, response. The woman didn't know anything about shaking hands, and when Gavin grabbed her hand, it felt cold and limp, as if he were shaking a wet sock.

Eve introduced him to everyone by name, but they clearly had no English, so he didn't bother trying to make small talk.

They had bought some of those white buns, which sat on the coffee table, ready to eat. Eve handed him one and he gave it the sniff test. It smelled of pork.

"Peel off the paper first," she warned.

Sure enough, stuck to the bottom was a thin layer of paper that tore easily when he tried to pick it off.

Eve stuffed one into her mouth, so he had to try his. The dough was a spongy mass of flavorless gut-filler, but at the center was the true reward, a hot, gooey mass of sweet pork.

"Yum," he said. He could get used to those.

Some questions were thrown his way, and thus began an arduous translation process.

The older generation spoke Cantonese, which the father translated into Mandarin. Eve translated that into English.

It seemed like a game of telephone tag until Gavin realized that the generations truly couldn't speak to each other. Eve knew no Cantonese, and her grandparents knew no Mandarin. Nobody but Eve spoke English.

So a whole lot of translating went on. It was almost like he was witnessing the death of an ancient culture.

He asked a few questions of the older generation. Nobody really wanted to discuss Mao.

So he turned to Eve in an effort to get to know her better.

His first question stemmed from his intense enjoyment of her British accent.

"Where did you learn your English?" he asked.

"I went to university in Singapore," she said, enunciating each word perfectly, as if trying to please him.

He had no idea that she had a college education, but it gave him a whole new respect for her.

"What did you study?"

"Literature."

He loved the way she gave the word a foreign sound.

"And how did you learn your French?" he asked.

She was blushing. "I spent a year at Montpelier."

As if he was supposed to know what that meant. It sounded like she was referring to a French city, but he didn't know where it was.

"I've been to France many times," he said.

"That explains your excellent French," she said.

If he had the capacity to blush, he would have at that point. The truth was, he only knew a few phrases and could hardly string together enough words to form a sentence.

"I've always wanted to live in the West," she said suddenly, while perched on the edge of the couch, hands on knees, dark eyes glittering with hope and promise.

Gavin had a good response to that. He wanted to say, "Come with me, baby." But it hardly seemed the time or place.

A question generated by the grandparents worked its way toward him.

"My grandma wants to know if you're a doctor."

"What makes her think that?"

It took a long time and several embarrassed titters along the way to get word back to him.

Apparently, Gavin had dropped something on the floor when he handed her his jacket.

"What was it?"

The grandmother retrieved it from a table by the front door. It was the hypodermic needle, still in its wrapper.

"Yes. It is true," he said. "I am a doctor." That didn't seem to garner much respect. But he proceeded anyway. "I came to give Eve a vaccination."

He took the needle and syringe and began to open the wrappers.

The entire family shrank away from him as if he were wielding a butcher's knife.

"I'm sorry," Eve said with a nervous laugh. "It is not convenient."

"What do you mean? You need your shot."

She stood up, hands still on her knees, ready to edge away.

"Others need the shot far worse than I do," she said.

"Nonsense. Everybody needs a shot."

She shook her head, and Gavin could tell that there was no way to force it upon her in front of her family.

He would have to try later.

"Yeye could use a shot," she suggested.

"Who's that?"

"My grandfather."

Gavin sized up the bent old man. He'd be lucky to find any muscle on the old geezer.

Everyone watched with alert eyes as the old guy sat on the couch and his wife rolled up his sleeve for him.

Gavin had no option but vaccinate the old guy. He positioned himself next to the man and pivoted slightly to line up the shot.

"Ever had a bad reaction to a flu vaccine?" he asked as he used an alcohol pad to clean the area of the man's arm where he would administer the shot.

Word came back that the old man had never had a flu shot before.

Gavin squirted out a few drops of fluid to leave 0.5 cc in the syringe, then grabbed the thickest part of the old man's deltoid muscle of the upper arm.

He honed in on the spot and jabbed the needle full force into the skin at a ninety-degree angle, puncturing it with a slight popping sound.

The man bucked slightly, but Gavin held the arm tight. Using his thumb, he squeezed in the full dosage of the syringe.

The man was a lucky old bastard. He would survive the epidemic.

As he removed the needle, Gavin's eyes fell on Eve. She had been seated on the arm of the couch, her face pale.

Was she simply afraid of needles? If so, what a stupid reason to put one's life in jeopardy.

But that was why Gavin had become a doctor. To save the less fortunate than himself.

He applied pressure to the injection site and slapped a Band-Aid on top.

"There. That should keep you."

The old man turned to Gavin. Despite his piteous expression, he had gratitude in his eyes. That needed no translation.

Before he left, Gavin had one more request of Eve.

"I need a date," he said. "I've been invited to a pool party tomorrow at the American consul general's residence."

"I can arrange a date for you."

"No, Eve. I'm talking about you."

"I'm sorry," she said. "Tomorrow is my grandmother's birthday."

He could see that the power had shifted back to Eve's side. There was no competing with a grandmother's birthday party.

He stood to go, and she rose to meet him. It was as close as the two had come all week. He could smell her beautiful, chestnut brown hair. Her eyes were locked on his in an innocent, schoolgirl sort of way.

He would have reached out to fondly touch her face, but four pairs of eyes were locked on them.

"Then I have one last request. The power is out in my kitchen."

"Why didn't you say so earlier?"

She was safely back in her liaison role.

Gavin felt deeply disappointed. The distance between them had never been greater.

To Gavin's surprise and chagrin, the American consul general was his immediate neighbor. He lived in the villa with the swimming pool that he had observed the day before.

It was the property with that ephemeral beauty swimming alone in the early morning hours.

It was now Sunday afternoon and the gorgeous creature lay stretched out on the rim of the swimming pool. If this were par for the course in China, then Gavin would be a happy man.

"Let me introduce you to my wife," Patrick said, leading him around to the far side of the pool.

So the woman was more than par for the course. She was the diplomat's wife.

"Honey, meet our neighbor."

Gavin looked at her tan, glistening skin. Now he could put a name and voice to the exquisite body.

He gazed into her perfect, almond-shaped eyes. Light green twinkled in her irises as she fixed her attention on him.

He flexed his abs and tightened the string that held up his trunks.

She peeled off the edge of the pool, leaving a moist outline where her shoulders had rested on the stone. She swung around toward him, giving him a full view of her sleek calves. Her hips hunched into a taut, sinewy position. And she leaned forward to rise to her feet.

Her face came up to meet his, a disarming smile on her lips.

"I saw you yesterday," she said, and pointed up at his bedroom balcony. "While I was taking my morning swim."

Her voice had a breathless quality that he found seductive. If only she weren't married.

To dispel the sultry atmosphere, and to relieve the tension that had built up within him, he decided to assume a jocular attitude. "Yes. I'm new to the neighborhood. Trying to meet my neighbors."

She lifted the hand that she had been trailing in the water, wiped it across the fabric top of her bikini, and held it out for him to shake.

"Shawnee," she said. Was she Native American? That could explain her beautiful skin.

"Gavin Peak," he said, shaking her still-wet hand.

"Gavin Peekaboo," she said teasingly, and poked him in the belly.

Was she some kind of child?

Patrick led him over to lounge chairs that looked far more comfortable than the edge of the pool.

Patrick ordered some watermelon tequilas from the male attendant who stood dutifully by, then turned to face Gavin.

"I understand that you're some kind of a hero."

Gavin was caught off-guard. He liked the diplomat, but there was a constant gamesmanship taking place under the surface.

"I'm talking about your medical intervention on that flight from Los Angeles."

"Oh, that." Gavin had long since forgotten the incident. But somehow the news had made waves in Guangzhou.

"How did you hear about that?"

The consul general shrugged. "When you do something remarkable, word gets around."

Gavin spent a few minutes dwelling aloud on the uncomfortable position he had been put in. "I was worried about a lawsuit in case I misdiagnosed her injuries."

"I'm sure you acted out of good faith and made the correct diagnosis."

"Well, if any lawyers come knocking, I've given you the straight dope."

"I believe every word of it. Oh, and by the way, how is Mr. Pu?"

Once again, the questions caught Gavin off guard. Clearly the consulate had its sources. Were they keeping tabs on the politician or on Gavin?

And were those watermelon tequilas ever coming?

"Mr. Pu was in good health," Gavin said. "He even beat me, not to mention beating his own handicap."

"You know, I've lived and worked here for over two years and the party secretary has yet to return my calls."

"That's strange."

The consul general shrugged. "That's politics. And yet you, you arrived only this week and you're playing golf with the man."

"Well, we certainly didn't talk politics."

"Hmm. So, if I may ask, what did you discuss?"

Gavin met him eye-to-eye and grinned. "That's for me to know…"

The consul general cracked a smile. "I didn't invite you over to discuss business."

Gavin appreciated the doublespeak. The consul general was both dismissing the topic and letting him know that he had some sense of why Mr. Pu had taken the meeting.

"But enough with the interrogation," the consul general said lightly. "Except for one thing."

Where were those tequilas anyway?

"Here's my question. A few days ago, Orchid Mountain gave my wife and me a flu shot."

"Great."

"And yet you never showed up to get yours." Then the consul general leaned toward him and pointed at the Band-Aid on Gavin's upper arm. "Where did that come from?"

"Oh, that. I got my injection at the office."

"That's interesting. Because I asked around, and the vaccine isn't generally available to the public."

"Flu season *is* coming."

"I know that, but the CDC informed us that U.S. companies haven't released their versions, and China hasn't begun issuing theirs yet."

Gavin was in a tight spot. How long could he withstand this interrogation?

"You know," Gavin said finally. "I'll have to look into how my company obtained the vaccine. I just assumed that we got it early as we handle viruses every day. You don't want crossbreeding to take place in the lab."

"Crossbreeding," the consul general said, musing. "No, you wouldn't want that."

Gavin stood to leave the pool party, happy to have access to the head of the consulate, but uneasy that he had had to withhold information from the man.

How soon before the consul general learned that Gavin's company had created the virus?

"Oh, here are the drinks."

To Matthew Justice, it felt like the perfect day for a picnic, and the aroma of roasting hot dogs gave the event the ultimate touch of summer.

The grounds of the consulate were deep green, along with yellow touches of pampa grass here and there. The basketball court swarmed with overly competitive high school boys. And sun umbrellas stood at full staff.

Detachment Commander Rodriguez patrolled the back door, a locally brewed craft beer in hand.

Over by the grill and flipping hot dogs was Sergeant Kyle Ortman, with whom Matt socialized and shared driving tours of the Pearl River

Delta.

Their favorite trips were to the bandit towers built over a century earlier by overseas Chinese who sent home money they had accumulated working in the great cosmopolitan centers of the world.

Matt and several of the Marines had experienced the wonder of climbing up inside the tall mansions. The ground floors consisted of gated guardrooms or kitchens. Then each floor unveiled itself like a new present and delighted with its added grandeur in tiles, furniture, and views. The towers remained as living museums with their German clocks, Mexican silver, and early 20th Century American kitchenware.

"I read in the newsletter that there's a trip to Kaiping next weekend," Matt suggested.

Kyle quibbled, "Is it any better than Taishan?"

"Some say."

Kyle twisted his lips noncommittally. "Come inside. You're sweating buckets."

Matt followed him and the platter of steaming franks into the near-empty eating area. "Where is everyone today?" Matt wondered aloud. This was to be the Marine's last fund-raiser before their big birthday bash.

"Oh, some are sick and stayed home."

"Flu season," Matt said somewhat dismissively.

"Yeah. A lot of people couldn't make it."

"A lot? How many?"

Kyle looked around the near-empty room. "I'd say half the staff had someone sick in their family."

"With colds?"

Kyle looked at him strangely. "Yeah. Why?"

"Fevers?"

"They said 'high fevers.'"

Matt had to finish his hot dog fast.

"I think the World Health Organization needs to know about this."

That sent Kyle doubled over with laughter. "Talk about an overreaction."

Matt forced a smile. But no, he would call Nils Andersson as soon as he finished eating.

Matt was fast becoming the eyes and ears of the WHO in Guangzhou. And yet, what could the international organization do?

He stuffed the last of the hot dog into his mouth and loaded up a second plate of food.

Then he threw a stack of Chinese ten yuan bills into the basket.

"Hey," Kyle called after him. "You coming to the Marine Ball on Friday?"

"If I can get a date."

Matt trotted outside and across the grassy grounds to the consulate entrance.

He handed the full plate of food to the Marine guard who was missing the hot dog roast.

"Gotta work," Matt said.

The thankful Marine buzzed him in, and he climbed up to the economics office two steps at a time.

He dialed Geneva and waited, all the while thinking about the mysterious vaccine and the woman already in isolation.

"GISRS."

Oh, yes. The Global Influenza Surveillance something.

"Nils, we have a problem."

"*Ja*, I know." Nils breathed in, not missing a beat from their last conversation. "Social media and web postings. We've noticed an uptick in concern in the public."

"I just came from an office party, and many of the people are home, sick."

"What are their symptoms?"

"High fevers."

"Well, just this morning I sent several team members from the WHO office in Beijing to fly down there and begin reporting on patients. I'm afraid that's the best we can do for now."

For Matt, that wasn't good enough. "Why don't you simply contact the Chinese government?"

"We have, and got nowhere. Remember, their policy is that any disease outbreak is a state secret. There is a news blackout until the Ministry of Health announces it."

"Yeah, well they haven't announced anything."

"Remind me the name of the biotech firm where that female patient worked?" Nils said.

"The woman in the isolation unit? The president of that company is a good friend of the consulate. Kind of a hero around here."

"His name?"

"General Gavin Peak. His company is FutureGenetics."

"Thanks. We'll follow up with him."

"Is there anything we can do to avoid getting sick?" Matt asked, feeling increasingly desperate

"Within China? Good luck."

Matt rubbed the slight pain in his left shoulder. At least he had had his vaccination.

CHAPTER 3

Contagion

It was Monday morning, and Gavin Peak showed up promptly at work. His golf outing with the party secretary had proven successful, giving him a virtual green light to ramp up production of the vaccine.

Along the corridor to the elevators, there was a long line of employees, each with a sleeve rolled up. At the beginning of the line, they entered an office where a team of nurses was giving shots.

Gavin caught up with Zhou and Vincent Fong, who were organizing the line and keeping people calm.

Several already wore facemasks. Did they realize that a mask didn't stop small droplets containing flu viruses?

"Get your shot?" he asked Zhou.

"Already got it."

"This morning?"

"No. Last week."

He was surprised. He had only gotten his shot on Friday.

"And you, Vincent?"

"Last week, too."

"Interesting. Vincent. I want you in my office at once."

Gavin took the elevator up to his office admiring the efficiency of his staff. It was almost like running a hospital.

Gavin's chief operating officer appeared at his office door.

"Vincent, starting today we'll begin ramping up vaccine production significantly. I want twenty million doses by the end of the week."

"Our facilities are somewhat limited. We have other products in the works."

"Mothball them. I want every square foot of our floor space dedicated to pumping out vaccines."

"We may need to expand beyond our campus, General. There are large, commercially available, climate-controlled warehouses outside the city."

"Lease them. We can't let storage and transportation get in our way."

"Right, General."

When Vincent left, Gavin felt as if he had just passed a gallstone. His company was on its way, flying high now.

And that was precisely why the investors hired him. He was a doer, not a thinker.

"General, it's a call from Geneva," Billy said, covering the mouthpiece of his phone.

"Geneva?"

"It's Dr. Nils Andersson, from the World Health Organization."

What the hell?

Swiveling toward his phone, Gavin did a quick mental calculation. It must be Sunday midnight in Geneva.

He picked up the handset.

"Mr. Peak," the voice said. "Our disease surveillance team has detected a curious outbreak of an unknown pathogen in southern China."

Gavin braced himself. This was the moment of truth. Would he come clean? Or would he try to shield his company from financial ruin?

"Outbreak, Nils?"

"As you know, we're constantly on the lookout for possible toxin exposure and potential epidemics. One of the things we look for is clinical characteristics that have never been seen before. Another indication of trouble is that related symptoms suddenly appear in widely dispersed populations of the world."

"And...?"

"Through your consulate and our computer monitoring system, we've uncovered such a phenomenon taking place in Guangzhou."

He horribly mangled the pronunciation of the city's name, but Gavin let it go. He'd have more than his city name to defend if his lab was ever implicated in the outbreak.

He tried his most ingratiating and innocent approach. "I haven't been aware of that. How can I help you?"

"Number one, we're trying to give you a heads-up so that you and your people react appropriately. But more importantly, I wanted to know if you, with your expertise in biomedical research and vaccine development, have any special insights into what might be going on there?"

Okay, he wasn't being implicated. And given that he had already feigned ignorance, his hand was forced.

"Well, thanks for the heads up. I haven't heard about this, but I'll certainly look into it. Now, I have to say, I'm not surprised."

"Why not?"

"Well, this *is* southern China." He let the insinuation speak for itself.

"Of course. It's southern China. But what worries me is that over the past few days, the WHO has discovered similar symptoms in Vancouver, Los Angeles, and Sydney."

That was fast. Gavin tried to imagine the immigrant populations in those various cities. Perhaps tourism and business connections contributed to the spread.

Now Gavin was asking the questions. "What, exactly, are the symptoms, and what's the mortality rate?"

"Hospitals report that symptoms include sore throat, high fever, and coughing."

That was exactly what Gavin had seen in his firm's isolation ward.

"And as for mortality, it's close to ninety percent."

Ninety percent? Gavin calculated quickly. The contamination breach had been on Tuesday. It was now Monday, six days later. There were already cases around the world. Nobody had yet died in his ward, but with a mortality rate of ninety percent, their imminent death was nearly certain. He made a mental note to check on his victims out back in the next day.

"Well, keep me informed," Gavin said. "I'll keep an eye open for signs around here."

"We could use more than that," Nils said pointedly. "We need to isolate the bug and create an antidote."

A light went on in Gavin's head.

"I'll check with my lab and see what they're working on. Maybe they've already got something."

"If so, we'd need to fast-track it. We know this one travels quickly, and it could get nasty."

"I'm with you there. So long, Nils."

Gavin hung up feeling like he was not yet under suspicion. But the risks to his company and him personally were high if the vaccine didn't pan out. Patients dying in Los Angeles at a rate of ninety percent was hard even for him to believe, and the image made him shudder. But, of course, once his company's vaccine hit the market, the world would be grateful to him, much like it celebrated Jonas Salk for the polio vaccine.

At that moment, a tailor walked into the office, a tape measure around his neck.

"What's this all about?"

"We're taking your measures, General," Billy said as he escorted the man into position beside Gavin.

"What for?"

"A tuxedo."

"Why a tuxedo?"

"The Marine Ball, General."

Damn. He'd packed his uniform and medals in his FedEx shipment. "When's the ball?"

"Friday."

Gavin held out his arms. They'd better get the chest right.

Now all he needed was a date.

He hated the distraction, but honored the Marines and wouldn't miss their birthday celebration. The only question was, who to invite?

His hormones stirred when he thought about Eve. She was still his number one, but was a hard one to nail down. Then there was Zhou. He had already taken her out and there were no sparks. His mind grew wobblier as he cursed his lack of options. He even wondered if Sunny was out of isolation yet.

Damn it. Nobody was going to spoil his next evening out. Whoever he chose would have a hell of a time.

"Billy, get me two tickets and book me a room at the hotel for the night of the ball."

"Four Seasons on Friday. Right, General."

At that moment, the tailor's hand got stuck measuring his crotch.

Tuesday morning as he arrived at work, Gavin Peak saw more employees than ever wearing surgical masks.

Yet there was no fear in their eyes as they went about their normal work.

After clearing out his inbox, Gavin's first order of business was to tour their makeshift isolation ward with Dr. Chen. He couldn't believe the ninety-percent mortality rate that the WHO specialist had told him about. Were his patients on the verge of death?

Gavin and his chief scientist met outside, but Dr. Chen waited until they were safely out of hearing range before filling him in on the latest news.

"First the interesting news. Our old welder, who has lived alongside the other rescue workers, has shown no symptoms of the flu."

"But clearly it's communicable. Look at the extent of the outbreak."

"Person-to-person communicability has yet to be determined," Dr. Chen reminded him. "For all we know, the outbreak is due to the aerosol dispersion from the explosion."

"But the welder was exposed to that by the billions of units per square meter."

"True," Dr. Chen agreed. "That leaves only one possible explanation."

"Some people have a natural immunity," Gavin completed the thought.

The two men paused to contemplate that. What demographic rule or earlier exposures allowed for preexisting immunity? Or was it genetic, the luck of the draw?

Dr. Chen stopped walking just outside Building 27. "Before we go in, I must warn you. Two of the men are already dead."

They looked at each other in full understanding of the implications. The disease had at least a fifty-percent chance of killing the exposed population.

It should have been a moment to celebrate the scientist's achievement. He had managed to create a pathogen that was both highly transmissible to humans and extremely lethal.

But Gavin's attention moved quickly toward self-preservation. "Did you sanitize the bodies?"

"As best we could. We sprayed the corpses with Lysol and put them in double body bags. Then we sprayed the bags."

"Plans to cremate them?"

"With their families' permission."

Gavin hesitated. He didn't want the families even touching the bodies, for fear they would contract the disease. But how could he explain the cause of death without revealing what had killed them?

"Should we cremate the bodies here?" Dr. Chen asked.

Gavin nodded. He expected some serious blowback from the

victims' relatives, and lawyers.

For the first time, he began to seriously doubt that he was on the right track. Nobody wanted death.

And there was nobody he wanted to save more than his friend Eve. He had to find a way to convince her to get vaccinated.

Even from outside, the building stank. Maybe it was the single toilet, or blame it on the poor ventilation, but Gavin could barely make it in the front door.

Their improvised isolation ward looked like a BSL-4 lab, but it smelled like a jail cell.

Just standing in the suit-fitting room, they could see the two remaining men beyond the decontamination room and its two sets of locked doors.

Gavin and Dr. Chen had brought in beds and chairs to make the place more livable for the victims, but lab tables still stood around the perimeter, and the room's smooth tiles had an antiseptic feel.

The patients saw daylight as Gavin and Dr. Chen entered the building, and came up to the door behind the chemical showers to peer through the glass at them.

The welder with the messy white hair was snarling at them like a caged animal. The other poor victim, no longer in his suit coat, looked as white as a sheet and was wracked by a deep, rattling cough.

Gavin was moved. He was a doctor, after all, not Josef Mengele performing deadly experiments on prisoners in a concentration camp. His first reaction was to reach for antiviral medication or antibiotics or at least to find the poor guy a ventilator. But if his quick diagnosis was correct, even with medical support the patient had no more than a day to live.

Gavin found himself hoping for some sort of treatment for the disease, until he realized that such a cure would greatly reduce the value of the vaccine.

He looked away from the healthy man and his dying cohort. He was in the unenviable position of letting nature take its course.

He grabbed Dr. Chen and they quickly took their leave.

Stepping outside into a sudden gust of wind, Gavin was even more convinced that he had to get Eve vaccinated.

But was the vaccine effective?

"Meet me in my office in fifteen minutes," he said. "I'll want a rundown on the test vaccinations in the neighborhoods."

Exactly fifteen minutes later, Dr. Chen entered his office with a pile of papers on a clipboard.

"I want to know how our test population is faring in the city."

Dr. Chen was beaming with confidence. "First let me report the extent of the damage."

Gavin nodded uncertainly.

"The outbreak began one week ago today. According to my sources within the Guangdong Department of Health, this specific virus has been identified as a new influenza strain with unknown origins. So far, my sources within the Guangdong Health Department reported five thousand cases."

"And our test sample?"

"No cases of flu as yet."

"That's great! Wouldn't you say that the vaccine is effective?"

Dr. Chen held up a hand. "We have to wait another week for the vaccine to take effect. Until then, we can expect cases among our test subjects."

"I can't wait a week," Gavin said.

"That's your decision," Dr. Chen said. "But if you wait a week, we'll begin seeing a divergence in cases between our placebo subjects and those we vaccinated. It should make a dramatic difference."

Gavin would love to see that split in the line graph, but he could see those five thousand reported cases getting out of hand. Even by ringing known cases by inoculating immediate family members and known contacts, the number of people they would have to vaccinate would be well over a hundred thousand. He didn't know if they had the doses ready to prevent so quick a spread.

"Do we know the reproductive ratio?" he asked, referring to the rate at which a disease spreads from one person to others.

"Not yet. These are the first reported cases. The city should know the ratio within a week."

For Gavin, it was important to know how transmissible the disease was. A basic reproductive ratio any higher than 1.0 meant the disease could take off in the human population and not die out.

Dr. Chen seemed unconcerned. "Remember that the initial infection began just a week ago. Already five thousand are infected just by aerosol exposure."

"That isn't good enough. I want you to send a team out to interview the family members and friends of our rescue workers. We can draw conclusions from that."

Dr. Chen nodded. "Consider it done."

"One last thing. Have you been able to keep the test under wraps?"

"We have been discreet so far. We believe that nobody knows that this relates to our new virus."

"I've seen several employees wearing masks downstairs. Do they know?"

"Not at all."

"Good. Keep it that way." Gavin sat back with satisfaction. "You're dismissed."

With that, the meeting was over.

He swiveled to his view of the mountain ridge. Large-winged gulls were flying in a jumbled flock that quickly changed direction. Whatever diseases they were carrying had nowhere near the potency of the new virus. Unless they had that, too.

As soon as Dr. Chen left, Gavin received a call from Billy.

"General, you have another interview request for later today."

Gavin rolled his eyes. There were certain social aspects to being the head of a company that he simply didn't enjoy. In the military, he didn't have to justify the existence of his unit to anyone. But now he needed to project a positive image of his company to the world. It was time to become a salesman. He needed to come up with more and different ways to appeal to the local press.

"What's the rag?" he asked.

"General, it's the *Wall Street Journal*."

It was a tricky interview with the Asian edition of the *Wall Street Journal*, particularly because the story might be reprinted in New York.

As with Nils in Geneva, Gavin Peak had to dance around the issue of where the disease had originated, but he assured the reporter that his scientists had started to explore the issue.

Images of the last two remaining victims in the quarantine unit still fresh in his mind, he was just reaching for the phone to call Eve about getting her vaccination when Billy rang.

"General, the American consul general would like to speak with you."

Gavin had barely been able to relax after the probing interview.

"Put him on."

"Gavin!" came the diplomat's voice. "We've got the WHO trying to get China to agree to letting their disease investigators in, and the Guangdong government isn't playing ball."

"Meaning what?"

"The Chinese have to invite the WHO to investigate and so far, they're stonewalling us. This is unprecedented."

"Investigate what?"

There was stony silence on Patrick Kind's end of the line. Then, "Rumors have hit the streets. We have a major outbreak of a new form of disease in local hospitals. Already a handful of patients have died of fluid buildup in the lungs."

"That's awful."

"Something is holding up Mr. Pu at the Guangdong level."

Gavin froze. What was the consul general getting at?

"Gavin. I can't get through to Mr. Pu. I want you to talk to him and get him to agree to investigators."

Gavin's grip eased on his phone. He wasn't being charged. The U.S. Government was calling upon *him* to do something that they couldn't do. "I'll try my best."

Gavin hung up feeling like he had just dodged a bullet. But this was only the beginning of what would be a firefight.

All he knew was, he had to set up a meeting with the party secretary. But not to invite in the WHO.

Rather, they had reached another critical juncture. Gavin had to sell him the vaccine.

As soon as he hung up with the consul general, Gavin asked Billy to set up a private rendezvous with the party secretary the next day.

"How about at his downtown club?" Billy asked.

"Set it up."

At last Gavin had a free moment to reach Eve. With each passing minute that day, he had grown increasingly worried about her catching the flu.

"Eve?" He finally got her on the phone.

"Mr. Peak?"

"I need to meet with you this afternoon. There's no time to waste."

"Okay. I finish work at five o'clock. How about four o'clock."

"This isn't for business. It's personal. I'll meet you at Orchid Mountain Villas at five."

Eve hesitated.

"It's important."

"Fine, Mr. Peak. I'll be at the Starbucks on Shamian Island this evening at six o'clock."

He hung up and checked his watch. It was already 3:15. He needed time to pick up another needle to inoculate her before Billy would take him to the island.

Gavin was driven by Billy as far onto Shamian Island as the road allowed.

When he stepped out of the minivan, Gavin was met by a bewildering array of sights and sounds. On the south bank, he could hear tennis balls ponging and players grunting. That activity seemed to come from the large courtyard behind black metal gates.

The smell of cooking noodles filled the air, but he was looking for coffee.

"Where's the Starbucks?" he turned back and asked Billy.

The little guy was being honked at by an obnoxious driver in a Mercedes.

"Halfway down the island," Billy said.

"Meet me back here in an hour," Gavin said, and slammed the door shut.

"Halfway down the island" sounded vague.

Gavin walked past a few huge Western-style buildings with historical markers that read: "International Club" and "Former American Consulate." Looking like a Greek revival bank, the old consulate was certainly designed to impress.

A few steps later, he saw what Billy meant in terms of "halfway down the island."

A long garden stretched down a tree-lined length of buildings. The garden, that appeared to form the spine of the island, was festooned with fountains and life-size statues of ordinary citizens of the past and present, Western and Chinese.

He seemed to have stumbled upon a small piece of Europe in the middle of China. Maybe he should have read a few guidebooks before moving there.

As he walked eastward in the shade of tall, old banyan and fichus trees, he passed French colonial architecture with round white pillars that gave the feeling of spaciousness even though one could barely slide a putty knife between the buildings.

The long, formal garden consisted of different segments. After a colorful flower bed, he crossed a square where a father and son played badminton. Next, he walked over a glossy chessboard with chess pieces the size of small children. A young man in a sweat suit was jogging on a narrow oval between roses and a long reflecting pool. Ahead was an ambling Chinese trail.

Still, there was no Starbucks, so he walked on. It felt like he was witnessing the calm before the storm, a storm that only he could predict.

He heard mothers scolding children, children crying out with delight at a new sculpture or garden, and a virtual aviary of birds calling to each other. A vendor rang his bicycle bell for deliveries. Brides and grooms, models, girlfriends, and families with children were all taking photos. There were even statues of photographers taking pictures of people taking pictures of them.

Clearly this had once been a vibrant and wealthy section of the city. It certainly was a romantic spot to meet up with the lovely girl from Orchid Mountain.

He had always pictured himself as an attractive figure in China because of his American citizenship and all the benefits that life in America entailed. For the first time, he imagined the possibility that a Chinese woman like Eve might actually prefer to live in China.

Inside a wall that encompassed a Catholic church, a lively market had formed around several tables. Gavin wasn't sure what was being sold. Meanwhile, people wandered in and out of the church without much reflection.

He briefly considered what religion Eve Yang might be. If the scene was any indication, churches were mere curiosities.

Then he came to a mansion within a courtyard. Hanging over the front door was the distinctive green Starbucks logo.

Most of the tables in the courtyard were occupied by young couples casually sipping their drinks.

He saw no Eve, and checked his watch. It was already six o'clock.

He felt for the needle in his suit coat pocket. This time, he wouldn't let Eve talk him out of giving her the shot.

He looked for her down the long garden. Ahead lay an Anglican church, Victorian style buildings, and lots of color and commerce.

Was there a second Starbucks down there?

Then he saw her, short but walking with authority under the moss that hung from the ancient trees. She wore a hideous T-shirt that read, "Crap Your Hands."

He was going to have a talk with her about that.

She waved when she saw him, and Gavin felt a flush of warmth toward her. He knew her from numerous phone calls and had even visited her family. She was his anchor to life in China.

Then he noticed a gangly guy with red hair walking slightly behind her. Who was that?

Eve stopped short of embracing Gavin. Instead she put her feet together and bent forward to offer her hand to shake.

Gavin shook it, deeply disappointed.

"I want you to meet my friend," Eve said, and pivoted toward the redhead who was leaning over her.

Before she could say his name, the young man stepped forward.

"I'm Matt. Matt Justice, with the American consulate."

The young man's official position momentarily threw Gavin off balance.

He wanted to get Eve into a quiet corner of the garden and give her a shot, but he sensed at once that this was neither the time nor place. Shooting up in public might attract police attention in China. And sneaking a trial vaccination into an unsuspecting subject seemed even worse. But doing so before a diplomat might go on his record.

So Gavin slipped the needle back into his pocket, and shook the young man's hand.

"Shall we get coffee?" Eve proposed, and gestured to the chic coffeehouse.

Matt Justice had his arm around Eve, and Gavin felt instinctively like the odd man out.

"I'm sorry," he said. "I won't be able to stay."

Eve knotted her plucked eyebrows. "I thought you had something important to tell me."

Damn. She was like some literal tape recorder. Didn't she know why he was there?

She certainly wasn't helping him out.

"No. It's no longer important."

He rose to his full height and confronted what looked like his romantic rival. The healthy glow on the guy's face made Gavin feel all of his sixty years.

"I know you from that flight from Los Angeles," Matt told him.

"You helped that poor flight attendant."

"Well, that was my duty," Gavin said, looking for a graceful exit.

"Of course. You're a doctor, after all." Then Matt leaned in closer. "Listen, I've been trying to reach you about an employee of yours in the isolation ward at Nanfang Hospital."

Gavin didn't want to hear anything about Nanfang Hospital.

"You must have the wrong company," he said. "We don't have anyone in the isolation ward."

That stopped the Foreign Service Officer short. He fingered his lower lip for a moment, then pressed on. "We were also wondering where you got your flu shot since you didn't get it at Orchid Mountain."

Gavin looked at Eve. Was she part of this inquisition?

"I don't know what you're talking about. Now if you'll please excuse me, I must be going."

He left with the two staring at him. But he couldn't get away from them fast enough.

And if Eve didn't want her damned flu shot, it was her funeral.

He walked away bitterly, feeling denied in several ways. But most deeply, he had lost the connection he felt with the one person in China who recognized and affirmed their common humanity. And if she denied him, what did it say about him?

All he wanted to do was go home.

He reached for his phone. "Billy? Pick me up now."

Nils Andersson sat in Geneva contemplating the alarming reports on his computer screen.

Five days earlier, a single phone call out of southern China had sent his detective antennae twitching, and he had been hot on the case ever since.

From his perch at the World Health Organization's headquarters in Switzerland, he was itching to bring his clipboards and survey teams out to the field. But China had yet to allow any international investigators to help them sort out what was clearly a burgeoning health crisis.

The recent red flag raised by that single phone call by Matthew Justice of the U.S. Consulate in Guangzhou was subsequently supported by the social media and web monitoring software that Nils had been watching with mounting alarm all weekend.

By Tuesday, the computer was lighting up with key words such as "flu," "hospital," "vaccine," and "sick" all across southern China.

It was exceedingly strange that General Gavin Peak, head of a biotech firm in Guangzhou, had no idea that such an outbreak was happening. Maybe he didn't have his finger on the pulse of the city, but Nils hoped the guy would serve as an important conduit of information in the future.

Although Nils was restricted from traveling to China, several WHO and CDC office workers were already living and working in Beijing.

Upon receiving such dire signals from Guangzhou, on Monday he had dispatched some of the WHO office staff from Beijing to Guangzhou to follow up on patients and report back to Geneva.

By Tuesday, they were able to report hospital records showing hundreds of cases of what was generally diagnosed as pneumonia. Although the government released no official figures, the simple hospital checks revealed anecdotal evidence that pointed to a possible health crisis of widespread proportion.

Guiding the field reporters with a survey approach, Nils had been able to draw a general picture of the typical patient. Patients had presented with cold or flu-like symptoms which rapidly turned into breathing problems, a drop in blood pressure, and, in some cases, seizures. The disease affected men and women alike, and sometimes children.

But he needed more information.

He got Yukiko Eto on the first ring.

"How's it going in Guangzhou?" he asked.

"It's pronounced Guang Joe."

"Okay. Thanks."

"It's pretty hidden here. I don't see panic in the streets. A few more facemasks have popped up in the past day. The hospitals have begun to shut their doors on us. We're getting data from private clinics and some city hospitals. Military hospitals are impossible."

"Okay. I need for you to change tactics," he told her. "I want to know what family members also have the disease."

"You mean talk directly to the families?"

"You have their addresses on your survey forms."

"Our team will have to fan out. This is going to call for more drivers and translators."

"Let me worry about the budget. Don't hold back. I want you to interview, interview, interview."

Gavin Peak was tired of being cheated and mistreated by those around him. By that, he meant young Miss Eve.

But a trip to the Canton Club in downtown Guangzhou on Wednesday morning put all that behind him.

He was there to see Mr. Pu and sell him a vaccine.

"Good morning, General Peak," a beautiful young woman greeted him as he mounted the steps from his car to the Canton Club.

How did she know his name?

"Mr. Pu is waiting for you at the swimming pool."

So Mr. Pu had told the staff about him.

"May I show you to the elevator?" the woman asked, her red-painted lips stretching across a broad smile.

"That would be wonderful." All Gavin could think about at that moment was her string of pearly white teeth.

Everything about the club had the classy, aristocratic feel of a bygone era. The photographs of Prince Philip and Henry Kissinger, the rosewood furniture, and the gold-plated china in glass cabinets spoke of history, taste, and enormous wealth.

They took a small, dark elevator up to a floor with plush carpeting and no labels on the doors.

If one had to ask for directions, one shouldn't be there.

The young woman hesitated just outside the elevator. "The swimming pool is at the far end."

He wouldn't mind if she took him all the way, but then it occurred to him that staff might not be permitted.

As Gavin walked down the quiet hallway, he wondered if Mr. Pu hadn't meant for them to swim together. Never mind the expectations, Gavin hadn't brought a suit.

Loosely wrapped in a white robe, a pot-bellied club member slipped out of a doorway. Not a word was exchanged, but a sense of mutual entitlement passed between the two.

Gavin felt uncomfortable stepping out onto the tiled deck of the swimming pool. He was wearing street shoes, and contemplated leaving them by the door.

But there was nobody in the large, sky-lit room to look askance at him, save Mr. Pu dogpaddling in the middle of the pool and a slender attendant standing by the spa room in a white dress, towel in hand.

Mr. Pu was no swimmer, but he seemed to own the pool. Without his glasses on, maybe he didn't notice Gavin's presence.

Gavin waited for the guy to complete his lap before he stood up to form a black blob on the man's consciousness.

"Mr. Peak, take a seat," the old guy called out. "I'll be right there."

Gavin moved a rolled-up towel off the nearest lounge chair and sat down, arms crossed to wait for his nibs to grant him an audience.

When the small mountain of flab pulled himself out of the water, Gavin was there to hand him his horn-rims.

"Come to sell me vaccines?" Mr. Pu said, toweling off.

"With the current outbreak in southern China," Gavin reminded him, "the virus is difficult to contain. The longer you wait, the worse the situation will grow."

Gavin didn't know what sort of lottery system the Chinese leadership would employ to choose who got the vaccine first, but that was their problem.

"I've got thousands of doses ready to transfer to you," he went on. "Just say when."

Mr. Pu sat down opposite him on another lounge chair and faced him squarely. "How much are you charging?"

"With high development costs, we're talking about fifteen dollars a dose."

Mr. Pu's expression was frozen. Was that too high?

"Mr. Peak," the party secretary said, "I want your company to survive long-term. I want you around to produce larger batches as required."

That showed faith in FutureGenetics. But what did it have to do with the price of the vaccine?

"I think you should charge enough to ensure your survival," Mr. Pu said.

"I'm always willing to charge more," Gavin said.

"Then name a price."

Gavin could hardly believe he was being bargained upward. But then, Mr. Pu had a population to serve. "Twenty dollars a dose would ensure our long-term sustainability."

Mr. Pu nodded. "That would be acceptable. But how effective is the vaccine?"

"We're performing studies as we speak. I should have results in the next few days."

"We aren't buying anything without knowing its effectiveness."

"Can you afford to wait any longer?"

"I can wait forever if it doesn't work."

Gavin saw his point.

They seemed at an impasse. Gavin was in a hurry, and the party secretary was being prudent. Wait too long, and prudence eventually became folly.

"I suggest you send me samples," Mr. Pu said at last. "I will ask the relevant bodies to begin clinical trials."

Clinical trials. Those two words were the death sentence for any hoped-for drug. It was the medical equivalent of being buried in committee.

This unexpected turn could result in months of delay. But what could he do?

"As I said," Gavin proceeded bravely, "we are performing our own tests and they should be concluded within a week."

"Don't worry," Mr. Pu tried to assure him. "We will fast-track the trials. They won't hamper the sale."

Although that sounded highly improbable, Gavin didn't want to argue with him. "I'll send samples to your office later today," he said. "Our laboratory is ready to meet your every need."

Mr. Pu was looking tired, perhaps from his swim.

"One thing that I need to ask of you," Gavin tried to sneak in. "Patrick Kind, the American Consul General, is trying to bring World Health Organization disease investigators to the city. I told him that I would ask you."

"I have received no such requests from the American consulate."

That was interesting. Gavin would have to determine later who was lying, Mr. Pu or the consul general.

"Fine. I just thought I would ask."

The young woman in the white uniform cleared her throat by the spa.

"You may go now," Mr. Pu said. "I want the results of your study, including how it was conducted and what the final numbers are. Then I will assess."

Gavin couldn't wait for the numbers himself.

Mr. Pu stood up and waddled toward the attendant. Then the two disappeared into the spa.

Gavin lingered a moment longer.

He needed a date for Friday, and the club workers were looking pretty fine. Couldn't he just ask one of them to the ball?

Before he left the chlorine-scented confines of the Canton Club's swimming pool, he needed to call Dr. Chen about supplying Mr. Pu with samples of the vaccine for clinical trials.

He reached into his pocket for his phone and turned discretely toward the wall. Then he placed the call to Dr. Chen.

"Pu wants sample vaccines so they can run clinical trials," he reported.

"What?" It was the loudest Gavin had ever heard his chief scientist speak.

"Calm down. He said it wouldn't delay the approval process. He's basically looking to our test results to make his decision."

"Oh. I know why he wants the vaccine," Dr. Chen said, suddenly mollified, if not humored by the request.

"Yeah. I think I know why, too. Just send some to his office today."

"We have lots of boxes. I'll send one over."

Gavin put his phone away with a smile.

The party secretary wanted to be vaccinated right away, even if that meant getting vaccinated before everyone else. It would make a great testimonial for an ad, if it weren't so underhanded.

One day after asking Yukiko Eto and her team to fan out across Guangzhou, Dr. Nils Andersson was staring at their data online.

The evidence was clear. Those who had died hadn't caught the disease from other family members.

That pointed to one thing and one thing only, sudden exposure to the disease.

So Nils worked the maps. He wanted to know all the military research facilities in China. Maybe there was a factory leak nearby, thus poisoning the city. Such information wouldn't be public knowledge, but the British and American embassies were helpful in that regard.

Soon he had maps plastered to his office walls. They showed places where there were chemical and biological weapons depots and research facilities.

While Guangzhou had many medical schools and research centers, none was military in nature. He had to go clear to the city of Zhuhai near Macau to see military researchers hard at work.

So the possibility of a leak seemed limited at best.

Nils' one, big digital map of Guangzhou was filled with red dots. Whenever a researcher found a case, he or she marked it down on a special tablet that transmitted the GPS coordinates to Geneva. His computer filled in the map electronically.

From the red dots across the city, the pattern was clear. The swath of cases extended from the southeast of the city to the northwest, with few cases outside of that area. Granted, people moved around for work and pleasure, so there would always be outliers, but the trend was clear.

Interestingly, the shape of the affected area didn't correspond to the natural geographic or demographic features on the map. There were no rivers or highways that defined that specific area. The ugly scar across the city seemed like a random, bloody slash across the map.

Just as he was entering the office that Thursday morning, Gavin Peak was approached by Billy.

"Blow wants to see you thirsting," Billy said, his voice muffled by a surgical mask.

"What are you saying?"

Billy removed the mask. "Zhou wants to see you first thing."

"Send her in. And Billy? No masks in this office. We have to set the right tone."

He stood to meet Zhou, and she approached his desk slowly. Her eyes lingered on him as if she were about to call him out on something.

"You do like this job, don't you," she said. It was more of a statement than a question.

"Yes. Never a dull moment. Please take a seat."

Her eyes didn't leave him as she sat opposite him.

"How much will we charge per vaccine?" she began.

"I told Mr. Pu twenty dollars per dose."

She seemed unimpressed, but wrote a note on her pad.

"I was thinking of raising it to twenty-five," he said, remembering Mr. Pu's concern about keeping FutureGenetics afloat. "Why not run those figures through your computer and let me know how that sits for maintaining long-term viability in this business."

"What do you consider 'long-term?'" she inquired.

"A year for this vaccine. Maybe two."

She nodded. "I'll run a price elasticity on demand analysis right away."

The math talk was a turn-on coming from her. Especially that bit about "elasticity."

"I'm not sure the demand is that flexible," he said. "The question isn't how much will a person pay to not die. It's how much do we charge before the government comes after us for price gouging."

"I'll run a regression analysis of cost-per-unit against increasing overhead costs and compare that to governmentally acceptable price points."

"Bingo." They were definitely on the same page.

She knew what to do, but remained glued to her seat.

"Anything else?" he said, half hoping there was more. He knew nothing about her ethnic origins or family life, her education, her hobbies, or her foibles. All he knew of the poised female was what she presented to the world: a mathematical mind, darkly wild features, conservative dress, and no ring on the fourth proximal digit of her left hand.

"I suppose I have to ask," she said. "Is there any news on the vaccine's effectiveness?"

"Not yet. I'm meeting with Dr. Chen next."

"Well, let me know. I have to balance the books," she said.

He watched her leave. Her tall, straight bearing contradicted the uncontrollably wild hair that swung across her square shoulders. It brought to mind those women who exuded great power, the Amazons.

He was used to dominating a conversation and telling others how to suck eggs. Only now, the shoe was on the other foot.

He had risen above others through the ranks of the military, in the national laboratories, in the boardroom, and in bed. Everybody was either superior or inferior to him. He preferred to be the one on top.

It was the first moment of parity he ever experienced with a woman. And it unsettled him that it gave him pleasure.

Dr. Chen appeared in Gavin's office precisely at ten, clipboard in hand.

"I'm here to report on my interview with the family and close friends," Chen said, "of our brave rescuers who are dying in our quarantine unit."

Gavin eyed him closely. Was the scientist succumbing to emotion?

He waved for Dr. Chen to continue, and the scientist resumed in a less passionate tone.

It was ten days since the leak and five to nine days since the rescue workers would have become contagious. Family members began showing symptoms as early as a week ago. At least three people acquainted with each rescuer had already been hospitalized. One, a spouse, had died.

"So that gives a reproductive ratio of 3," Gavin concluded. "That's pretty good, about twice the ratio of ordinary seasonal flu."

"I have even better news on the city front," Dr. Chen said. "The number of cases has increased to 30,000."

That sounded remarkable to Gavin, in a macabre sort of way. "What does that mean to you?"

"It means that even if the initial 5,000 cases were caused by exposure to the virus through the air after the explosion, these newer cases had to have been transmitted directly from the initial victims. Human-to-human contact."

"At a 5-to-1 ratio," Gavin said.

"Consistent with, and slightly better than, our subjects in the quarantine unit having transmitted it to their families."

Gavin reflected on the reproductive ratio of 5. The disease didn't have a high rate of communicability like the measles, which had a ratio of around 15, meaning every 1 case was transmitted directly to 15 people. But 5 was well above the normal rate for flu transmission, which was usually between 1.0 and 1.5. To him, the total of 30,000 already affected by the new virus should set off alarm bells around the world.

He began to do the math. If the disease was communicated in an average of 4 days after exposure, within 4 days, the initial 5,000 cases would have spread to 25,000 more cases. Within 8 days, 125,000 more would be affected. Within 12 days, Guangzhou could expect 500,000 new cases. And within 16 days, there would be 2,500,000 more sick in the city.

Thousands of Guangzhou residents flew to the United States each week, whether for business, leisure, or school. Assuming 1 infected person reached the United States in the first few days, within two weeks, 500 Americans would come down with the flu, assuming no super-spreaders were among them and discounting the fact that many more than 5 people would have caught the disease on the plane flying to America. Of course, more than one affected person would have traveled to the United States in the past 10 days. He could imagine that there were 5,000 to 10,000 cases in the States already.

He hoped to God the vaccine would prove effective.

"How about our neighborhood study, the ones that we vaccinated? Is the vaccine proving effective?"

"Of the one thousand in our study, a quarter were placebos. Five days after we vaccinated them, nobody was showing symptoms. Now it has been a week, and ten subjects show signs. Nine of those had taken the placebo."

"The vaccine is taking effect!"

"We may not have vaccinated everyone in time, but you're right. Our data are beginning to indicate complete effectiveness in infants, children, and grownups."

"Who was the one subject that got sick?"

Dr. Chen shrugged. "The one subject that we vaccinated and still got sick has been running a fever for five days now. He was likely already infected before he was vaccinated."

"So far, the numbers look good," Gavin said. "I want you to fill Zhou in on the effectiveness right away, and give me a report every day from now on."

Already the vaccine seemed to be one hundred percent effective if administered in time. That would be an excellent result to report to the party secretary.

He leaned toward his phone and got Billy.

"Set up golf on Saturday with Mr. Pu."

Nils Andersson couldn't sleep. He lay in bed knowing that his disease surveillance workers in China were spinning their wheels. Hospitals had closed their doors to any more inquiries, and the government was clamping down on media access.

What concerned Nils was that this was happening as the official number of reported cases declined dramatically. And so had the internet chatter. In fact, in the past day, there were no hits for the typical key words. Was nobody "sick" in China?

Someone was blocking the keywords that the WHO typically searched for. What were the Chinese hiding?

Nils needed another strategy. And he thought he knew what.

He rolled over and reached for the phone on his nightstand. "Get me the team leader in Guangzhou."

A minute later, he was talking to Yukiko Eto on the streets of Guangzhou.

"We need a change of approach," he said. "But first, with all the data showing a decline in cases, what's your personal reading?"

"There are definitely more cases," she said, her voice tired. "We see a steady stream of ambulances to the hospitals. I would estimate that more than half the population wears facemasks in public now."

"So here's our new approach," Nils said. "I want you to go back to the families of the original victims you documented and find out if there's any transmission to those who lived with or cared for the sick. Is the next ring of contacts getting sick?"

Despite her obvious fatigue, Yukiko was willing to go back and re-interview families of the bereaved.

Nils knew it was hard work and difficult to approach grieving families, but with hospitals denying her access, there was no other way to collect data.

"Good luck, Yukiko. I wish I was there," he said.

"No you don't."

It was Thursday noon, the soft opening for the Canton Fair.

And Matthew Justice was there to report on it.

The exhibition center was a few miles downriver from the consulate and occupied huge exhibit halls in a sprawling area the size of 3,400 tennis courts.

Matt didn't need to be reminded of the scope of the fair, where Chinese sold toilet brushes and TVs to the world, and at the International Pavilion where foreign manufacturers sold their goods to the world. He already watched Honeywell selling air conditioners to Saudi Arabia and New Zealand selling honey-flavored toothpaste to Indonesia.

The key items to watch and interview people for was the level of international participation, and the prices in the pavilions where China sold wholesale to the world.

In the words of his boss, Bart Parsons, China's competitive advantage that made it the factory for the world was their low prices. But this year, that might have changed. With disinflationary pressures in both China and the rest of the world and low global demand, this might be the year when China ceased to be the bargain basement of the world, causing inflationary reverberations from Moscow to Main Street.

When Matt thought about it, bringing jobs back to America due to seismic shifts in the world economy could have more far-reaching effects than a disease epidemic.

Electric shuttles ferried people across the vast complex. The halls had high ceilings that sucked up individual sounds, and walls of glass that let in iffy daylight. Skinny Chinese dancers and singers performed on vast indoor stages. And between the halls, tranquil courtyards featured winding rivers with flawless topiary gardens.

Matt clutched his phone closer, leaned over, grabbed the rolling bag that he used to collect brochures, and dove into the crowd.

God, he loved his job.

Before he got down to interviewing salesmen, he wanted to make sure his evening was lined up.

"I'm just checking to see if you're ready for the ball tonight."

"Oh, yes. The dance." Eve's voice sounded scratchy.

"Are you okay?"

"I'm fighting a sore throat," she said. "I don't think I should go to the dance."

Matt felt deflated. He didn't want to let his Marine buddies down. The food and alcohol wouldn't be bad. But most of all, he had harbored images of dancing the night away with his sweetheart to the latest DJ tunes.

But he was concerned for her. "Are you working today?"

"Yes. I'm at work. I'm just a little tired."

"How about this," he said. "Instead of the dance, get some sleep tonight and tomorrow, and we'll take a walk on Sunday."

That sounded fine to her, and they hung up on good terms.

At least she didn't have a fever. And she was the one who had arranged flu vaccines at Orchid Mountain.

She *was* vaccinated, wasn't she?

Gavin Peak leaned forward in his executive chair that Friday morning, itching to propel his company to action.

"Vincent, get marketing to hit the pavement and work all our clients, from China and the United States to Europe and Australia. I want orders, orders, orders."

"General, just yesterday we were pursuing all our contacts and getting no response. Today, the phones are ringing off the hook. We're getting inquiries from all over the world."

Inquiries were fine, but the world couldn't afford to wait for some country to run clinical trials. What Gavin needed was an initial sale. It was up to China to provide both the blessing of their government labs and the first major orders. "Any feelers from Beijing?"

"The central government's policy is to allow purchases to be made on the city and provincial level. So far, we've heard from Shanghai, Hubei, Zhejiang, Fujian–"

"You can stop right there." It all sounded great to Gavin, but without knowing the population sizes of the areas mentioned, he couldn't begin to calculate the quantities his company would need to produce. "Are we still building capacity to meet demand?"

"We're behind a week or two, but we'll catch up soon."

From Gavin's knowledge of how influenza spread to span the globe and seasonal changes spread it to the Southern Hemisphere, they'd be taking orders all year. "I want you to prepare for massive ordering. Build for the long term."

"We are, General."

Vincent sounded busy, so Gavin let him go.

He sat back and looked at the ceiling of his office. It must be what astronauts felt like taking off for space.

Next up was his daily briefing by Dr. Chen.

Gavin had to admit, he was getting impatient to start selling the new vaccine. As determined by Vincent Fong, they already had enough doses sitting in warehouses around town.

It would be way too early to notice harmful side effects that a clinical trial would bring out. But with the virus already claiming lives, it was too late to quibble over details.

Dr. Chen's report was encouraging.

"There were more deaths of those taking the placebo, and no illness from those taking the vaccine."

"I'd declare that an unqualified success," Gavin said. "Let's get ready to move out the vaccines."

"And do you have buyers?"

"We'll know tomorrow." He swung his hands as if he were hitting a tee shot.

It promised to be a good golf game indeed.

"General?" It was Billy on the line. "I have made the room reserves at the Four Seasons for tomorrow night."

There was that nagging Marine Ball to attend, and still nobody to go with.

Gavin picked up the phone and called Eve.

"I'm feeling unwell," she told him, with a slight cough.

Gavin set the phone down, bewildered. Was that just another excuse? It was such a shallow, forced cough that it could have been faked.

Why did she continue to resist him?

Nils Andersson stared at his computer screen. Green dots were appearing all over the map of Guangzhou. Most overlapped the red dots of the initial outbreak of the disease.

The green dots represented new cases reported in follow-up visits by his WHO team to the families of the original victims.

According to the team, the disease had definitely been transmitted from the original victims to their family members and caregivers. What he was looking at was a contagious disease that could be passed from person to person.

The second wave was definitely bigger than the first. That meant the ratio of reproduction of the disease was high. For every initial case, there appeared to be on the order of five new cases.

This thing wasn't just contagious. It was virulent in a way that he had never seen before.

He thought about that original phone call from Matthew Justice. He was calling about the population getting flu vaccines. Were they off the mark and it was something other than the flu?

Clearly those in contact with the victims were becoming sick through some form of contagion. If it were anthrax or some other sort of toxic agent, the residue would last for long periods of time, sickening others. If it were a bacterial infection like the plague, it might be transmitted from rats and other rodents to humans by way of fleas or sweeping up rat droppings. If it were a virus such as SARS or bird flu, the disease would be transmitted through droplets of water, usually from coughing or sneezing.

He was still puzzled. Any of the three explanations could be true.

If it were a deadly toxin, he couldn't think of the causes without going to bioterrorism. If it turned out to be a bacterial infection, the vector must be eradicated.

And if it was a virus, he was even more concerned. Viruses could spread on a worldwide scale and continue spreading within communities.

But he could never rule out bioterrorism. He picked up the phone and dialed the director of the World Health Organization.

He needed her to pressure the Chinese and allow him and a team of medical doctors and bioterrorism experts to fly to China and conduct a full investigation on the ground.

On the way to the Marine Ball, Gavin couldn't help but notice the vertical landscape of downtown Guangzhou. Buildings that struck sleek lines curved, angled, and shot toward the lighted haze of the nighttime sky.

The Four Seasons was no exception. It occupied half of the tallest building in the city.

He and Zhou looked like a comfortable pair locked arm-in-arm as they entered the glass lobby.

"All right," he said. "Have you picked out a new nickname?"

She looked at him unblinking. "You don't like 'Fanny?'"

"Are you kidding?"

Fanny.

"Maybe you should give me a new name," she suggested, her creative powers clearly having reached their limit.

He stared at the wild-featured beauty, whose long hair defied control, whose dark skin spoke of distant places, and whose tall, thin bearing complemented his powerful stature. He wanted to call her something from *South Pacific*, but Bloody Mary was the only name that came to mind.

"Quick. I need a name before we walk inside."

He drew a blank. "It's up to you."

He ushered her through the lobby to a metal detector, and from there to a line of waiting Marines.

The five men and one woman were in their dress blues with ribbons, medals, and white belts. They were all young and could have been his kids, if he had any.

The first in line had three stripes up and three down on his jacket sleeves. If the Marine was any older than the others, it was by months.

"Good evening, Sergeant," Gavin said, shaking his hand. "I'm General Peak. Gulf War."

"Welcome, General. I'm Detachment Commander Rodriguez," the sergeant said. "Glad you could make it."

"Wouldn't miss it for the world." He turned to Zhou. "And this is…"

Zhou stuck out her hand. "Beatrix."

What the hell?

How had she come up with that name?

She should have stuck with Fanny.

Beatrix.

For the next few Marines in line, he took over and made the introductions.

"This is my friend Bea."

God that sounded awful. It sounded like Aunt Bea from *The Andy Griffith Show*.

Okay, there were three more in line. He tried a new variation on the Beatrix theme.

"General Peak's the name," he told them.

Their eyes adjusted from polite and welcoming to intense respect. "And this is Trixy."

He cringed as soon as he said the name, and he was nauseous by the end of the line.

And there stood Consul General Patrick Kind followed by his wife.

There was no way Gavin could bring a "Trixy" to their ball. He had to think fast.

The diplomat shook his hand in the warm and friendly manner that old acquaintances do after a long absence.

"I'll need a word with you later," Patrick whispered in his ear.

Gavin smiled evasively. No doubt the consul general was wondering whether Mr. Pu would admit WHO investigators.

He tried to deflect the diplomat by turning to Zhou. "You remember…"

Patrick Kind's face lit up. "Fanny!" he said. "I remember you from the Chamber of Commerce bash."

"That's right, sir," she said.

The diplomat's obvious enthusiasm for Gavin's date got him thinking. Was this a swinging kind of town?

Then the consul general pulled him close.

"Where's your uniform? This event is full dress."

"In my shipment, I'm afraid."

The next couple was bumping up against Fanny, er Zhou.

Patrick turned to his stunningly beautiful wife, whose skin looked more tanned and lustrous than ever. "Shawnee, you remember our neighbor, Gavin Peak."

All Gavin could do was stare into her green, almond-shaped eyes and think about her tawny limbs stretched out poolside.

Fanny nudged him from behind.

"Good to see you again, in the flesh," he said, whatever that meant. "And here's my friend, Fanny."

They got through the firing squad slightly wounded, but still standing.

After his flustered encounter with his neighbor's forbidden fruit, Gavin made a beeline for the bar. There, the barman filled two tall glasses of beer for Gavin and his escort.

Gavin raised his glass and Zhou bravely raised hers. Their eyes met.

"You like beautiful women, don't you," she said. Again, from her, it sounded like a statement of fact.

"She's very sexy," he admitted. "But I don't think she's very smart."

"The spouse of the American consul general?" she said.

"Maybe she was slightly intoxicated when I first met her."

Zhou didn't seem to buy either of his characterizations.

"Oh, look. The ballroom doors are opening."

Gavin found his numbered table and the place cards for Zhou and himself. He barely had time to meet his tablemates, a group of science teachers from the American School, before the lights dimmed.

The colors were presented and the ensuing ceremony followed a prescribed order used by Marines every year at every post around the world.

Gavin occasionally glanced at Zhou. Her eyes glittered with admiration.

When at last the oldest Marine was introduced, the table for the fallen Marines was honored, and all speeches were made, the lights came up and waiters floated in with steaming hot food.

Gavin could see empty seats around some tables. What a pity that they couldn't make it.

One table over, he spotted the pesky American who had tried to convince him to play golf at his resort on Hainan Island.

Gavin sought to avoid him, but the guy was closing in fast.

"General Peak," the man said.

Gavin couldn't even remember his name.

"Harold Priest. Remember, we met at the AmCham Fall Ball?"

"Oh, yes. Of course, Harold."

"You aren't in uniform tonight," the man said. "Where are your stars?"

"Did I tell you I'm a general?"

"Yes, at the ball."

"My uniform hasn't arrived yet."

"You look wonderful in this tuxedo."

Would the man go away?

Harold was slipping him his business card. "I want you to come play golf in Hainan. No, I'll take no excuses. I have a private jet that can pick you up anytime. Just give me a call."

The idea of a private jet sounded intriguing. Gavin could get FutureGenetics to pay the expenses.

"And don't worry about the cost," Harold said. "The trip's on me."

Gavin gave the man some more of his attention.

"Golf, huh?"

"Imagine the Florida of China. Tropical breezes, coconut groves, the sound of the sea. I'll roll out the red carpet."

Gavin slipped the business card into his coat pocket for future reference.

Maybe the Marine Ball was going to pay off after all.

Just before dessert was served, Gavin spotted the consul general heading his way. Shawnee wasn't in tow, so Gavin braced for business.

"Have you talked with Mr. Pu?" Patrick Kind said, slipping into a vacated seat beside him.

"I did speak with the party secretary on Wednesday," Gavin reported, remembering his meeting at the Canton Club's swimming pool. "But I got nowhere. He told me that the American Consulate never requested WHO investigators."

"You see," the consul general said, "the WHO already has some of its fulltime staff down here from Beijing. They aren't disease investigators, but they're under instructions to find the source of the outbreak."

"I see," Gavin said noncommittally.

"They think it originated in Guangzhou and have started interrogating family members of the deceased."

"Is it getting to that stage?"

The consul general sat back and regarded him from a distance. "How is it that you can chat with the party secretary about health investigators and run a biotech firm and still not be aware of how critical this has become?"

Okay, Gavin had to stop feigning ignorance. "Listen, I can only tell you what Mr. Pu told me. I put the question to him, and he said that he had received no such requests. End of story."

Gavin didn't want to admit that he would be playing golf with Mr. Pu the very next day.

As much as he enjoyed hobnobbing with highflyers, Gavin was still getting used to the games they played. And it was becoming increasingly difficult to keep the diplomat at bay.

"Well, the World Health Organization has preliminary findings," the consul general said.

"Such as?"

"The source of the outbreak appears to be somewhere in Science City. Police and hospitals in that area are combing through their records for the past few weeks."

Okay. This was hitting way too close to home. At what point would Gavin come clean, if ever?

A piece of the Marine's birthday cake arrived just in time. Gavin dug in and worked the creamy sweetness around in his mouth.

The diplomat waited for him to finish, then said, "The WHO staff here are only able to track hospital records and interview the public," he said. "They aren't scientists and they aren't doctors. We need bona fide health investigators on the ground to determine what brought this disease upon us."

Gavin knew the process of looking for the culprits of a disease. First, investigators would determine the vector, whether by touch, food, water, or through the air. Then they would find the reservoir from which the disease was coming. If it was a virus, usually that meant rats, migratory birds, waterfowl, pigs, chickens, or related species.

These animals or birds could harbor the disease without symptoms for years before a rodent bite, home slaughtering, or poorly cooked meat allowed the virus to jump species to a human host.

Once the World Health Organization was armed with those facts, they could call for trapping the rodents or culling the poultry, thus removing the reservoir of viruses.

And once people stopped coughing and sneezing on each other and transmitting the disease through fomites such as handles, handshakes, dishes, and doorknobs, they could rely on vaccines to eventually block the spread of the disease in the general population.

But that was not how the disease arrived or was spread. There were no rodent or avian reservoirs. There was no skipping across species to people.

There was only Dr. Chen in his laboratory, brewing the new strain of influenza. And the explosion had done the rest of the work, transmitting it to thousands of victims across the city. Now the virus had migrated to other continents where it could spread virtually unchecked.

Every year, 125,000 to 500,000 people died worldwide from seasonal flu. This year the number of deaths would double, at the very least.

Gavin took another bite, but had lost his appetite.

The consul general leaned in close so that others couldn't hear. "I don't want to remind you how serious this has become. The world needs China's cooperation."

"I get that," Gavin said, irritated at the guy breathing in his ear. "I'll see the party secretary tomorrow, and I'll deliver the message personally."

The diplomat sat back with a triumphant smile. "All we need is a formal request from China to the World Health Organization to come on over and have a look-see."

"You know," Gavin reminded him, "the Canton Fair opened this week, followed next week by the Boao Forum."

"I am painfully aware of those upcoming events."

"Well, the party secretary is, too."

The diplomat's silver tongue was silenced, and he seemed to appreciate Gavin in a whole new light. Gavin had become a full-blown intermediary between the two large countries in a great international stalemate.

"Tell Pu I don't care about the fair or the forum," the diplomat said, his voice dry and hard. "Tell him that people all over the world are dying, and we have to stop it in its tracks."

"Relax, Patrick. Of course he knows that."

"Well, impress upon him the *urgency* of the matter."

Gavin welcomed the role of negotiator, but didn't like being dictated to.

"Patrick, enough. I get it."

With that, the diplomat gave him a broad smile. The ball was in Gavin's court and both men knew it.

But Gavin wasn't going to see Mr. Pu about increasing inspections. Far from it. He was going to seal the deal on the vaccines.

As the lights dimmed and a peppy beat arose from the huge speakers on stage, the diplomat shook his hand and took his leave.

The music kicked into high gear, and the floor began to vibrate.

The consul general had the first dance, and Shawnee melted into the big guy's arms. They made a lovely couple except for the annoying fact that she was so damned attractive.

Gavin looked around at the other faces at his table, and people were transfixed.

He located his wine glass and raised it to Zhou.

"You'd like to dance with her, wouldn't you," Zhou said.

Gavin downed a full, gut-warming swig.

Eventually, others joined in the hip-hop that seemed to be the DJ's favorite.

The youngest Marine had a cute little Chinese girl twisting her hips in a tight skirt, and several Western women began to gyrate through the latest dance moves.

In the flashing light, Gavin saw tuxedo jackets come off and women flash their legs as they crouched in high heels.

A Marine hopped in front of the screen and pointed upward in a *Saturday Night Fever* pose.

Disco lights were changing from red to green to yellow.

And in their glow, Zhou began to look highly desirable. Nobody on that stage could hold a candle to her for her poise as she quietly enjoyed the music with an easy smile.

"Care to dance?" he offered.

"You know how?"

What she didn't know.

She was great at eye contact, and they locked eyes all evening until their intentions were crystal clear.

Long after the music stopped, he was showing her more moves of his own in their hotel room.

And that's how they spent the night.

From the Four Seasons the next morning, Billy Liu drove Gavin Peak to the Luhu Golf Club for another Saturday game with Mr. Pu.

FutureGenetics was fielding inquiries from around the world and Gavin was ready to tout the vaccine's effectiveness to the Guangdong party secretary.

If Mr. Pu accepted his findings and purchased the vaccine, it would open the floodgates for sales in China and many countries around the world.

However, the news was sure to make international headlines, and touch off investigative reporting. And where would the press turn for their information?

Patrick Kind had warned Gavin that the WHO had narrowed the initial outbreak down to Science City, where Gavin's company was located. And at Patrick's insistence, Gavin would continue to ask Mr. Pu to invite WHO investigators into China. Gavin could feel the inevitable squeeze coming, both from the WHO and the press.

What he needed was a story. He needed a plausible, but not damaging, explanation for the outbreak starting at his company.

So, as the minivan jerked in and out of traffic openings, he placed a call to Dr. Chen.

"We have a problem," Gavin said.

Dr. Chen yawned audibly over the line.

"The WHO has zeroed in on Science City."

"I thought the WHO wasn't invited by the Chinese."

"Something slipped out. Somehow they caught wind of the outbreak and they're going to come knocking on our door before we know it."

"Okay. So we tell them what we've been doing."

There was no way Gavin would do that. Whether it was out of a sense of duty to mankind or his scientific reputation or the need to protect his company, he didn't know. But whatever his rationale, he wasn't going to let Dr. Chen ruin it all, just to take credit for the vaccine in scientific publications. "Chen, we need a story."

He waited and watched through rain-streaked car windows as the thick layer of clouds gradually thinned out, revealing a hint of blue.

"So here it is," Dr. Chen said, his voice less sleepy than before. "We can describe our two-step approach. We used techniques employed by a University of Wisconsin study and Erasmus University research, where both labs genetically engineered a lethal and aerosolized form of H5N1."

"What the hell? Why did they do that?"

"Their point was to find the gene markers that were most deadly and easily communicated. They thought that governments should be prepared for a worst-case scenario."

"Is that what gave you the idea to engineer the virus?"

"Their publications were my starting point, yes."

"Shit. That makes us sound like we were trying to kill half the world."

"Then there's the pressing need for our research. We can say that we were responding to recent outbreaks of H3N2 in the swine population of southern China."

"Go on."

"It's well known that H5N1 is endemic in birds in southern China. The virus mutates naturally all the time and is already shown to kill half the humans who get it, yet isn't easily communicated to humans. However, a form of human-to-human transmitted flu, namely H3N2, has been discovered in the pig farms of China. If that H3N2 combines with H5N1, it's only a few mutations away from becoming an easily transmissible, as well as deadly, strain of H5N1."

"…and that's what we isolated and were trying to eradicate."

"Precisely."

"I like your story. It's solid. Is it true?"

There was no response on the other end.

"Don't tell me. I don't want to know."

With that, a story was born, one which provided cover against the WHO or Pu or whoever went looking for the source.

"So have you sold the vaccine to the Chinese yet?" Dr. Chen wanted to know.

"I'm arriving at the golf course right now."

After some terrific sex with Zhou at the Four Seasons, Gavin was feeling at the height of his powers. And by the fourth hole, his score threatened to annihilate Mr. Pu.

Already the guy was shooting daggers at his cheap $75,000 golf clubs. Pretty soon, he'd take it out on Gavin.

They played another hole, and low-and-behold, Gavin's driving game and putting abilities suddenly deserted him.

They strolled toward the bench under the magnolia tree where they had sat before, and Mr. Pu shooed the caddies away so that they could talk.

The clouds had completely cleared and sunlight heightened the intense colors of the golf course.

Mr. Pu swung his arms to loosen his shoulders, then he puffed out his chest and sat down. "So what are the results of your vaccine study?" he said at last.

Gavin was bursting to tell him, but wanted to build the suspense. "Do you really want to know?"

Mr. Pu nodded, his face all business.

"Okay. I'll tell you. We completed our study of a randomized sample of infants through adults. It showed a one-hundred-percent effectiveness rate. It's a winner."

Mr. Pu stared at him in disbelief. "It prevented the flu in every case?"

"All one thousand of them within two weeks, and sometimes sooner."

Mr. Pu closed his eyes. It would come as a great relief to his country.

"I want to congratulate you, Mr. Peak," Mr. Pu said. "Our Center for Drug Evaluation has run clinical trials and approved your vaccine."

Boy, that was fast. The Chinese government must be good at post-dating reports.

"So you'll take shipment of the vaccine?"

"I will. My province and particularly Guangzhou needs immediate vaccination."

"Our price is a consistent thirty dollars a dose, no matter what the quantity."

Mr. Pu raised his massive black eyebrows. "Thirty dollars?"

Gavin nodded definitively.

"Bold. Very bold."

"As you suggested, we need to ensure our long-term survival as a vaccine producer."

Mr. Pu gave one of his Yoda-like smiles.

"We'll start with forty million doses," he said.

Gavin gulped. That was a good start.

"And we'll buy more after that. Can you handle that quantity?"

"We're totally geared up," Gavin said, wondering if they could get out even a fraction of that amount. That was a lot of vials of vaccines.

It behooved him to make one last good-faith effort to press Mr. Pu on Patrick Kind's request to let the World Health Organization in.

"Listen, I'm getting pressure from the American consulate," Gavin said. "They've been requesting that China invite health investigators from WHO to track down the origin of the disease."

"And…"

"So I guess I'm asking you now."

Mr. Pu looked at him more closely. "Are you asking me or is the consulate asking me?"

"I'm asking you on their behalf."

Gavin held his breath. He didn't want the party secretary to officially invite in the WHO. Despite the vaccine-creation story he had concocted, his decision to cover up the explosion was still a risk. His actions could eventually be revealed and he had everything to lose. Nothing less was at stake than his dream of vaccinating the entire world against the deadliest influenza virus.

And, even if Mr. Pu decided to extend the invitation through him, Gavin decided to ignore the request. The World Health Organization would just have to fret from the sidelines.

But to Gavin's amazement, Mr. Pu didn't go there.

"I have a duty to preserve public order and protect economic interests," Mr. Pu said. "No investigators."

And that was that.

It was a pleasure playing golf with the party secretary.

Gavin Peak lay in bed the next morning. After all, it was Sunday.

He had considered a six-day workweek earlier. Now he had the company running seven days a week, with all hands on deck.

He checked his wristwatch. It was 8:00 a.m.

He rolled over, grabbed the telephone, and called the office.

"Zhou," he said triumphantly over the phone. "We got an order for forty million doses by the end of the week."

He was met with stunned silence.

Finally there was a response. "I thought they wanted twenty million."

"I underestimated the demand. Pass the word. Have Vincent hire whoever he needs, rent whatever space is required, buy trucks if necessary. This is bigger than you or I ever imagined."

"And what did he bargain you down to?" she asked.

"Down? I asked for thirty dollars a pop, and he bought it."

"That's double private sector prices for ordinary influenza vaccines."

"This, my dear, is no ordinary flu vaccine. It's going to save the world."

"You like making money, don't you."

"You bet I do!"

It was hard to stay calm and at home for the rest of the day.

First he made a quick pen-on-paper calculation. Forty million doses at thirty dollars a dose came to a cool 1.2 billion dollars, at least half of that pure profit. And a good chunk of that profit went straight into his profit-sharing plan.

He couldn't lie in bed all morning, so he got dressed and moved down to his living room.

There, coffee in hand, he looked over *Forbes* magazine, half expecting his neighbor to appear in his good-neighborly fashion and extort the news about Mr. Pu out of him.

Patrick Kind's pointed observation that the outbreak was being tracked down to somewhere in Science City still bothered him, and he reviewed the plan of attack he had developed the day before with Dr. Chen.

He would reveal that before his arrival in Guangzhou, his firm had discovered a new, deadly strain of H5N1 avian flu that had mingled with the highly contagious H3N2 in pigs, and that the resultant H5N1 strain had jumped to humans. They had successfully isolated the virus and developed a vaccine against it. By the time Gavin had arrived in China, production of that vaccine was well underway.

The outbreak of the disease must have arisen from poor handling during the virus production process, and he was looking into it with firm resolve to punish those who mishandled the live virus.

That was all there was to it. *Mea culpa*, hands raised in surrender. There was nothing the diplomat could do to him. This was a Chinese company and the U.S. had no jurisdiction there.

Sorry, Yanks.

That was his story, love it or leave it.

But it wasn't the consul general who stopped by.

The doorbell rang mid-morning, and when he opened the door, Gavin was surprised to see Shawnee standing there with a plate of cookies.

The blatant attempt at neighborliness to force information out of him was laughable at best. He dearly enjoyed looking into the woman's eyes, but she had him all wrong.

"Mind if I come in?"

He hadn't expected her to be so forward. He glanced at the driveway next door, and there was no car.

"He's at the office."

"On a Sunday?"

"Doing the Lord's work."

So she was the religious type. That gave a new twist to his understanding of her otherwise loose behavior. Did she feel protected by God?

Then she laughed and stepped through the doorway, needling him with an elbow. "I'm just punking you."

She did have a wilier personality than he had expected.

She was already inside, looking around the immaculately clean house and untouched furniture. So he let her in.

Besides, he hadn't had freshly baked chocolate chip in eons.

He began to reach for a cookie, and she turned a shoulder toward him.

The two were caught touching each other, and her eyes shot up to his.

"First things first," she said.

He had no idea what she was up to, but was certain it had nothing to do with cookies.

"Ooh, your pool," she cried, looking out the floor-to-ceiling windows. "It's bigger than ours."

She set the plate down on the foyer table and ran downstairs to the patio door.

Before he could stop her, she had removed her cotton blouse and was dangling it in one hand.

She seemed like some sort of crazed pool rat, and he had no idea what to do with her.

"Do you mind if I try it out?" she asked, turning around, her naked breasts on full display.

Gavin nearly choked on his cookie.

Before he could formulate a response, she was out the door and running toward the water.

"I guess she likes pools," he said under his breath.

He had been reading an article on the ten richest people in the world, but that could wait.

He kicked off his house slippers, threw his sweater over a chair, loosened the top buttons of his shirt, and headed after her.

"Jump in! Jump in!" she chanted.

She was already naked and standing in the middle of the pool, her arms splayed out overhead.

What one did for one's neighbors, he grumbled to himself. But he stopped well short of removing his clothes and throwing himself into the pool.

"Just tell me what you're doing here," he said.

"Come on, sport," she said.

"Enjoy the pool all you want," he said, taking a pool chair. "I'll just sit and watch."

A sly smile crossed her lips, then she turned and dove into deeper water.

Gavin's mind was spinning. Was she drunk? Screwy? How did Patrick deal with her? And was he watching?

His eyes shot up to Shawnee's house. Nobody appeared in the window or on the balcony. Maybe it was just like she said. Patrick wasn't home and she loved pools.

After swimming a few laps with outstanding form, she eased out of the water. By then, Gavin was convinced she was simply an expert swimmer who liked to try out pools.

Until she sat next to him on the hot cushions.

"Ouch," she said, and scooched her bottom off the chair. She stood in front of him, dripping wet, her breasts inches from his face. He saw why she didn't need a swimsuit. She needed nothing to maintain her form, and it only interfered with the sun.

"Okay, Shawnee," he said. "What's all this about?"

She spoke to him in a low voice and ran her fingers through his crewcut. "Patrick wants me to ask you how the party secretary responded."

So that was what this was all about. She was some sort of spy. And a kooky one at that. Did she even know what a party secretary was?

From the moment Gavin had stepped off the airplane in Guangzhou, even in his greatest fantasies, he never anticipated a situation like this.

"Shawnee," he said to her breasts. "I—"

He couldn't let her down.

Besides, she wasn't doing this because she craved his attention or wanted his passion.

But it could be.

"This is going way too fast," he said.

"What is?"

"Er, you and me."

"Poor Patrick," she said, and sat down in his lap. "He only wants to know."

She squeezed out the water from her blonde hair and it dribbled on the grass between her feet.

Gavin didn't know if he should lay a hand on her bare skin to steady her, but suddenly she was off-balance, and he had to grab something.

And that was how he ended up with his hands around her hips.

She flinched slightly, then turned to face him. "Let's make love," she said in a tone that came from deep in her throat. "Then we can talk."

He looked into her green eyes, the almond shapes squinting against the sun. How and where did she have in mind? He was open to suggestions.

But rather than respond to her invitation, he got a firmer grip on her and rose to his feet. They stood facing each other, her hands clasped together against his chest.

"The party secretary said 'no,'" he finally said. "He has 'a duty to preserve public order and protect economic interests.'"

A pout formed on her lips. She was either a superb actor, or she had genuinely looked forward to making love. Gavin didn't want to guess which, just yet.

Finally she raised her eyes to meet his and there was a playful smile on her lips. Then she turned and skipped back up the hill, picked up the clothes she had littered on the patio, and disappeared around the corner of the house.

"Thanks for letting me use your pool!"

Maybe that was what happened to multi-millionaires.

Sunday morning found Matt seated beside Eve in a taxicab.

It was Eve's idea to spend the morning along the Pearl River.

"Zhujiang?" he asked, referring to the river walk preferred by most young lovers.

"No. I'm thinking Haizhu," she said.

So she was going for the traditional, the ancient part of town.

He leaned forward and gave the cab driver the destination.

The taxi swung wide to the west on the elevated tollway and began to approach the old part of the city from the northwest. The overhead expressway carried them over the wide train tracks of Guangzhou West Station and past the tan apartment buildings of west Guangzhou.

The weather was clear for the moment and Matt could see the high green slope and outline of Baiyun Mountain in the middle of the city.

When the ramp finally took them down to river level, they were met by the smell of fresh fish. On the wet pavement of the market, trucks hauled the day's catch out to restaurants and grocery stores. Fresh alligator tails and shark fins would be available by noon.

Eve gave a slight cough that clearly hid a deeper respiratory problem.

Matt had been mildly concerned ever since she had missed the Marine Ball, but attributed it to an abundance of caution.

Yet it hadn't gone away.

"Are you okay?" he asked, prepared to turn the taxi around and head back home.

She said nothing, and her wan smile gave him little confidence.

They were passing Shamian Island, where they had bumped into General Peak and enjoyed six-dollar cups of coffee at Starbucks earlier that week.

The island, once just a sandbar, had been built up for defensive purposes during the Opium Wars by foreigners trying to protect their homes and offices.

Just beyond the island was a huge customs building that overshadowed what had once been a lively scene of boat dwellers, factories, and commerce that had made Guangzhou one of China's busiest and most important trading ports.

The taxi cut inland toward People's Park, the former seat of regional governments and home to emperors for over a thousand years. From under the overpass, he could barely see inside the area, that had been razed by the Nationalists and Communists and turned into an open urban park.

The road quickly directed them onto a bridge that soared over the river. The sky suddenly felt open, the light brighter. They crossed the north branch of the Pearl River onto an island where the river began the final leg of its 1,500-mile journey from far western China and northern Vietnam to the South China Sea.

Back across the river on Shamian Island, he saw the towering White Swan Hotel, aptly named. Though there was nothing graceful about it, it did seem to float on the water.

The leafy urban park on the western point of the Haizhu District had two dozen women practicing synchronized dance to modern music.

"Want to join them?" he asked, remembering how she enjoyed dancing in the forest early in the morning.

She smiled and shook her head.

He peered through the fog and spotted a river cruise ship, a police boat, and a cargo ship like the ones he had seen in Hong Kong.

Two middle-aged men holding rescue buoys swam for exercise in the heavily polluted water.

Matt was reminded of news that morning of two ferries colliding in Hong Kong Harbor, killing dozens. Life could end so quickly.

He looked at Eve, who had stopped walking and was watching a couple play badminton under a banyan tree.

The tranquil scene seemed to put her mind at ease. For the first time, he saw her in a new light. She seemed to possess an old soul. Whereas Matt had many plans for the future, was she clinging to the past?

He reached over to caress her.

The weather wasn't warm, but her forehead was burning hot.

"Do you need to go home?" he asked.

She nodded, her heart too heavy for her to speak.

"Should I hail a cab?"

"Let's walk," she said in a small voice.

So they strolled down old streets on the large island in the middle of the Pearl River.

There were no neighborhoods in the traditional Western sense.

Instead, Matt observed endless shopfronts and shoppers busily bustling in and out of stores, plastic bags in hand. There were few sidewalks, and pedestrians ruled the street. The amalgam of steaming food and damp stonework and the sounds of people hawking and spitting and cheerily talking in loud voices was uniquely Chinese. In a sense, they were venturing deeper into Guangzhou's, and Eve's, past.

At one nondescript corner, she guided him around the bend onto a more sedate street named Jiangnan Avenue. The buildings leaned toward each other over the narrow lane and cast the pavement in shadow. Bright and modern storefront displays made up for the darkness.

Eve shouldered him close to the first window.

An adoring shower of light sent a mannequin's chiffon bridal dress aglitter.

Eve paused to study the display. Two traditional red Chinese wedding dresses hung from displays off to the side. But it was clearly the modern American bridal dress that had caught her eye.

The juxtaposition of Western ideals with the clinging tropical air of China were hard for Matt to reconcile.

But Eve soaked it up. Her eyes were as big as the mannequin's, and twice as bright. She seemed like a trapped creature, caught between two worlds.

"Let's move on," he said.

"Okay."

The next shop also had three wedding dresses on display, these all Western. The designs seemed interchangeable with the last store.

Down the rest of the street, all the stores were boutique bridal shops.

Had Eve taken him down that road on purpose?

He studied her more closely as she reached toward a small rack with a stack of free wedding magazines. From the rapture on her face as she took a magazine and flipped through the pages, he could tell that she was totally sold on the concept of a Western wedding.

Was this just Eve being herself, or was she trying to tell him something?

Either way, one thing gave him hope. She wasn't entirely a creature of the past.

And then she collapsed in his arms.

"Eve!"

He caught hold of her by the shoulders before she hit the pavement. "What's wrong?"

The smile was still on her lips as her eyes fluttered closed.

"*Chuzu che!*" he yelled. "Taxi!" He hoped his voice would carry to the nearest road.

"Do you need a doctor?" he asked her.

"I'm fine," she said, her voice weak. "I just need some sleep."

One of the green cabs pulled up to the end of the alley.

Desperate, he tried to move her there, but her legs were sluggish. He ended up half-carrying her to the end of the street, afraid that the cabbie wouldn't wait for them if she looked ill.

It was a struggle, but he got her into the back seat of the cab and circled around to get in the other door.

"Take us to Nanfang Hospital," he said.

Nils Andersson had been sorely disappointed by word from his big boss, the director of the World Health Organization.

Despite intense media pressure from around the world and his argument about a possible biological terrorism component to the epidemic, she had remained unmoved. As long as China refused to request a WHO medical team, none would be provided.

So he did all that he could do. He studied the world map on his screen. Initial cases, represented by red dots, had been recorded in major population centers around the world, mostly those that had direct flights from Guangzhou. In the Western Hemisphere, there was a handful of cases in Vancouver and even more in Los Angeles and New York. In the Eastern Hemisphere, red dots appeared in Tokyo, Hong Kong, Hanoi, and Sydney. These were his index cases, the first arrivals of the disease to their countries.

Then he overlaid the red dots with green dots, and the clusters grew larger and spread to further cities. Clearly the disease continued to be transmitted at a horrific rate.

Scientists from several laboratories had looked at antigens found in the blood of the victims, both living and deceased. They all came back with the same results. There was no evidence of anthrax, ricin, or other toxins.

But the level of antigens was astounding. Clinical observations of patients showed sudden fluid buildup in the lungs that led to a lack of oxygen transfer to the blood, leading to rapid decline in health and, in well over fifty percent of the cases, death.

The number of deaths in America alone stood at 329. All told, there were 12,317 deaths linked to the disease worldwide. From China, there were no official figures.

In the few cases where victims pulled through, it was because of heroic methods of direct blood transfusions of oxygenated blood and other techniques that pumped the fluid out of the lungs and cleared the tiny sacs where oxygen transfer took place.

A small percentage of patients, however, had shown a better natural response to the infections and were able to pull through on their own after days of hacking coughs and high fevers.

From hospital tests in several cities around the world, doctors had found a culprit. It appeared to be H5N1 bird flu.

Nils pulled up the map of the red swath across Guangzhou. All the cases had occurred at the same time, and the pattern clearly indicated dispersal by wind. Toxins could be carried by the wind, but could the H5N1 virus?

Air transmission of the flu virus depended upon droplets that contained the virus. Aerosolized particles could be of different sizes. The largest droplets fell to the ground within a meter. The smaller droplet nuclei, perhaps 1-4 microns in diameter, could remain suspended in the air for a long time, travel long distances through the atmosphere, and reach all the way to one's lower respiratory tract.

Nils leaned toward diagnosing a new, mongrelized form of influenza that the medical community had never seen before. But investigators sometimes jumped to conclusions.

He had to get more data.

So once again, he reached for the phone to call the director of the WHO. But this time he wanted to go around Chinese authorities. What the organization needed was the most intense political pressure they could put on China's secretive leaders.

The WHO had a weapon in their arsenal to move governments that they rarely used.

But this time, they must.

CHAPTER 4

Pandemic

Gavin Peak had renewed respect for Zhou that Monday morning as he stood by her side watching product move out of their warehouse.

Her head was screwed on straight, whereas Shawnee…

For a moment, he pitied her husband, Patrick. But to each his own.

Gavin turned his attention back to the operation at hand. The vials of vaccine were packed in cardboard boxes that workmen struggled to carry out of the chilly storage unit and onto waiting trucks.

The vaccine wouldn't last long unrefrigerated. He hoped the trucks didn't have to travel far, because they were not climate controlled and the day was already sweltering hot.

"Where are they going first?" he asked.

"Dongshan," Zhou said.

The name didn't ring a bell.

She must have read the confusion on his face. "It's the military and Communist Party housing area in the city."

Gavin had wondered what lottery system the Chinese would use to determine who got vaccinated first. Now he knew. The Communist Party won the lottery every time.

In any event, his product was on the street, and demand was high.

The Canton Fair was a two-week event, with booths switching over the weekend from hard goods to soft goods. It should have been an exciting time, but Matt's heart wasn't in it.

Wearing his white-colored visitor's badge on a lanyard, he wandered aimlessly through the professional displays set up by each company that wanted to play a major role in their industry.

The lighting was warm, the carpeting inviting, and the Chinese salesmen and saleswomen at their most appealing, calculators in hand, contracts ready to sign.

The radios were high tech, the toilet seats were brilliantly painted, the exotic lamps made of rubber and rock. He saw cars on spinning platforms, farm machinery idling, and an entire exhibition hall just for motorcycles. He checked out the saws and shovels that might soon appear at the local hardware store. There were colorful vases of bath salts and a hundred different kinds of fake stones to clad the exterior of his house. If he had a house.

It felt like the entire world was for sale and vying for his attention.

Along the way, he eavesdropped on conversations. Was the producer price index too high, causing manufacturing costs to push prices up? Were companies that operated on razor-thin margins able to find ways to increase prices without losing their prime customers?

Matt would, after all, have to write a report.

The easy laughter of last year's fair had been replaced by frayed nerves, over-the-shoulder glances at competitors' booths, and hushed phone calls back to headquarters.

He saw ink flowing, but haltingly.

A middle-aged Chinese man approached him, so they talked. His display looked just like an Ace Hardware store. The guy's company specialized in wooden ladders, and all his models lined a wall, ready to test. But Matt wasn't there to test products, only to learn about the market.

He slyly turned on his phone's voice recorder as the man spoke in polished English.

"I had a factory of two hundred people last year. This year, I let half of them go. Then I had to lower their wages. The Chinese yuan is coming down, so the cost of importing raw materials is way up. Then, my main buyers are holding off because their markets are weak."

"Who buys your products?"

"America, Mexico, the Middle East, and Africa." The guy shook his head gloomily. "I combine contracts to raise the bulk, and still there's no room to negotiate. I have a son at UC Santa Barbara. I'm not sure how I'll pay for his spring semester."

Just then the man spotted a buyer from Bahrain that he recognized, and rushed over to shake hands.

Matt left the two to correct the international trade imbalance.

He jockeyed back into the stream of 180,000 mostly foreign visitors carefully guarding their checkbooks. He only had 24,999 more exhibits to see, not to mention all the meetings and forums due to take place that day.

How could he condense all that he saw before him into a single economic report for the U.S. Government?

It was shaping up to be one busy week.

And then his phone rang.

It was Nils Andersson calling from Geneva.

"Good morning, Switzerland."

"Is it morning? I haven't slept in days." Nils sounded all business. "What's up?"

"Matthew, are you near other people?"

Matt was looking at a good five football stadiums worth of people from all over the world all under one roof. "Yeah. Why?"

"We have a raging epidemic on our hands."

Matt was aware of the World Health Organization's latest attempts to probe the city with a team of bureaucrats from Beijing masquerading as disease detectives.

The Swedish doctor explained. "This appears to be an influenza virus. And it's more virulent than we thought."

"So this is just the flu?"

"The WHO Director-General just held a press conference. She believes that from samples of patients taken around the world, this is all the same pathogen, an H5N1 influenza strain that has never been seen before. She has just given the new disease a name. It's called Highly Pathogenic Pneumonia Virus. HPP, for short."

"Just how bad is it?"

"At least fifty percent of the city you live in will catch the disease."

Matt looked with different eyes at the foreigners sniffing around the exhibits.

Nils hesitated, as if for effect. "And half of them will die."

Matt's thoughts naturally turned to Eve. He had to get her out of the hospital where other patients could infect her with the deadly virus.

"I have a friend in the hospital," he whispered. "I have to get her out of the city."

"Nowhere is safe," Nils responded in his deep, accented voice. "According to International Health Regulations, this constitutes a PHEIC, a Public Health Emergency of International Concern. The WHO has declared it a worldwide health threat. Since it has spread beyond the Western Pacific Region, it is now a full-blown pandemic."

"So what can we do to stop it?"

"The good news is that pressure from Geneva has worked. The WHO just got the green light from China's Ministry of Health. I'm coming to Guangzhou today."

"You're crazy. You're the only person I know who wants to come here. My guess is that everyone else will try to leave."

"There's no way to leave," Nils said in his matter-of-fact voice. "The WHO has just issued an emergency travel advisory. All flights out of China are effectively banned."

Frantic, Matt called the consulate driver.

He had a million things to do, all at once. He had to get away from the public. He had to get word to the consul general. And he had to yank Eve out of the hospital.

"Where are you?" the driver asked over the phone.

Matt looked around in bewilderment. He had no idea where he was.

Panic suddenly took hold and he broke out in a sweat. Was he near the river? He hadn't been paying attention to his location and had no visual map in mind.

He flagged down the first person to pass him, a young woman in Indian or Pakistani dress.

He handed her his phone. "Can you tell my driver where we are?"

Calmly, and with great command, she told his driver the nearest entrance to the fair.

"Simply stand over there," the woman told Matt, and pointed at a nearby doorway. "He'll come along soon."

Matt wanted to thank her by telling her to leave the city with all deliberate speed. But, instead, he mumbled an embarrassed thanks, wiped off the phone, and ran for the door.

Just as arranged, the sedan pulled up to the pavilion, and Matt jumped in.

"Take me to Nanfang Hospital," he said.

Behind him, a long line of recently registered visitors swarmed into the Canton Fair.

"Don't go in!" he wanted to scream.

But with other countries' borders effectively closed by the WHO, where could they go?

He had to share news of the WHO press conference with the

consulate.

It took little effort to get through on an emergency basis to the consul general.

Patrick Kind detected the urgency in Matt's voice at once.

"Calm down, young man, and speak in complete sentences."

Matt took a moment to compose his thoughts. "I just got a call from Nils Andersson with the WHO in Geneva. The WHO Director-General just made a major announcement at a press conference. This outbreak is far worse than we discussed this morning."

"Go on."

"What's affecting this country and others is a new influenza virus that has never been seen before. The Director-General has given it a name. It's now called HPP, which stands for Highly Pathogenic Pneumonia Virus. And the worst thing is, they predict a fifty-percent probability of death for anyone who catches it."

He paused a moment to consider what that meant for Eve's prognosis. She was strong. She was healthy. And hadn't she taken the vaccine?

"I've already approved two medical evacuations this week," the consul general said.

"Well, Nils just informed me that the WHO Director-General has declared this a worldwide health threat and issued an emergency travel advisory, effectively banning all travel out of China."

He waited for the consul general to react, but was put on hold.

Classical music played over the phone while the consulate car crossed the Pearl River into the heart of Guangzhou's New Town.

Eventually Patrick Kind came back on.

"I just got word," he said. "The State Department has issued a travel warning for China and an evacuation order for all nonessential personnel."

"Well, it's a little late for that."

"They'll try to arrange military flights to pick up consulate personnel."

Matt was right. Everyone was trying to evacuate the country.

"How in the world did this get so bad so fast?"

Matt could tell from the consul general's steady voice that he wasn't speaking out of exasperation. He wanted to know what Matt knew. Matt had become the consulate's point man for a raging pandemic.

"I wish I knew. But Dr. Nils Andersson at the WHO just got China's permission to fly in to Guangzhou. He's coming here immediately."

"I have a wife to take care of," Patrick said. "I may be gone."

"Don't worry, sir. I'll stay put and run this thing down if it kills me."

"Young man. Keep your eye on the ball, and work the problem. We'll beat this."

Matt hung up more determined than ever to help contain the outbreak. Even the Chinese finally recognized the need to end its secrecy. This was a time bomb that could explode in every city in the country, and every country of the world.

He already saw signs around him.

Starting from south of downtown Guangzhou, they had to drive to the far north of the city to get to Nanfang Hospital.

The traffic wasn't just awful. It was at a near standstill. It looked like every car in the city was on the road. They filled all lanes heading in the same direction. And he knew why. The entire city's population was leaving town.

His attention turned to Eve. Like the city's collapse into panic, his thoughts about her were overrun by fear.

She *had* taken the vaccine at Orchid Mountain, hadn't she?

The traffic was going nowhere.

He picked up his phone and jabbed in the number of Orchid Mountain.

"Get me the nurse, please," he requested as calmly as he could.

"*Wei?*"

"This is Matthew Justice, one of your tenants."

"Hello, Matt."

"I'm calling to ask you about the vaccine you administered ten days ago."

"Yes. We have run out of doses. I'm sorry, we can't–"

"It's not about more doses. I'm wondering if Eve Yang got her shot."

"Our Eve?"

"Yes."

"No. She refused to take her vaccine."

The phone nearly slipped out of Matt's hand.

"You mean she never got the vaccine?"

"Not from us."

Matt was about to hang up in frustration when a thought struck him. Maybe he could go to the source.

"Who produced that vaccine?"

"I already told you. I don't know the company."

"Fine. I remember you told me that. But let's work backwards. Who told you that the medicine was coming to Orchid Mountain?"

"I got a call from a Chinese man. He said he was sending over a box of vaccines and that we should administer them to the tenants and employees of Orchid Mountain."

"Do you know who he was?"

"I never met him before. I have to–"

"Wait. Who delivered the vaccines?"

"It came in a truck."

"A truck? Can you describe the truck?"

"No. It was a bus."

"What kind of bus?"

"Not a city bus. One of those minibuses. I remember now. It was blue and green."

"Did it have any identifying marks on it?"

"I suppose it had a name…"

"Think hard."

After several seconds, the nurse said, "I have to go now," and hung up.

Matt was left shivering in the car's air conditioning.

Eve had not taken the vaccine, and he had no way of finding out where to get some for her.

Then the whole logic of the situation hit home. She was sick. It was too late for a vaccine.

The slow crawl through all the landmarks of the city seemed to take forever. At times, Matt simply wanted to get out of the consulate car and begin running. But then the traffic would clear for a short distance and the car would spurt ahead.

At long last, the car reached Nanfang Hospital.

Matt got out and advanced on foot toward the imposing white building. Sleek, black cars with the word "POLICE" in big, bold letters ringed the hospital.

He jogged around to the emergency room where he had brought Eve the day before. He remembered bitterly that security guards had forced him to let her go as medics took her into the building. Now policemen were posted at the emergency room door, and they were giving him the eye.

So the government was shutting down access to hospitals.

He circled the perimeter of the building where Eve had been swallowed up.

Policemen stood at every door.

Matt considered rushing one of the young men in uniform and pushing him out of the way so that he could run up the stairs and get to the isolation ward. But there would be policemen inside, and he wasn't even sure that Eve was at the isolation ward.

He ended up leaning against the concrete railing of a bridge that arched over a small pond. He pulled out his phone.

She hadn't answered all day, but maybe she would now.

He scrolled through the long alphabetical list. Nobody meant anything to him now. Until he got to her name, buried deep in the Xies and Yangs and Zhangs.

"Eve, please pick up." He nearly prayed into the phone.

There was that horribly funky music as he waited for her to pick up.

There was no announcement that her number was unavailable. No voice told him that all lines were busy. There was simply that old, empty music.

He hung up and turned to face the windows of the hospital. All he saw was gray sky reflected back at him.

And then, against all reason, he raised a hand over his head and began to wave.

He waved so that she could see him, and exposed his face to the full view of the hospital windows.

"Eve!" he called out. "Can you see me?"

Eventually, a young guard gently escorted him off the hospital grounds.

Early Monday morning, Gavin Peak received a call from Vincent Fong. As he listened in the darkness, with Zhou's legs wrapped around him, the urgency in Vincent's voice began to register.

"General, the Chinese Army is at our headquarters."

What the hell? Gavin jumped out of bed. The shit had finally hit the fan.

"Okay," he told his chief operating officer. "Calm down and tell me exactly what happened."

He switched on his bed lamp and checked his watch. It was 5:00 a.m.

Zhou was now awake and scrutinizing him as she lay in the four-poster bed.

"The situation is this," Vincent began again. "Chinese paramilitary forces are at our front gate. They are in full battle gear. Their guns are drawn. And their tanks, water cannon, and mounted machine guns are pointing everywhere. What should we do?"

"Well, why are they there?"

"We don't know at this time."

"Then find out and call me back," Gavin thundered, and slammed down the phone. Was the army there under Mr. Pu's orders to take over the company?

He rubbed his temples to forestall a headache.

Zhou pulled him back onto the bed. "What is it?"

"Don't worry. You can go back to sleep."

She remained silent, but didn't move to a more comfortable position.

"What is it?" he said, irritated.

"Tell me what happened."

He explained as patiently as he could that there were military forces at the headquarters gate. "I need to get dressed and head over there and sort things out."

"Before you do that," she said, reaching for her phone, "let me find out more details."

He watched his chief financial officer dial a pre-programmed number and confer with someone on the other end.

Zhou sounded like a totally different person when she spoke Chinese. She ceased to be the sweet, willing bedtime companion and turned into a shrill, demanding dragon lady.

After a minute of brutal conversation, she put her phone away and gave him a reassuring smile. "It's nothing."

"Who did you call?" he demanded to know.

"A source," she said cryptically. "You don't want to know."

Gavin began to wonder who she was really working for. But she was on his payroll, damn it, and she should be up-front with him. God, he hated things going on behind his back.

"You need to stay put," she said, sitting up and rubbing his shoulders.

"I'm the CEO, and I'm heading to the office."

"No. I recommend you don't go anywhere today." Like her hands, her voice was soft, yet firm.

"Why not?"

"Trust me," she said, her voice now a whisper. "There is no urgency, and you need your rest."

"Yeah. You just want me back in bed."

"I'll keep you busy," she said, luring him to relax with one of her fondling techniques.

"Well, I am waiting to hear back..."

It wasn't until 10:00 a.m. that the phone rang again and Gavin got more news from the office.

It was Dr. Chen who had arrived on the scene. "Not to worry, sir. I talked it over with the army commander. They're simply here to set up barricades, protect the facility, and pick up vaccines."

"Why the need for protection?"

"Haven't you heard the news?"

Gavin sat up in bed and disentangled himself from an aggressive Zhou.

"What news?"

"Turn on the television."

Gavin finally shrugged off his lover and stood up in the middle of the bedroom, sunlight beating against the curtains.

He found the television remote and turned on CNN.

There was a massive "Breaking News" headline with urgent music, then a stiff-faced anchor from Hong Kong delivering the word.

"A stark new warning from the World Health Organization. The UN body discovering a new virus, named Highly Pathogenic Pneumonia, responsible for the deaths of nearly a thousand victims, mostly within China. The organism believed to have originated in the city of Guangzhou in southern China. It has spread across China and the surrounding region, cases now appearing around the world. It is currently responsible for the deaths of eleven Canadians, five Americans, nearly thirty citizens of Hong Kong and elsewhere in Southeast Asia. This HPP virus, its abbreviation, highly contagious and lethal. The WHO advising everyone in affected areas to stay home, to avoid public places and to wash their hands frequently. A direct quote from the World Health Organization: 'If you know an affected person, do not go near them or touch them. Notify local public health officials immediately.' In addition, the WHO recommending a complete travel ban to and from China until the disease is brought under control. All citizens advised to shelter in place."

Gavin jumped back to the phone. Dr. Chen was still there.

"Looks like television is doing all the advertising we need," Gavin said. "Is Vincent able to keep up production?"

"He is. And it helps that the People's Liberation Army is here to safely distribute the vaccine for us."

"So, should I come in to the office today or not?"

"Well, there is one wrinkle."

"I don't like the sound of that."

"The Chinese national Ministry of Health," Chen said, "has overridden Guangdong local rule and invited the WHO to come into the country and begin epidemiological investigations."

Gavin reminded himself how dangerous such an investigation might be. True, the WHO had identified the new virus, and damn them, got to name it, but sending in detectives to find the source of the outbreak threatened to expose FutureGenetics' initial contamination leak.

"You've got our story straight?" Gavin asked his chief scientist.

"As we discussed."

"Then stick with it. You discovered the virus. You made a vaccine. We're the heroes in all of this."

"Still, with all due respect, I suggest this might be a good time to lie low."

With Gavin's neighbor breathing down his neck, sending his wife over to seduce him, World Health Organization investigators waltzing into town, and military at the gates, "lying low" made for sound advice.

"Or I could take a brief vacation to, say, Bali."

"I'm afraid Indonesia won't accept flights from China."

Damn that travel ban.

Then Gavin remembered the open invitation to the golf resort in Hainan. Hadn't he been offered a private jet? An under-the-radar trip to Hainan suddenly seemed like a smart move.

He muttered into the phone, "Send Billy to pick us up."

"Us?"

"Yes. Zhou and me."

"Uh, I'm sorry. That won't work."

"Why not?"

"Billy isn't feeling well."

"Shit. Then how can we get to the airport this time of day?"

"You're in luck. Our minibus is delivering vaccines in your vicinity right now. I can get it to your door in five minutes."

"Thanks, man."

Before he asked Zhou to pack up, Gavin had to make sure there was a plane.

He dug out the business card of one Harold Priest.

"Send a plane?" Harold said, his voice full of glee. "It's already at the Guangzhou airport. When can you come by and hitch a ride?"

"Now would be a good time."

"That's grand. Go straight to the Private Charters desk. I can't wait to see you at our resort!"

Gavin turned to Zhou. "Honey? Pack your bags. We're flying to Hainan."

Matt Justice wandered in a daze from the hospital into the congested neighborhood known as Tonghe. He was looking for his driver when a small bus streaked his way at high speed.

He jumped onto the sidewalk just in time to avoid getting nailed. Still glaring at it, he noticed the name on the side of the bus.

The blue and green lettering formed the logo of FutureGenetics.

The colors triggered a memory. It was the minibus that the nurse had spotted when it delivered vaccines to Orchid Mountain!

Sitting in the bus was a young Chinese woman and none other than the president of that company, General Gavin Peak.

It didn't take long for Matt to put the pieces together. What he was looking at was arrogance and a callous disregard for human life. And he wasn't merely thinking about the reckless driver.

General Peak must have known about the virus long before anybody else did. Patrick Kind had informed the country team that Peak was wearing a Band-Aid at his pool party yet denied knowing anything about the disease. And Peak had denied any involvement to Matt on Shamian Island. But Peak's company had delivered the vaccine long before it was available on the open market. Peak had also denied that his company had sent a worker to the isolation ward at Nanfang Hospital. Additionally, he hadn't identified the disease to the hospital. And he had preferred to drag his feet rather than ask the party secretary to formally invite the WHO to investigate.

The man sitting in that minibus was weeks if not months ahead of the public health community in knowing about the disease.

And to whose benefit? Since they had their hands on a virus long before the competition, FutureGenetics had a head start on creating a vaccine. After the onset of the pandemic, the company stood to rake in billions of dollars from sales of the vaccine.

Which got Matt thinking about the epidemic itself. As Nils Andersson had told him that morning, the virus had "never been seen before."

FutureGenetics was a biotech firm with the capability of isolating and genetically altering viruses. Had they created the beast? And if so, had they released it into the world to create a demand for their product?

Matt thought so, as he pounded down the street in search of a taxi to follow that bus.

His company hiding the existence of the virus to the public had enabled the disease to spread, thus increasing public fear and spurring higher demand. Clearly, General Peak was guilty, at the very least, of having caused the deaths of thousands of people.

What Matt was looking at sitting smugly in the cool, modern bus was not an American hero who rescued people on airplanes. He was the CEO of a company that perpetrated the biggest fraud the public had ever seen.

General Peak may well be responsible for Eve collapsing in his arms.

The scheme was breathtaking in scope.

And wrong.

It was hard to keep the minibus in sight as it zigzagged without regard for human life through the heavily populated neighborhood.

But Matt Justice was in hot pursuit.

Gavin Peak stared out the window at the neighborhood. The minibus was taking Zhou and him through one more of those narrow alleyways that he had come to know on his walk up to Eve's house.

Only today, they were heading for the airport. For some reason, the main highway had become a parking lot, so they were taking the scenic route.

For the first time, he noticed that white surgical masks had blossomed across the city like mushrooms after rain. He should have been in the mask business, too.

He was confident that Vincent and Chen could run the operation in the meanwhile and find some excuse for his absence. Even though the WHO had a proven record for always tracking diseases down, he was sure that Chen's story would safeguard the company.

What worried him most was the Ministry of Health. The apparatchiks in Beijing had pulled rank on the Guangdong authorities to let investigators in. Mr. Pu's protection was crumbling. What else would the national party do?

Demonize him and nationalize his business?

Just in case, he needed an escape plan, and sneaking off undetected to Hainan was a safe move, for the sake of his company.

He had use of a private jet. If things got truly dicey, maybe he could get Harold Priest to let Zhou and him enjoy its use to, say, visit another country.

After winding through several back streets of the new, but cluttered part of town, the FutureGenetics minibus came to a screeching halt at a small, anonymous intersection.

Gavin looked out the windshield and saw why they had stopped. The road ahead was clogged with vehicles.

With nowhere to go, the bus driver had an idea.

If they walked fifty meters down that road, they would get to the Tonghe metro station, and there they could take the subway to the airport.

Gavin hadn't taken a subway in years and was reluctant to try one now, but he had little choice.

He and Zhou grabbed their suitcases and headed out for the metro station.

He had read that Guangzhou's metro system was world-class, but the smell of urine that immediately greeted him on the street was not encouraging. Soon that smell melded seamlessly into food smells as the roadside became crammed with restaurants, presumably there to feed hungry commuters on their way to and from work.

The gathering throng of panicked individuals and families began to climb a flight of stairs. He thought that subways were underground, but nothing surprised him anymore.

"Gavin Peak!" he heard a man shout behind him.

The accent was American. But who had seen him?

"Wait a second!" it came again. Then the man yelled something in Chinese.

A wave of voices swept toward them through the crowd.

"Keep moving," Gavin told Zhou. "Someone's after us."

Thanks to her thrusting her suitcase into people, they made headway in the crowd.

Gavin glanced back from the top of the stairs and saw a sea of bobbing heads.

One man with a mass of red hair stood out. The young man caught his eye. It was the fellow from Shamian Island, Eve's friend from the American consulate. What was his name?

Oh, yes. Matt Justice.

Gavin picked up his pace and hurled his weight and the hefty suitcase against the wall of bodies in front of him.

The steps immediately changed direction and led down six long flights. Daylight disappeared and was gradually replaced by fluorescent light.

Ahead, he heard the clunking of turnstiles and the murmur of hundreds of people. If Guangzhou had an efficient metro system, that didn't mean it was spacious and suitable for meditation. It was the busiest train station Gavin had ever seen in his life.

Policemen dashed all over the place, trying to create order out of chaos.

Gavin and Zhou stood in line waiting for access to a computerized ticket machine.

Once there, Zhou touched the screen for their destination: Guangzhou Baiyun International Airport. She pressed the "2" symbol for two tokens.

"Sixteen yuan?" she said, offended. "It costs only thirty to take a cab."

"Just pay it," Gavin said, checking over his shoulder. He had no time for his chief financial officer to try and save money.

She handed him one of the tokens, which was a plastic disk with raised writing on one side. How did it work?

He had no time to find out.

The American was screaming his name as he entered the crowded station, but Gavin couldn't stop and chat.

Policemen stood at each turnstile, ensuring a smooth flow of passengers onto the subway platforms.

People streamed through the gates ahead of Gavin, flashing ID cards. But he saw and heard no tokens dropping.

It was his turn and he tried to jab his token into a small square screen. There was no slot.

So he switched to the turnstile that Zhou had just passed through, but the gate closed on him.

The policeman frowned at him.

"There's no slot," he complained.

"Just swipe it," Zhou called back.

He looked over, and his old turnstile was standing open. The plastic disk must be a magnetic ticket, not a token.

He ran back to the turnstile and scooted through before the next person came up from behind.

He looked around to get his bearings. All the signs and announcements were in Chinese and English. Which was nice, as long as the passenger knew the name of the end station and the station where they intended to get off.

He relied on Zhou to take him to the right platform.

"Let's stay away from that guy," Gavin said, pointing over his shoulder.

So Zhou grabbed him by the arm and dragged him through the crowd to the far end of the platform.

A Washington Metro-style train came zipping up. He and Zhou stood on arrows behind the sliding doors and waited for the train to come to a stop.

People burst out and they fought their way in. It was not even rush hour, but the system seemed overcrowded. The majority wore facemasks that muffled their voices, but didn't hide the panic in their eyes. Where was everyone going?

Gavin and Zhou were finally on Line 3, but he could tell from the flashing dots on the map that it wouldn't take them all the way to the airport.

They made way for passengers to come and go around them as they stood by the door, ready to jump out when it was their turn.

People were nervously conversing with each other despite the strangers all around. The car was brightly lit with a television screen quietly flashing advertisements.

The train reached its terminus and they had to get off. He could barely hear Zhou's voice above the crowd, but he heard the words "Turn right."

They exited out the right door and everyone pushed across the platform to another waiting area with more arrows on the floor.

A young man in a yellow jacket barked out orders for more people to squeeze into the waiting train.

Despite their best efforts to get people out of the way, Gavin and Zhou missed the first train. But they were well positioned to catch the next.

This one was newer, with plastic hand straps hanging from the ceiling. Gavin needed one to keep his balance in the crush of people.

One stop later, they got off.

It was the airport.

Matthew Justice raced into the airport terminal and looked around.

With international flights listed as "Cancelled" on the Departures board, many would-be international travelers clogged the terminal, wondering what to do.

Check-in lines for domestic flights were brimming with anxious-looking travelers.

General Peak was nowhere in sight.

Matt checked his wallet. He still had his credit card and residence permit. He could purchase a ticket and follow General Peak wherever he went.

He pulled out his phone and called the consulate.

This time, it took longer to reach Patrick Kind, but soon the two were talking.

"I've followed General Peak to the airport. I believe he's trying to flee the country."

"Good luck with that," Patrick Kind said. "With this international travel ban, I can't even get nonessential personnel home."

"I'm going to track him down and turn him over to the Chinese authorities."

"Young man, if you find him, do not apprehend him. He might be on legitimate business."

"Legitimate business? I think his company knew about the

outbreak long before it happened. And they told nobody."

"That's a strong accusation. How can you back it up?"

"It was FutureGenetics that distributed the vaccines to Orchid Mountain. They knew about the outbreak before the government announced it."

"So that's where the vaccine came from."

"And probably where the outbreak began. The WHO has narrowed the source down to Science City, where FutureGenetics does their research."

"Are you implying that Gavin's company *caused* the outbreak?"

"Yeah. And now that there's a panic, they're profiting from it."

"So that's why Gavin didn't help get WHO investigators on the ground. I tried everything to get him to persuade the party secretary. Gavin was our intermediary, and he failed to get their approval. I even sent my wife... Never mind. Maybe he was trying to fend off investigators."

"Wait! I see him at the counter with the red carpet."

"That's for private jets."

"Sir, I'm going after him."

"If you do, remember that his company is distributing the vaccines. Do you really want to stop that process?"

Matt started pushing through the crowd. "He's a villain, sir. Plain and simple. There's no getting away with this."

"Listen," Patrick Kind said. "We need that vaccine. The consulate is hunkering down and trying to acquire doses."

"Don't count on getting any of it," Matt said.

"If you catch him, remember to keep the vaccine on the market."

"You're assuming the vaccine even works."

"What are you suggesting?" Patrick Kind said.

"Was it even tested? What if he's a quack?"

"Oh, my God. I'm calling the WHO right now."

General Peak and his stunning travel companion had just jumped onto a golf cart and were speeding away.

"It looks like I'm flying commercial," Matt said.

"Where to?"

"I'll have to find out."

"Good luck," Patrick said.

Matt began walking briskly after the cart.

"On my end," his boss said over the phone, "I'll develop a legal case against Peak. After all, people are dying on American soil."

"Get the FBI or Interpol involved."

"I will," his boss said. "If you find him, get him somewhere where we have jurisdiction and can interrogate him."

Matt hung up. Interrogate him…or worse.

With Zhou's help, Gavin found the check-in process for private jets quite easy.

Red carpet treatment began just inside the terminal doors. Literally, a red carpet was laid out there, as well as at check-in and, as he would soon find out, at the security line, VIP Club, and at the gate. It was like walking on rose petals.

"Would you like to take a golf cart to the waiting area?" the pert young customer service agent asked.

Gavin took one look at the overcrowded passenger terminal. A golf cart had already pulled up behind them.

He and Zhou seated themselves, their legs hanging off the back of the cart.

As the cart silently gathered speed, he watched passengers trip over luggage and reel in their wake. Meanwhile a tall, young lady in a tight red dress raced after them pulling their bags.

Behind her, the consulate man with the carrot top pulled into view.

Gavin gave him a friendly wave, but had a plane to catch.

Matt Justice watched the golf cart zip away down the terminal.

Was that General Peak waving at him?

There was no way Matt could catch up with the cart. He'd lose it quickly in the overcrowded terminal.

How could he find out where General Peak was headed? He looked back and saw the red carpet in front of the check-in counter.

Above the carpet read, "Private Charters."

"Excuse me, ma'am. Can you tell me where that couple is headed?"

The petite young check-in officer looked up at him. "They are taking a private jet, sir."

"Where to?"

The agent reviewed her records, sifted through some tickets, and came up with an answer.

"Haikou," she said with a sweet smile.

So the villain was fleeing the mainland, heading off to a tropical island destination.

Matt leaned forward as calmly as he could despite his rapidly beating heart. "How can I take the next flight to Haikou?"

The young woman checked her computer. "There's a Hainan Airlines flight leaving in thirty minutes."

"For Haikou?"

"That's correct."

Matt whirled around and looked through the flood of travelers for the check-in line for Hainan Airlines.

The golf cart pulled Gavin and Zhou around to one side of the terminal and stopped.

Half a minute later, the woman in the tight red dress came crashing to a halt with their luggage.

A baggage handler took the suitcases and led Gavin and Zhou to a secluded room. There, big square chairs were spread around evenly on a plush red carpet. The room was illuminated by tall windows that peered out onto a small garden

"This is the VIP lounge," Zhou explained.

"I don't need a lounge," Gavin said. "Can't we just go?"

"They have to handle our passports and paperwork."

"Yeah, about the passports. Why do we need passports to fly within China?"

"It's just a formality. I think they need to make a copy and use the photo for identification."

Gavin hadn't liked surrendering his passport at the check-in counter, and he wanted it back now.

Just then a bright flash of lightning illuminated every corner of the room. Gavin looked at the rain-laden clouds. What a poor choice of days to fly in a small jet plane.

They were served Coke and water and plates of watermelon, oranges and tomatoes.

Time passed and they remained alone with the gleaming woman in red with no luggage or passports.

"It's all being taken care of," Zhou tried to assure him.

Gavin could use a real meal, but they weren't allowed into the terminal.

Then with a clap of thunder, the clouds burst open. Rain washed down the tall windows in hypnotizing patterns.

The wait was preying on his nerves. "Do you think they're calling the police?"

Zhou seemed to take it as sarcasm. "Don't worry."

Gavin decided he was going to continue to worry until they were safely in Hainan at Harold Priest's golf resort.

Eventually, they were given back their passports and led to a private security gate where a female officer stood up, took their documents with two hands and bowed.

Gavin had brought a plastic water bottle in his bag and the guards sternly asked him to remove it.

Gavin quickly reached for the offending bottle and handed it over to the security officer.

The man looked at it closely, then cracked a smile and offered it back.

Gavin was not amused. He just wanted to get out of there.

The woman at security declined to wand them and pat them down as they did in every other airport.

Then the woman in red led them to another door.

When she opened it, they were hit by the loud sounds of ground operations mixed with a gust of wet wind.

Gavin shielded his eyes and saw a bus waiting for them several yards away. He'd have to brave the weather.

Such were the inconveniences of private plane travel.

Gavin got wet from the heavy drizzle, and his shoes dampened the red carpet of the bus. He and Zhou sat on red velvet seats facing each other over a glass-topped table. The woman and baggage handler stood the whole way out to the airfield.

Gavin felt like a prisoner.

But instead of being taken to a maximum-security prison, they were driven straight to a Learjet.

Gavin huddled against the rain and mounted the stairs of the plane.

Inside he smelled leather, a scent that always put him at ease.

He wiped rain droplets off his blazer and chose one of the two forward-facing seats.

While the baggage handler took their luggage to a storage

compartment in the rear of the cabin, the woman in red handed out bottles of water and the latest newspaper.

Gavin just hoped they served hot food.

The male flight attendant looked twice at Matt Justice as he took his seat.

Sweating and red-faced from his sprint through the streets of Guangzhou and subsequent dash through the airport on a hot and humid day, Matt had no doubt he looked like a flu victim suffering from a high fever.

But his Western face garnered him a bottle of water and a *China Daily*, the English-language mouthpiece of the Communist Party.

He glanced at the headlines.

It amazed him that the Chinese put all that effort into making up stories, translating them into English, and putting their alternate universe into print each morning just for the occasional foreigner like him.

What didn't amaze him was the lack of real news coverage. Where was the flu epidemic? Where was the travel ban?

Instead, the front-page stories told about health tourism and canceling anniversary events over the Daioyu Islands as a "strong signal" to Tokyo.

He reached for his seatbelt, and immediately had to adjust it. It was set for a much slighter person.

There he sat, his face coated in sweat, in an airplane in the rain in Guangzhou.

Thunder emanated from the generally gray sky. His phone was off. He was slowly losing touch with the outside world.

Through the drizzle, he saw the zigzag face of the Guangzhou airport. Baggage handlers in flip-flops threw suitcases onto his plane's cargo ramp.

He looked around the airfield for a private jet, "tarmac jewelry" as he called such extravagances. But only large commercial airliners occupied that part of the airport.

In the cabin, many last-minute arrivals were still on their phones.

Hokey Chinese flute and piano music played over the PA. It sounded computer-generated, and cycled through the same four songs. But it was comforting for Chinese passengers because it was familiar.

Out of duty, Matt checked the emergency card in the seat pocket in front of him. The plane was an Airbus 319. Not quite a 320.

There was no calming word from the cockpit.

They simply took off.

Gavin and Zhou took the luxuries of the private jet in stride.

Aside from the comfort of the extra-long seats and sidewall speakers, what he appreciated most was the anonymity.

He had left Matt Justice in the dust.

"Just out of curiosity." He turned to Zhou. "Where is Hainan?"

The airplane had individual touch screens that she could pop up. She switched hers on and selected the tracking map.

Gavin saw the whole of China, shaped like a giant hen with its head up and tail feathers out. Just below the hen in the South China Sea was an oval egg.

Zhou pointed at the egg. "That's Hainan Island."

Gavin estimated the distance they would have to travel. In the small jet, it might take several hours.

"And where's New Delhi?"

"Why do you ask?" she said, her eyes taking him in fully.

"I'm thinking about paying a visit to our new acquisition there," he said. "We can apply some of the business practices we learned here."

"Such as…?"

"I heard about a new superbug they're trying to fight off. Maybe we can engineer such a thing ourselves."

Zhou gave him a wicked look.

"In any event, I think it's time to leave China," he said.

"Why do you want to leave?"

She seemed reluctant to leave. It was almost as if he were dragging a truculent child away from home.

"Because I'm not sure we're wanted here any longer. Now, where are the nearest countries?"

Slowly and deliberately, she pointed out Vietnam to the southwest. Then she pointed south to the Philippines.

She fell back in her seat and put the television away.

Apparently, she didn't like the idea of her country not wanting her anymore.

Gavin closed his eyes and pictured what he had left behind. He had only been in China for two weeks, and already he had a pricey vaccine in high demand and the army on his side defending his facility.

With the clarity of distance, he saw that while it was a mess at the moment, the world would be far better off for it. And so would FutureGenetics.

"Gavin," Zhou said, waking him from his daydream. "We slept so late, we forgot our shareholders telephone call."

"Damn it. You're right."

She checked her watch. "I could still set it up."

He looked at the phone mounted on the wall of the airplane.

"Sure. I'll give everyone an update."

It turned out to be midnight in New York, but surprisingly his investors were hanging around waiting for news. The three mystery Chinese investors had also made room in their schedules to listen in.

"Everything is coming up roses," Gavin began his summary of the company's past two weeks. "We've got sales in the tens of millions and we're able to meet demand. At this point, we're beating all expectations."

"Uh, General," came one of the voices from New York. "There's a severe outbreak in many cities around the world. New York has barred all direct flights from China."

"Yes, if you're worrying about my health, don't," Gavin said. "I've already taken the vaccine."

"And you're confident that it will protect you?"

"I'm living proof," he said. "We've been running tests for weeks now, and the vaccine has proven completely effective."

"Tests?" came a more skeptical investor on the West Coast.

"Yes. The Guangdong Department of Health has run clinical trials and given us the green light. In addition to that, we have been monitoring the effectiveness of our vaccine in the general public since the outbreak began, and the results are conclusive. Gentlemen, you have nothing to fear if you buy our vaccine."

"So what are your next plans?"

Gavin sucked in his breath. "At the moment, I'm not in Guangzhou. For the next few days, you'll find me at the Hainan Pro Golf Resort on Hainan Island."

"A well-deserved rest, I'm sure," the first investor said.

There was only loud breathing on the Chinese side.

"In fact, I'll be landing soon, so I must cut this meeting short."

He heard a chorus of bravos and other congratulations, then handed the phone back to Zhou to hang up.

He had been starved for feedback from those who stood the most to gain from his success. And the response was everything he wanted.

A brief look out the window of his descending plane told him they'd be in paradise soon.

Matt Justice woke up as his commercial airliner made its descent into the city of Haikou.

At first it looked like they were going to land on water, then land appeared, and shortly thereafter a runway.

As the landing gear hit the ground, everyone woke up and lurched forward, along with the contents of their respiratory tracts as they cleared their throats.

Haikou was a new city for Matt, and he looked out the window at the grassy field surrounding the runway for signs of what to expect.

He had been to the southern end of the island once. In fact, he had spent the weekend there at the resort outside the city of Sanya with friends from the consulate.

Whereas Sanya was built-up, thanks to a tourist economy based on tropical weather and pristine beaches, Haikou was more of an industrial port. As the closest city to the mainland, it handled all the fruit and vegetables locally produced for the Chinese market.

But he wasn't getting container port vibes. Instead, blue sky dominated the horizon in all directions.

Haikou's airport was large and modern, with a long terminal of gates, and only one other plane parked there.

It was a private jet.

A glossy brown marble floor led Gavin and Zhou to a small line of people waiting behind a railing.

Their hostess was the only one at the end of the line expecting someone.

She greeted them with, "Are you General Peak?"

He looked around. Were there any other General Peaks?

Zhou shook the lady's hand and the two conversed briefly in Mandarin.

Then the woman turned to Gavin. "I'm from the Hainan Pro Golf Resort. Welcome to the island."

She looked like an islander with her pleasant disposition, broad features, long and loose black hair.

She turned away and clumsily used her phone to call for the resort's driver.

A few minutes later, they loaded up their luggage and Gavin and Zhou peeled off in a gray minivan with air conditioning.

But they immediately came to a halt. They were stuck in line behind a blue cab. Two separate parties seemed to be fighting over who got to the cab first.

Gavin's driver, a tall, pudgy man with small, oval glasses and thick lenses, backed up and drove around the stopped cab.

But the maneuver didn't work. He was immediately pulled over by a young man in a green uniform.

Gavin turned away so that the boy-soldier couldn't see, and thus remember, his face.

Flustered, Gavin's driver jumped out to see what the matter was. But the uniformed man stood, legs apart, directly in front of Gavin's minivan.

"I'll have a talk with him," Zhou said, and jumped out, too.

Apparently, the soldier was waiting for the first taxi in line to go first, so Gavin's vehicle must wait.

Then Gavin recognized the man getting into the blue cab. He was lanky with red hair.

Matt Justice had followed them all the way to Hainan.

Gavin had the entire palm tree-dotted island in front of him, an empty airport behind him, and he was prevented from leaving.

Eventually, the boy-soldier headed off to see what was happening with the taxi, and Gavin's driver and Zhou piled in.

They took off at once.

Gavin looked out the back window and saw Matt Justice finally jump into the cab.

"You can drive faster," Gavin said.

Zhou translated, but the driver appeared not to understand Mandarin.

After several wild arm gestures, she got him to pick up speed.

They curved around palms and bushes out of the well-landscaped airport. Ahead, the terrain was as flat as a coral reef.

Gavin estimated that they had a one-minute jump on the blue cab. He couldn't shake Matt Justice in Guangzhou. Was there any way he could elude the guy in Hainan?

They drove past empty fields, some lofty, half-finished apartments, more fields with occasional palm trees, and some densely populated two-story blocks.

"We're entering East Haikou," Zhou said.

Gavin looked for signs of the pandemic.

The tree-lined streets and pedestrian overpasses had a relaxed, mid-day atmosphere. There was light traffic made up of nice new cars waiting politely in line, a motorbike or two where the drivers wore neither helmet nor facemask, and the occasional bicycle sticking to the shady side of the street.

Then they passed out of the city and onto open land.

He looked back. The cab was limping along and had just entered town.

Ahead, he saw the sea beyond a long line of palms.

Suddenly they were traveling along the shoreline, and a few five-star hotels popped up.

Then there it stood: the Hainan Pro Golf Resort.

And standing out front was none other than Gavin's buddy from the American Chamber of Commerce, Harold Priest.

Matthew Justice thought better of pulling into the impressive golf resort that Gavin Peak had entered. Instead, he asked his cabbie to ease past the front gate.

He could stay next door and investigate on foot.

So his blue cab pulled into the neighboring hotel, the Sheraton Resort.

Matt looked around the lobby. The resort hotel was much the same as the Sheraton he had stayed in on the island's southern beach. The white walls and huge round pillars seemed inspired by the colonial style of the Raffles in Singapore.

He was the only one checking in.

The bellhop took him up an elevator and led him through two dark hallways of rooms. Midway down a third corridor that was strewn with housekeeping equipment, they stopped at an anonymous-looking room 3019.

The first thing he needed to do before looking for General Peak was to wash his hands. He had scrupulously avoided touching his heavily sweating face all afternoon, and now, with his hands clean, he would be free to wash his face.

Except the sink was already full of water, and there was no lever to pull up the drain.

He opened the room door and found a young housekeeper. He summoned her into his room. She acted suspicious until he showed her the problem.

Her dark round face suddenly lit up when she understood. She reached a hand into the full sink. There, she pushed down on what apparently was a spring-loaded plug, and the water began to drain.

She smiled at him with a "voila"-like expression. Problem solved.

He decided against closing the drain in the future.

Hungry, he raided the fruit bowl and cookie jar on the coffee table. A dragon fruit, Asian pear, and five cookies later, he was ready to set out and find General Peak.

Gavin Peak's initial impression of a man usually proved accurate. Harold Priest was a vapid groveler and Gavin had little use for him.

Except that Harold had put a private jet and golf resort at his disposal.

As he looked around the place, Gavin was interested, but not surprised, that nobody else was there.

"Designed by Greg Norman, the Great White Shark," Harold said, baring his teeth.

Gavin gave a wan smile.

"General, I'll tee off with you at eight o'clock in the morning," Harold said.

"Fine," Gavin relented. The company would be dreary, but the golf course sounded tolerable.

"I was just wondering if your jet is available to fly to New Delhi."

For the first time, he saw Harold balk.

"I'm afraid my plane doesn't have that kind of range."

Gavin didn't think so, but wondered if it could hop out of the country and refuel on the way.

"I'd like to get out of the country the day after tomorrow. Do you have any suggestions?"

If Harold was disappointed that Gavin's stay would be so short, he didn't show it.

"Might I suggest flying commercially out of Sanya International Airport? I can arrange morning train tickets for you."

"Train? How far away is Sanya?"

"A mere one-plus hour train ride. It's the way to go."

"Fine. Buy us tickets."

"As you wish."

"Now, before dinner, I think we'll take a swim."

"Swimming pool, ocean, it's all yours."

"We'll take advantage of it."

He and Zhou were shown to their private villa, a bungalow with a view of the sea beyond a manicured lawn and palm trees.

"Will this be satisfactory?" Gavin asked his chief financial officer-turned lover.

She gave him a look. Was it even a question?

As Gavin kicked off his shoes and put on his swimming trunks, he thought about calling the office. Despite the horrendous traffic they had encountered on the road, he wondered if distribution was in full swing. Were orders still coming in?

Then he felt Zhou's firm hands massaging his shoulders.

She could read his mind. There was always tomorrow.

After a couple of high-pressure weeks in China, he could take a day or two to relax.

Together, they headed across the lawn to the beach.

He couldn't wait to dig his toes in the sand.

Matt Justice wanted to get a good look at the resort next door. But his room faced the courtyard, and he would have to go down to the shore to see the Hainan Pro Golf Resort.

He had no swimsuit or change of clothes. But he was in the tropics. At least he could go barefoot.

In the densely planted courtyard, signs pointed to a beach.

As advertised, the courtyard opened onto an endless, white sand beach twenty yards wide and fringed with palms.

Matt remembered that two weeks earlier had been a seven-day Chinese holiday, Mid-Autumn Festival combined with National Day. He didn't want to think about how crowded the place had been.

That also explained the empty hotel. Since all Chinese vacationed on the same few days, the hotel business was either boom or bust. He shook his head. China had to work out a more flexible holiday schedule.

But beyond the scheduling problem, China admitted that they had overbuilt. In Matt's experience, Sanya hotels were only half-full in winter. And that was high season.

He smiled at himself. He couldn't hold back the economics officer inside him, always taking notes for a new report.

Hotel managers he had spoken with had told him that the real money came from selling food.

However, Chinese families would come and stay in the air conditioned comfort of their hotel rooms, eating their own packaged soups, and finally coming down to the beach at sunset, having never eaten at the restaurants.

So hotel managers had begun to rely on Russian business.

Earlier that week, Matt had read in the press that authorities cleaned up five tons of trash off the beaches of Hainan after the week-long Chinese holiday.

So when he reached the shore, the beach was spotless. The cleanup effort had worked.

How Eve would have loved the location.

A red warning flag was permanently installed over an empty lifeguard stand, though waves were only inches high. Any water was a hazard in a country that didn't know how to swim.

He sat in the sand under a tree.

A uniformed guard in a cone-shaped hat with earbuds and a cell phone meandered up to him and explained in Mandarin that the water was dangerous.

Matt assured him that he had no intention of entering the water. He didn't even have a swimsuit.

Smiling, the man seemed relieved.

"*Xian sheng*," Matt addressed him politely. "Do you work for this hotel?" and he indicated the Sheraton.

Pointing to his uniform, the man explained that he worked for the provincial government. His duty was to guard the beaches for all the resorts.

That explained the empty lifeguard stand and the permanent warning flag.

"Is anybody staying at the next hotel?" Matt asked, and pointed to the Hainan Pro Golf Resort.

"Only one couple," the man replied. "An old foreigner and a Chinese model."

Matt nodded. That was an apt description of Gavin and his consort.

Then, still smiling, the man disappeared back into the jungle.

Matt felt like he had made a friend.

Matt didn't want to be noticed, and he didn't particularly want to interact with total strangers in a disease-ridden country. So he stayed inside his hotel room and ordered Hainan Chicken from room service.

"Work the problem," Patrick Kind had told him.

Here Matt was a thousand miles from the outbreak. He was running away from the problem, not toward it.

But he knew someone who was aiming straight for it.

Nils Andersson had said was he was flying direct from Geneva to Guangzhou. Now there was a brave man.

They had last talked six hours ago. By now, Nils was surely en route to Asia.

Matt had little other information at his disposal. He picked up his phone to check for messages.

One SMS message stood out.

It was written in Chinese, followed by an English translation:

"Warning. If you exhibit any symptoms of HPP, such as a sore throat, fever, or coughing, you are required to report your case to the Health Ministry and self-quarantine immediately. For all citizens, travel outside the home will result in a 10,000 yuan fine and possible imprisonment."

Well, the Chinese certainly changed their tune. They had gone from complete denial to full containment mode. He could imagine the chilling effect that would have on the Canton Fair and the streets of Guangzhou. But did the "stay home" order apply to people in Hainan?

The message may have been sent only to people with a Guangzhou number. Since he was gone, it was unclear if it applied to him.

Then he checked the number of the sender and focused on the prefix. It read "10."

That was Beijing.

CHAPTER 5

Investigation

First thing in the morning, Matthew Justice checked his phone again.

Thank God there were no new SMS warnings from the Chinese government.

He had no mobile number for Nils Andersson, so he had to wait for the Swedish public health professional to call him.

It had been twenty hours since Nils had informed him that he was leaving for Guangzhou. Matt was sure that Nils would land soon. Then he would be busy meeting and working with the WHO team that was already on the ground.

There was one number Matt could call.

He dialed the American consulate.

It was Tuesday, a workday. But ominously, there was no answer. Clearly China and the WHO's "stay home" message had gotten through to the diplomatic community. Or had a military transport been able to evacuate the staff and families?

China was fully wireless, and there were no landlines among his friends at the consulate. So he tried their cell phones.

Again, no answer.

Had Guangzhou shut down its cellular service, or had everyone made it safely out of the country?

To find out, he went long distance and called the Operations Center at the U.S. State Department.

A female officer on the night shift took his call.

He calmly explained who he was and where he was, and asked what had happened to the rest of the consulate.

"Right now," she said, "the consulate is on a military transport heading to Washington."

"I must have missed the flight," he said.

"Don't worry, Matthew," she said. "Now that we have your name and location, we can arrange an evacuation flight for you, too. We have a CDC Gulfstream in Hong Kong ready to pick up stranded officers."

"That's awfully nice, but put it on hold. I've still got work to do here."

"You're sure about that?"

"If I don't do it, who will?"

He hung up, feeling lonelier than ever.

Nils wasn't calling. The consulate had evacuated.

It was just him and General Peak, *mano-a-mano*, in the jungle.

And then he heard what sounded like a fast-moving lawnmower in the distance.

He went to his window and looked at the sea.

A motorboat was cruising the shoreline. He watched it pass the Sheraton and curve toward land. It was approaching the neighboring resort: the Hainan Pro Golf Resort.

When Nils Andersson and his team landed in Guangzhou, he was met by the bizarre sight of an enormous, modern arrivals hall with nobody inside.

He stretched his sore back, then rolled his luggage right past the deserted Immigration desk. He felt like a ghost passing through the ethereal halls of another dimension.

Only the squeak of the team's shoes and the squealing sound of wheels against the polished floor made his arrival in Guangzhou seem real.

Nils was proud of his group. He had assembled his investigators long before the Chinese gave the WHO the go-ahead to enter the country.

Beside him walked Professor Tracy Woolman, a prominent mammalogist, Dr. Arjun Kapoor, the WHO's best epidemic intelligence officer, and Dr. Mindy Moore, an outstanding CDC virologist with whom he had worked in the field before and who had his utmost respect.

They had brought with them equipment stored in containers which they could set up anywhere as a field laboratory, complete with microscopes, blood testing equipment, biosafety cabinets, small power generators, and liquid nitrogen.

He had asked the pilot to remain in Guangzhou. Nils needed him to bring samples of the vaccine and blood samples of birds, mammals, and humans back to the lab to be analyzed with electron microscopes and genetic tests.

Waiting in the darkness of the otherwise empty arrivals hall was another team of four people, looking fatigued in the extreme.

Despite her surgical mask, he recognized Yukiko Eto at once.

The two embraced, Nils' bristly beard scratching her cheek, and he felt his energy pass from him to her. He was not only bringing a whiff of fresh air from the Swiss Alps, he was also bringing hope.

Yukiko introduced her team members, two Chinese women and one Chinese man, who had helped her research hospital records and track contacts for the past week.

Nils appreciated all their work, and let them know it. They seemed pleased by the recognition, from what he could tell behind their masks.

"But we'll still need your help," he said. "We don't know a thing about China and none of us speaks Mandarin."

They laughed and replied in English that they were all one team.

"Can someone please explain to me why this airport is so empty?"

Yukiko said, "Our travel advisory is working."

"But that was for international travel to and from China. Where are the domestic flights?"

She held up her phone. "Last night there was this. The national government issued an SMS. Anybody exhibiting signs of HPP is required to report their case and self-quarantine. Everyone else must confine themselves to their homes on possible penalty of jail."

It sounded like the country had resorted to a centuries-old solution, but he couldn't argue with the need. If influenza was already in the general population, it would continue to spread as long as there was contact between people.

"How long is the quarantine for?" he asked.

Yukiko shrugged. "They didn't say."

That was probably wise until scientists learned the pathology of the disease.

He looked out the glass doors. The only vehicles he saw were green trucks with red stars on the doors. Inside, sat soldiers with white surgical masks strapped to their faces.

"Friend or foe?" he asked.

"Depends," she said. "Right now, the People's Liberation Army is essentially our only taxi service."

"Have you set up a field office?"

She looked ashamed. "Until this morning, we worked out of our hotel rooms."

"And now the city is at your disposal?"

She nodded.

"Then take me to Ground Zero. I want to visit FutureGenetics."

Despite the SMS warning to remain indoors and the threat of a jail sentence if he was caught outside his quarters, Matt Justice was determined to find out who was just arriving at the golf resort where General Peak was staying.

He opened his room door a crack and listened. No one was in the hallway. So he grabbed his room key card, stepped out, and gently closed the door.

Then he crept to the end of the dark hallway toward the morning light that played on the glass door.

He opened it ever so slightly. Palm fronds rattled nearby and, in the distance, the lawnmower sound was winding down as it approached the shore.

He padded on bare feet down the steps to the courtyard listening for sounds of activity.

There were no voices, splashes in the pool, or clinking dishes.

The dense jungle path led him mysteriously, with piped-in music, past a children's pool. There were no children. In fact, there seemed to be nobody in the hotel but him.

Staying in the shadows, he eased past the adult pool. There weren't even chairs to sit on.

He continued to follow the signs to the beach. He could hear the distant lapping of waves.

Then a breeze hit him. He stepped out into the sun. The path was burning hot. He walked quickly before his feet caught fire.

At last he reached where sand met sea.

Nobody was on the beach.

Matt craned his neck to look for the motorboat, but the wharf was just out of view.

For a better look, he rolled up the cuffs of his pants and waded into the water.

It was warm enough, but he wasn't there to swim. He was there to reconnoiter the neighboring resort.

The phone rang in Gavin and Zhou's room, waking them with a start.

Gavin grabbed it first.

It was Harold Priest, the resort's owner.

"I think we may have to cancel this morning's golf."

Gavin looked at his watch. Had he overslept? It was already 8:00 a.m.

"Sorry about that," he said. "I overslept."

Harold laughed. "No. It isn't that. You have visitors."

Now he was fully awake.

"Who are they?"

"I'm not sure. But they're on the wharf right now."

Gavin thanked his host and hung up.

"Who knows we're here?" he asked Zhou, who seemed to prefer to remain asleep.

"Nobody does."

"Then who's on the wharf?"

He went to the blinds and pulled them partly aside.

Sure enough, there was a motorboat tied to the boat launch. Squinting in the sunlight, he made out a group of men pulling luggage ashore.

"Who is it?" she asked.

"Damned if I know. They're Chinese."

And they were heading his way.

He let go of the blinds and hunted for his clothes.

"Honey, get something on."

Gavin stepped outside to greet his visitors, three men staggering up with golf bags and suitcases.

At last they were close enough to identify.

They all had the obligatory dyed-black hair and black suits of Chinese businessmen. But one of them looked goddamned familiar.

The sun glinted off the bald forehead and large glasses of none other than...

"Mr. Pu."

It was the Guangdong Party Secretary paying him a visit, and likely escaping the streets of Guangzhou.

Ostensibly, Mr. Pu came for another round of golf with his favorite golf buddy.

Gavin ran out to help the group with their clubs and bring them into the tree-lined shade of his bungalow.

Zhou stepped onto the patio, ready to translate for them.

"Don't bother," Gavin told her. "They speak English."

She paused, looking at the men as if they had just ruined her vacation. But then, she was an officer of Gavin's company, so her expression changed accordingly.

With her eyes on Mr. Pu in particular, she bowed and returned to the air conditioning.

Gavin turned to the three men, who had already found chairs and were wiping their brows.

His main question was, how did these guys know he was there?

But he took a tactful approach.

"To what do I owe this honor?"

Nils Andersson was sure that FutureGenetics, as a leading biotech firm, could and would provide all the laboratory equipment and facilities he needed to set up a field office.

The driver of his troop transport truck pulled up to the manicured grounds of company headquarters.

The place was surrounded by tanks and heavy artillery that turned and aimed at him!

Meanwhile, other army trucks ferried goods out of the back of the complex and disappeared in the giant grid of Science City.

"What's going on here?" Nils asked.

Yukiko pointed at the main gate. "We've been trying to get in there for the past day, but the army is not letting us through."

"But this is all the same army," Nils protested.

"With two different missions," she said. "One of their jobs is to distribute the vaccine."

"So let them distribute the vaccine."

"The other job is to protect production of the vaccine."

"We aren't going to harm anything," he argued.

"Tell them that."

"This is ridiculous," he said, and jumped out of the truck.

He strode across the otherwise empty street while holding up his

WHO badge.

"World Health Organization," he told a soldier, who swiveled the truck-mounted machine gun his way.

Not being able to see the soldier's full expression behind a white mask made him seem all the more menacing.

"Let me talk to the president of FutureGenetics."

He heard small footsteps behind him.

"He doesn't understand you, and even if he did, his orders are to protect the perimeter at all costs."

He turned to Yukiko. "Then we have a problem."

At that point, the male member of Yukiko's team approached them. "Let me talk to him. Tell me what you need."

"I need to study the vaccine. None of our scientists have been able to study and test the vaccine. If we could only use their facilities…"

"I doubt they'll allow that. And we won't be able to discuss science with these soldiers."

"Okay, then the president of the company. I'd like to speak with Gavin Peak. I have already talked with him by phone."

The Chinese translator bravely confronted the soldier and passed along the name "Gavin Peak."

Though the guns prevented them from physically entering the complex, a soldier did carry their message through the gate and into the main building.

It was hot and the sun bore down directly overhead, so Nils returned to the truck and waited in the cab with his team until word came back.

Gavin Peak was still waiting for the three Chinese visitors to introduce themselves and announce the purpose of their visit when his phone rang.

"Excuse me, gentlemen," he said, and stepped inside the bungalow to take the call.

"Who is this? I'm in a meeting now."

It was Dr. Chen calling from headquarters.

"General," Chen said, with a slight cough. "We have visitors."

"Well, so do I."

"Sir, it appears that the World Health Organization's investigators have landed in Guangzhou, and they came straight to our office."

Gavin was confused. Wasn't there an epidemic to stop? "What do they want with us?"

"These are sharp guys. The best in the business. They want to talk to you."

"Well, I'm not there."

"Should I let them in?"

"Under no circumstances. We're under no obligation to assist them in any way, and that means studying our research or letting them use any of our equipment or facilities."

"I thought you'd say that."

"Give them the boot."

Then he considered Chen's situation more closely.

"Is the military still surrounding the place?"

"They're still here in a protective stance. If I tell the WHO to go away, the army will make them go."

"We're busy. Tell the WHO to get lost."

"General?" Again that cough. "We need the military for more than protection."

"Why's that?"

"They're helping fill the vials and box up the vaccines."

"Why?"

"This building is quarantined and half our employees are either gasping for air or dead."

"What happened?"

There was a long pause. Chen's incredulousness hung heavily in the air.

"General, we killed them."

It took half an hour, but eventually a soldier approached Nils' truck and began to speak in terse, crude language through his mask.

"The president is gone," the translator said.

That was a setback. Not much of a negotiator, Nils had lost his best excuse for entering the headquarters.

The soldier spoke again, this time more forcefully.

"Go away," the translator translated.

"Yeah, I got that."

Nils asked the driver to pull ahead and around the corner of an empty roundabout.

They were surrounded by large buildings on all corners of the traffic circle. One was a bank headquarters, another some sort of academic research institute, then a science and technology company. They all looked recently abandoned, and, with the countrywide quarantine in place, he was sure that they were.

The WHO had their pick of where to set up shop, but Nils was feeling the long shadow of the tanks and wanted to get further away from them.

He had the trucks crawl along the main road for a while until FutureGenetics was out of sight.

After a kilometer, they passed a large, friendly looking complex. It had a high red structure like an auditorium and sat up against a mountainside. Inside the fence sat a row of buses.

"What's this place?" he asked.

"American International School," one of the translators read.

"The gate looks locked," Nils said.

"Dr. Andersson, you forget," came back Yukiko's little voice. "We are with the army."

Two minutes later, they had rammed through the gate and pulled into the slots of parking spaces before the school.

"If we're in luck," Nils said, "they'll have a science lab."

"Allow us to introduce ourselves," the oldest and most robust-looking of the Chinese visitors requested of Gavin Peak, in English that sounded like Business English 101.

"My name is Yi Wentian. I am Secretary of the Central Commission for Discipline Inspection for the Communist Party of the People's Republic of China. I am a standing member of the Politburo and a chief advisor to the president. I oversee the Ministry of Public Security in China."

Gavin reached over and shook the man's hand. It did feel like an executioner's paw come to think of it, and he was likely good at golf, too.

The next man to introduce himself looked more fit and less thuggish. He had a towering stature that spoke of a mean tee-shot.

"My name General Wang." He nodded. "I Central Military Commission. Politburo."

Gavin saluted back. He should have recognized a fellow military man, and instantly felt a natural affinity toward the general. He forgave the guy his lack of English.

"That's okay," he told the man. "I don't speak Chinese either."

Which actually seemed to put the man at ease.

Then Gavin turned to Mr. Pu. "And this man needs no introduction."

He instantly regretted saying that, having perhaps disrespected the others, who might well outrank Mr. Pu. "But I must say, how did you gentlemen know that I was staying here?"

The three men looked at each other like contestants on a TV show.

Finally, it was the thuggish Mr. Yi who spoke. "General Peak, we are the three main investors in your company."

Gavin stared at Mr. Pu, who nodded.

God, what a scam! It was brilliant.

Mr. Pu, the man who agreed to look the other way when there was a containment incident at his company, who had him raise the price, who ran a mock clinical trial for the vaccine, and who was the government's first purchaser of the product, was actually a major stakeholder in the company.

Gavin had to give it to the Chinese. They really knew how to get things done, and make all the money they needed on the side. Why wasn't America more like that?

Then, the more he thought about it, the more he understood the involvement of Mr. Yi of the Ministry of Public Security. There would be no criminal prosecution of the handling of the leak, the official corruption taking place, or the prices that even Gavin found exorbitant. Mr. Yi could take advantage of his powerful position in the government to protect his investment in FutureGenetics.

General Wang was harder to figure out. Why would a military leader invest in a company that made vaccines?

Then the image Vincent Fong and Dr. Chen depicted of People's Liberation Army tanks defending his company's facilities brought the picture into clear focus. General Wang's soldiers were out in force protecting the production process and distributing the vaccines around the nation. In a one-party state, when things had to happen, it was the military that ultimately got things done. And General Wang reaped the rewards.

Gavin's hat was off to the three men. It was a humbling experience to think that he, alone, hadn't forged the company's success. It took a set of players behind the scenes to bring the controversial product to market and ensure its success. It was amazing what removing the constraints of democracy and the rule of law could yield.

Gavin's most recent conference call with shareholders had clearly tipped them off to his whereabouts.

But still the question lingered.

They had all brought golf clubs. Were they really there to play?

The mysterious men who had arrived next door at the golf resort were too far away for Matt Justice to identify. But they were carrying clubs and suitcases.

Matt counted the men. There were three total, along with a skipper who remained behind with the boat.

From where he stood in the water, Matt had little to go on, but that didn't mean he was without resources.

The same uniformed man from the evening before was approaching from that direction. Still equipped with his cone-shaped hat, earbuds, and cell phone, the guard had lost his characteristic good humor.

"Out of the water!" he ordered.

Matt took a few steps back onto dry land.

"*Xian sheng*," Matt addressed him in the politest terms. "Who are those men who just arrived?"

"Rich guys," the man said, frowning.

That was interesting, but to be expected, given the exclusive nature of the resort. But why the frown?

"It seems you know who they are."

"Everybody does. They're all Party big shots."

"Such as?"

The guard paused to study Matt. He seemed to be thinking, why was this foreigner interested in so many details?

"I'm just curious," Matt said. "Who are they?"

The guard stood back in the shade and glanced at the golf resort.

"Two guys from Beijing and one from Guangdong."

"Come on," Matt said. "What are their names?"

The guard's frown remained deep. "Yi, Wang, and Pu."

Those were all common names, unless you were talking about the country's top leadership.

"Yi Wentian?"

The guard nodded.

"General Wang?"

Again a nod.

Those were the two from Beijing. Then the third name suddenly clicked.

"Pu Aiguo, the party secretary of Guangdong?"

A final nod, and the grim-faced guard moved on down the beach.

Matt knew that the Party elite often came south to play golf. And coming there to escape the outbreak made complete sense.

What did any of that have to do with General Peak?

Matt was beginning to think of the tropical island as a rich man's refuge during quarantine, until it struck him.

One of the men was Pu Aiguo, Guangdong Party Secretary. Now, *he* had a direct connection with General Peak.

Matt fell against the nearest palm tree, his mind spinning.

The American hero, who had ridden so gallantly into town a couple of weeks ago, had immediately gained the ear of the Guangdong Party Secretary. That was no mean feat. In fact, the consul general had been trying for years.

What had the two discussed so soon after his arrival?

Matt searched his memory for conversations that the consul general had had with General Peak.

At the American Chamber of Commerce Ball, Patrick Kind had approached the general. Then, the two men had met at Orchid Mountain at the consul general's pool party. They had conversed again at the Marine Ball, and later by phone.

Sometimes, the consul general had inquired about the vaccine, and other times he had tried to get General Peak to pressure the party secretary, Pu Aiguo, to cooperate with the World Health Organization.

Why had General Peak been meeting with Pu in the first place? And why so often? What were they discussing?

Clearly from the start, getting Pu to invite the WHO disease detectives to China was not going to work. Did General Peak really press the case?

It now seemed obvious that General Peak would naturally meet with the Communist Party higher-up simply to curry favor for his business. But that didn't explain why Mr. Pu and some of the top Communist leadership had come down to Hainan to see him. What was behind their visit?

The answer seemed tantalizingly close.

The Chinese visitors to Gavin Peak's little corner of paradise had been sitting on his patio too long.

Gavin sensed nervous energy building on their part, and braced for them to reveal the true reason for their visit.

Why had the three chief investors of his company descended on him now? Did they have a new direction in mind for the company? Were they planning to upbraid him for mishandling the outbreak? Were they there to take his measure, express their support of him, or get rid of him?

Finally the minister of public security stood up and slapped his pants with vigor.

"Let's play golf!"

Once his team had set up shop in the American School, Nils Andersson began to worry whether they had the proper authorization to be there.

He got on the phone to Switzerland and asked them to iron out permission with the school's administration.

Then he got down to implementing his strategy.

Since the Chinese had allowed his group in, he needed to pursue two main goals.

One was to assist the Chinese health authorities in categorizing the cases, spreading messages to health care professionals and citizens about how to avoid catching HPP, and helping them measure the extent of the spread.

Secondly, he needed to investigate the source of the virus and stop it from spreading.

As for helping the Chinese monitor the disease, he named himself leader of the team that would visit the local Health Department and hospitals. He asked Dr. Mindy Moore, the virologist, to accompany him on the visits.

"My first stop will be with the Guangdong Health Department. I want to pave the way for our visit, obtain a sample of the vaccine they're using, and get a handle on what they need from us."

Yukiko selected the male translator to accompany that group.

"Then we'll make our first survey of the hospitals," Nils said.

"If they let you in."

"That's why we need to work with the local Health Department. They can identify which institutions will let us in to their isolation wards."

Yukiko nodded uncertainly.

"Now, to investigate the source of the disease." He turned to his epidemic and mammal experts.

"I noticed that there is considerable forest cover in this area. Including behind the FutureGenetics complex. I'd like you to climb that hill and do some recon of their activities. Also, trap a few of the birds and animals you find and we'll extract blood samples here at the lab."

Everyone agreed to the plan of action. Finally, they were doing what they had come to China to do.

The first stop for Nils Andersson and Dr. Mindy Moore was the Department of Health of Guangdong Province.

"Oof!" Mindy said, covering her nose and mouth.

The moment they walked in the entrance of the provincial health care administration, they were hit by a strong stench. It smelled like urine that had been floating in a squat toilet for far too long.

He looked around the dark lobby. For such a large building, nobody was there.

A directory on the wall listed the Office of the Director of the Guangdong Department of Health. It was on the second floor.

So that was where Nils and Mindy went.

"Down there," the interpreter said, pointing down the hall.

To Nils' relief, a light was on at the end of the hall.

All alone in the office, a middle-aged bureaucrat sat hunched over a computer monitor.

"Director?" Nils said, tapping on the doorframe.

It took half a minute for the man to look up and acknowledge their presence. He had a long face with thin eyebrows. When Nils thought about it, the poor man had little hair at all and hoped that wasn't from tearing it out.

Nils advanced respectfully into the office and introduced himself and Mindy as members of the WHO team in Guangzhou.

Fortunately, the man spoke perfect English, at least within the framework of his trade.

"My name is Dr. Wu. I am Director of the Department of Health of Guangdong Province. I have been expecting you."

This was going wonderfully. Not only was Nils meeting face-to-face with his Chinese counterpart, but also the director was a medical doctor.

"Where do we start?" Dr. Wu asked. Having wrenched himself away from his computer screen, he was putting himself at their full disposal.

Nils focused on the vaccine right away. If he accomplished nothing else in China, he needed to bring home a sample of the vaccine to test if it matched the flu virus that was going around.

"First, I need a vial of the vaccine so that the WHO laboratory can study the viruses targeted."

"Of course." Dr. Wu picked up his phone and placed an order somewhere downstairs.

The next item on his agenda was to advise on the containment strategy implemented by the Health Department.

Nils began by offering support for the SMS message sent out to the public. "In particular, I think it was important that people report their cases. Do you feel that you have a good handle on the numbers?"

Dr. Wu then explained the reporting system, coordinated from the local level to the national level via a common reporting form on computer.

Nils was impressed that the Chinese had begun to categorize cases into useful groups for observation purposes. Dr. Wu described the three case definitions: suspected, probable, and confirmed cases.

As he explained, the patients who were suspected of being infected by the disease had a high fever, coughing, and shortness of breath, and had been in close contact with poultry, rodents, or probable or confirmed human cases.

Those who fit into the suspected category were mostly health care workers who had helped a patient, or close family members who had cared for the patient.

Such cases were subject to a clinical assessment at the hospital and to having a blood sample drawn for the laboratory. Most were in isolation units in hospitals or being closely monitored by case trackers at home, limiting contact with others.

"Case trackers?" Nils asked.

Dr. Wu nodded. "The Central Government has supplied our province alone with a hundred thousand soldiers, armed police, and civil servants. They help us track individual cases and enforce quarantines."

"Okay." Nils had seen totalitarian regimes throw manpower at problems in the past. "Go on."

The next category of patients was those who were probable cases. To fit that description, the patient had to meet the conditions of a suspected case and either be dying or have partial lab results or chest X-rays that showed acute pneumonia.

"So pneumonia is the key indicator?"

"Present in all confirmed cases, but not conclusive," Dr. Wu said, then went on.

The last category, laboratory confirmed cases, was made up of patients or the deceased who had blood tests that proved positive for the virus.

Confirmed cases were being subjected to isolation for the patients who were still alive, and cremation for the deceased.

It was no joy to be in any of those categories, but at least the authorities had a method for reducing the spread of the disease.

"Do you use this information to target which population to vaccinate?"

"It is a struggle with other government departments," the man admitted. "Of course, the Party has bought the first batch, then the military. However, I have convinced the military to spare enough doses so that our Health Department can create a ring of vaccinated people around those who have contact with the sick."

That was standard practice and would work in the best of circumstances. "Do you have enough doses?"

"Yes. The numbers in the ring are high, but nowhere near the number of soldiers in the military."

"Can I ask what your numbers are?"

The doctor looked at his computer screen for the latest figures. "So far, our province has 55,072 suspected cases, another 46,911 probable, 41,482 confirmed cases, and 23,539 deaths."

Nils was stunned. He'd never seen so widespread a disease that was so lethal.

"Where did this virus come from?"

Dr. Wu shrugged. "We haven't had time to investigate that question."

"This one seems highly contagious. Have you calculated the basic reproductive ratio?"

Again, Dr. Wu checked his computer screen. "Right now we calculate it's at 4.5. But with our containment efforts, we hope to bring that down to zero."

Nils nodded his approval, and noted that Dr. Mindy Moore was writing down the statistics for her WHO report. He only hoped that the numbers never climbed so high in other cities and countries.

"And how about the sick? May I ask how you care for the infected?"

"Oseltamivir, zanamivir, or peramivir if they present within the first forty-eight hours. If patients have respiratory complaints such as shortness of breath or abnormal lung sounds, we send them for X-rays to rule out pneumonia. Then we treat them empirically with antibiotics for secondary bacterial infections. Ventilators are reserved for our sickest and most compromised patients. That's all we can do."

"Do you have any X-rays available to view?"

Dr. Wu thought about it, then pulled up one patient's X-rays.

Setting aside privacy issues, Nils moved in close to examine the progression of the disease.

At first, the patient's lungs were two healthy black shadows. Then two days later, the entire shadows were no longer black due to fluid build-up at the ends of the bronchioles where gas exchange occurred between the air sacs and capillaries.

Oseltamivir and zanamivir were medications given in pill form as Tamiflu and Relenza, and peramivir, a drug sold under the name Rapivab, was injected intravenously.

These drugs sometimes reduced the duration of influenza symptoms by a day if given within forty-eight hours of the infection. But they rarely kept people out of the hospital and, due to overuse of the pill form, the population of China was quickly growing resistant to them.

Was there more that doctors could do?

On a hunch, Nils remembered the demographic of those who died during the 1918 Spanish Flu pandemic. It was the healthiest among the population, many of them soldiers freshly returned from the war, who died of the influenza.

"If I may inquire," Nils said, "what is the age range of those patients who have died?"

Dr. Wu scrolled through the data. "The vast majority of deaths occurred in the range of 20 to 35 years of age."

Nils was right. There was a pattern that could help them create better outcomes. Death might result in those who were healthiest because their healthy immune systems were becoming overly aggressive in attacking the disease and thereby drowning the lungs with fluid.

"May I suggest a new approach to treating patients?"

Dr. Wu looked at him as if for the first time.

"What might be going on here is what in the literature is called a 'cytokine storm.' The body's immune system activates too many immune cells. There are drugs on the market that can reduce that reaction and let the body attack the virus-infected cells with normal force."

The director's face was gradually transforming from surprise to the recognition of a possible solution.

"We have TNF-alpha blockers that can reduce such an overreaction."

"You can even use the cholesterol-lowering drug Gemfibrozil proactively in HPP cases to reduce cytokine signaling and prevent the immune system from kicking in so strongly."

Suddenly, Dr. Wu seemed to have a whole new purpose in life and jumped back to his computer, presumably to order the new medicine.

And Nils, despite having given him the inspiration, was only an impediment to getting it done.

Recognizing this, Nils decided to wrap up the conversation as quickly as possible.

"On the prevention side, I have another suggestion."

Dr. Wu paused and turned to him, his eyebrows lifted.

"I suggest that you send out another SMS alert with a hygiene message."

"Saying…?"

"Wash your hands frequently and cover your mouth when you cough."

Dr. Wu nodded seriously and turned to type something on his computer.

"And finally on the question of eliminating the disease, I have just one request," Nils said.

The preoccupied doctor blinked and nodded for him to go on.

"I would like permission to visit some of the hospitals that are treating HPP cases."

Dr. Wu stood up straight and shook his head vigorously. "I'm afraid that the hospitals are closed to inspection. We need to prevent the disease from spreading."

"I understand that completely," Nils said. "That makes good epidemiological sense."

Dr. Wu spread his hands. "As you can see, my hands are tied."

They didn't look tied to Nils, but he didn't want to quibble with the metaphor.

"May I ask which hospitals in the province are handling HPP cases?"

Dr. Wu enumerated the various types of hospitals involved. "We are using military hospitals, teaching hospitals, cancer hospitals, traditional Chinese medicine hospitals, municipal hospitals, and private hospitals."

Nils focused on the military hospitals. "Say we arrived with a military force. Would we be allowed into a hospital?"

Dr. Wu gave the kind of laugh that tried to hide uneasiness more than express mirth. "The hospitals make that decision."

Nils smiled. "Thank you for your time. I have to say that I'm deeply impressed with your organized approach to disease monitoring."

"Thank you," Dr. Wu said with a bow. "We have learned much from the past. And I have learned much from you."

As Nils and Mindy left the director's office, a set of five vials of vaccines was ready for them to pick up.

Nils carefully lifted a vial out of the box. The glass was cold to the touch. Then he looked closely at the label.

There was no brand, year, dosage, or manufacturer's name on the label, only the words "Flu vaccine."

The ease with which the label could be counterfeited would undoubtedly lead to huge numbers of fake vaccines.

But equally disturbing was the lack of accountability. Nobody claimed to have made the vaccine.

Nevertheless, genome sequencing would soon tell them more.

Nils stepped out onto the sidewalk with Mindy. "What do you think of their containment approach?"

"In theory, it sounded fine. I'd like to see it in practice."

"Yes. Theory and practice don't always line up."

"But I did like your cytokine advice."

Nils studied the virologist. "Do you think it'll work?"

Mindy screwed up her lips. "They have nothing to lose by trying."

Nils nodded. That was the safest thing one could say, and the only thing they knew for certain. But the number of those affected was astronomical, and he hoped to God the cytokine-inhibiting drugs would work.

"Right now, we have to address prevention. And that means, we've got to refrigerate these vials, then get them to Geneva for testing."

They jumped into the cab of the troop transport and Nils leaned toward his translator. "Have them take us back to the American School."

The order was passed, and the truck gunned to life.

"After we refrigerate these vials, I'd like to see the index patient at Nanfang Hospital," he said. "If my gut is correct, the patient from FutureGenetics was the first admitted to the hospital for HPP."

"What makes you think we can get in?" asked the translator, whose efforts to gain access to hospitals had been frustrated for days.

Nils pointed to the soldier at the wheel.

"We may be foreigners, but we've got the army on our side."

Dr. Arjun Kapoor thought he and Professor Tracy Woolman made a strange-looking pair as they climbed up the ridge that cast a shadow over FutureGenetics.

Arjun was a tall, proud, and well-fed epidemic intelligence officer who was better suited to staff meetings and addressing the press.

Tracy was a short, bent research professor whose hair was a combination of blonde and gray and who vastly preferred spending time with rodents and monkeys than with the human species.

Alone on the heavily wooded route, they had stepped away from the footpath here and there to place various kinds of traps behind trees.

Half the traps contained seeds and were designed to lure birds whereas the other half were cages containing oranges and nuts, food that rats and squirrels might enjoy.

Professor Woolman was needed for her brains and experience in trapping animals, and Arjun was there for his brawn.

Their activity would have appeared highly suspicious if anyone were there to observe them. But like most of the city, the forest was deserted.

Nevertheless, they moved furtively and spoke in whispers for fear of scaring off wildlife.

The purpose of their mission was to gather samples of the animal species that might serve as reservoirs for the nasty virus freaking out the world.

The theory was that perhaps the virus lived in these birds or rodents, causing only minimal discomfort to them, and that the virus had somehow jumped to human hosts.

Sometimes it was by birds or bats excreting on food eaten by animals that humans ate. Other times, people would slaughter the animal without protection or eat them without having properly cooked the meat, thereby allowing the virus to move into the human population.

However the virus got into people, once there, it clearly thrived and was usually passed on from person to person through sneezes or coughs that left droplets on surfaces or hanging in the air.

To someone who studied the vectors and fomites of epidemic disease transmission, the pathways were straightforward.

But finding the exact species at fault for harboring the virus took a lot of animal testing. And lots of animal testing meant trapping lots of different kinds of animals.

Hunting animals wasn't his favorite part of the job, but the promise of a solution to his problem was flying, fluttering, or scurrying somewhere around him.

The canopy above was full of life, evident mostly by the sounds. In particular, a chorus of locusts drowned out all other sounds when it reached its peak.

He saw no evidence of mammals, until Tracy pointed out half-eaten fruit and berries under plants, burrows built into the banks of creeks, and disturbed dead leaves that indicated a trail.

It was a busy world of animals, but he couldn't see how any of it connected to humans. If the epidemic truly began from these mountains in Science City, how had the virus ever jumped species to humans? Surely people weren't eating songbirds and rats, nor was animal feces ending up in the food chain consumed by people.

They had just set their last mouse trap when an opening in the trees revealed the valley below.

Arjun straightened his back to study the view. Small white buildings were arranged symmetrically behind the headquarters of FutureGenetics.

He saw air conditioning and filtering units behind many buildings, and quickly surmised the purpose of the structures.

"Laboratories," he said.

"Yes, but watch the trucks," Tracy said.

They watched army trucks back up to buildings on the perimeter.

Soldiers in surgical masks were carrying cardboard boxes to some trucks and plastic coolers to others.

"They're distributing the vaccines," she said.

She was right, of course. All the buildings couldn't be laboratories. But he was fascinated that there were so many buildings with air filters.

"They must have biosafety labs for experiments as well as virus production," he said. "And one of them looks damaged."

Tracy already had her binoculars out.

"It looks like fire damage," she said. "There's a gigantic hole in the roof."

She handed him the binoculars.

What he saw through the lenses brought on a deep sense of foreboding.

Laboratory equipment was still exposed to the outside world. The room had been used to reproduce viruses.

It didn't look like culturing in eggs, rather growing vaccines in live cells. And from the shattered Petri dishes and test tubes, black powder burns and the gaping hole in the roof, a large number of those viruses must have escaped.

Untold numbers of virions could have been set free in the wild, wet, blowing mass of air above the city.

His heart beating double time, he reached into his camera bag and pulled out a digital camera with a telephoto lens.

He took several pictures of the general layout of the complex, then zoomed in tight for close-ups of the damaged lab.

"Well, that explains a lot," he said.

They had come looking for the animal culprits behind the influenza outbreak and stumbled upon a possible human cause.

"Biosafety breach," Tracy said. "I wonder when that happened."

"If we can find out, my guess is it corresponds to the date of the outbreak."

Although logic indicated they had an answer to their question, scientific rigor dictated they collect the trapped birds and animals and study them as well.

One thing that Arjun had learned in his decades with the WHO was that one never jumped to conclusions. Every avenue was explored and every detail studied.

The world, including his wife and two kids back in Geneva, would suffer the consequences if he was wrong.

Nils Andersson returned with Mindy Moore to the American School with their hard-won vials of vaccine.

He climbed the front steps to the science laboratory that he and his cohorts had appropriated from the school, and Mindy placed the vials into the refrigerator and set it at five degrees Celsius. Not too cold, not too warm would prevent the vaccines from becoming damaged or compromised.

He wasn't surprised that Arjun and Tracy hadn't returned from their trapping and recon work. But he did want to see them before he headed off to Nanfang Hospital to find Patient Zero.

When they finally did rush into the science lab with their arms full of chirping, squeaking, fluttering creatures, Arjun asked him to wait.

Breathless from the experience and full of news to impart, Arjun and Tracy asked Nils to help extract blood from the specimens before they died.

Nils grabbed a capillary tube and went to work on bleeding the rat. First he put on goggles, a surgical mask, and gloves. Then he held the panicked rat firm with one hand. With the other, he shoved the capillary tube up the top of one of the critter's eyeballs, thereby breaking blood vessels.

Dark blood dripped through the tube.

Meanwhile, Tracy was busy calming her gray-backed thrush and azure-winged magpie before they inadvertently broke their own wings in panic, and Arjun was extracting blood from the squirrel with the same method Nils used.

The rat's organs also needed to be harvested. With no carbon dioxide and gas chamber available to euthanize it, Nils resorted to cervical dislocation followed by decapitation.

"I'll leave the dissection to you," he told Arjun and Tracy. "Make sure to preserve all organs."

"Vacuum flasks are fully cooled with liquid nitrogen," Mindy announced. "The laptop is set to print out labels."

Nils was proud of his team's efficiency.

Once the four specimens were euthanized, the team took a short breather.

Nils wanted to tell them what he had learned, but it was clear that Arjun couldn't wait to relate his news.

"We climbed up behind FutureGenetics and got a good look at their layout. There are roughly two dozen buildings out back, many with air filters, suggesting they are laboratories. However, we discovered that one of the lab buildings had been breached. There was a gaping hole in the roof and evidence of an explosion of some kind, black marks everywhere. From that angle, we could see into the lab. We saw rows of Petri dishes and test tubes. My guess is that it was a vaccine production lab. Guys, I think the company may have accidentally released the live virus into the air."

Nils found himself staring at the epidemic investigator. "Why didn't they tell anybody?"

Arjun shrugged. "They haven't stopped production. Soldiers are hard at work carrying vaccines out the back of the complex."

The only thing that came to Nils' mind was criminal negligence: the criminal act of not informing the public they had released a deadly virus into the air. To his knowledge, the company had never disclosed such a mishap. "Do you have evidence?"

Arjun patted his camera bag.

"Send photos to Geneva at once."

"We're wondering when the leak occurred," Tracy said.

"If the date of the breach correlates with the outbreak..." Arjun said.

"We'll have our culprit," Nils completed the thought.

He took a deep breath. He was far more used to rationally discussing key steps in finding and eliminating infectious diseases. He had no experience dealing with outright criminal behavior.

He almost forgot to tell the others his news: the staggering number of dead, the containment measures taken by the Chinese, and the possibility of life-saving treatment.

By the end of their meeting, the hopefulness of his news was overshadowed by the horrific malfeasance by the biotech firm, and the fact that so many people lay dead as a result.

"Mindy and I are leaving for Nanfang Hospital now. We hope to interview the FutureGenetics lab worker that Matthew Justice of the American consulate discovered in the isolation ward."

Suddenly, meeting with Patient Zero became all the more imperative.

"I want you two," he said, gesturing toward Arjun and Tracy, "to get the vaccine, blood, and organs ready for transportation. We'll be heading for the airport in the next few hours. Wake up the pilot and have him get the plane ready to take us back to Geneva. And the photographs? I'll get you an email address so we can send them for legal analysis."

Meanwhile, he and Mindy had a hospital to visit.

Half an hour later, thanks to nearly empty highways, Nils Andersson and his expert virologist arrived at Nanfang Hospital determined to see the index patient.

He could see at once that the tall building was ringed by police cars.

"Put on your surgical mask and gloves," he ordered Dr. Mindy Moore and their male interpreter. "Bring along the soldiers. We're going in."

Word spread from the cab of the personnel carrier to the soldiers in the rear, and by the time they rolled to a stop, several military boots had already landed on the pavement behind the truck.

Nils shifted in his seat and pulled on his door latch.

"It's show time," he said through his clean white mask.

His street shoes hit the ground hard, and he swung into line behind the masked soldiers who approached the hospital's emergency room entrance with authority.

The Guangdong Provincial Police kept a wary eye on the WHO team, but made no move to intervene.

Nils was interested that there was no public clamor to get into the hospital for treatment. Even if not sick, often the "worried well" showed up certain that they had caught the bug.

But the heavy silence in the streets that surrounded the hospital indicated a fear of hospitalization, and perhaps a fear of the authorities who might confine them there. Like a tomb, the hospital was the kind of place that once entered, people never left alive.

Inside, the hospital corridors were exceptionally quiet. Passing the emergency room, Nils saw no patients waiting for treatment or people in surgery. The floor was utterly abandoned.

Nils had imagined disease surveillance teams bringing in possible cases and the extensive examination of patients as they poured in from all parts of the city. Instead, the beds were empty and the equipment turned off.

It wasn't at all the picture that the director of Guangdong's Health Department had painted.

Were people too sick to seek medical attention, or too worried that they would catch something worse if they entered a hospital?

With no receptionist to guide them to the proper room, the team of three decided to climb the stairs until they encountered patients or medical staff.

What they found on the second floor was a totally different scene. The lights were off, but every room was occupied by hacking, groaning patients.

Yet there were no doctors, nurses, or visitors in sight. Nor were there physical barriers to isolate patients. In effect, the entire hospital was in isolation.

Had the medical staff panicked and abandoned post?

Then Nils heard the sound of footsteps and they cornered a nurse carrying blood samples.

Through his mask, Nils asked as politely as possible, "Where are the rest of the doctors and nurses?"

A simple shrug. "Many died. The rest ran away."

Nils was floored. "Why are *you* here?"

"All my friends are patients."

Nils blinked several times. The news was overwhelming.

He drew in his breath and inquired softly if she knew the first patient to have entered the isolation ward.

Her eyes crinkled with a smile. "You mean 'Sunny,'" she said, using the English name.

The isolation ward was on the third floor, she told them.

They thanked her and headed immediately for the stairwell, where they scrambled up the remaining stairs two steps at a time.

Again, the corridor was dark, but there were no patients in immediate view. Instead, a glass door blocked off what looked like an isolation unit.

With nobody guarding the door, they pulled it open.

Nils entered with some trepidation. These would be the confirmed cases of HPP.

But, to his deep concern, patients weren't confined to their rooms. Rather, they sat in a circle, coughing, wilting from fevers and playing mahjong.

How could that be?

Then he realized there was no need to isolate the mixture of men, women, and children from each other. They were all sick.

The masked team interrupted the game, and all players turned to look.

The interpreter asked for Sunny, and the group looked at a young woman in green pajamas who appeared to be their leader.

The woman stood up, perplexed.

An old man explained something to the interpreter, and after a minute of sorting things out, the young woman in the pajamas separated from the group and walked with the team to a room where she grabbed her smartphone.

Nils was even more confused when the woman began typing on her phone, and the interpreter replied via his smartphone.

"What's this all about?" Nils asked.

"She lost her hearing," his Chinese interpreter said. "We must ask questions by texting."

Nils might have been trained as a physician, but he missed all the signs of deafness. At once he was put into a more empathetic frame of mind. And the more he let his emotions ride with the situation, the harder it was to take.

The woman had been hospitalized for weeks, but seemed unaffected by the disease. The lights were off, food came infrequently, and she couldn't hear a thing. How could she hold up so well?

His first questions to her were about her health and well-being.

Once again, he was surprised when she began talking in Mandarin, full of force and disgust.

Mindy immediately turned her digital voice recorder on and began to take notes.

"She says that she has been in this ward for half a month and never suffered any symptoms," the interpreter said. "Other patients had come there and many had died. Sunny has become the *de facto* nurse."

"She worked for a biotech firm," Nils said. "What was her training?"

After a short discussion, Sunny looked at Nils and Mindy directly. "I have a degree in biology," she said in somewhat distorted, but flawless, English.

Nils nodded at her to show her that he understood.

"I worked for FutureGenetics when the accident occurred."

"What accident?"

Sunny reverted to Mandarin and her hand gestures became more animated as she described what could easily be interpreted as an explosion.

Nils looked at Mindy. She checked her recorder, then began to write down the interpreter's description of the event.

"The electricity had gone out, the laboratory door couldn't be opened, and she couldn't get out of the low-pressure lab. People on the roof of the building tried to cut a hole to rescue her before she died of suffocation. But they couldn't get through. Then a man with a blowtorch cut through the double set of doors into the lab. But as soon as he did, the electricity came back on and there was a sudden explosion that shattered everything in the laboratory, blew a hole through the roof, and ruined her hearing. But she was rescued."

"When precisely did this happen?"

The interpreter texted her the question.

Sunny tapped her watch. "Exactly fifteen days and five hours ago," she said in English.

"And what was in the laboratory?"

The story Sunny told took a while to get across, but the delay in translation didn't mask the sheer horror of the situation she described.

She told how scientists at her company, FutureGenetics, had designed a virus to be as contagious and lethal to people as possible. The theory was that it would be a virus whose vaccine would prevent people from getting the most dangerous forms of influenza ever again.

She had taken the vaccine two weeks before beginning work. She was to work in the lab that produced large quantities of the virus, incubating it in Petri dishes and test tubes, so that it could be used later in formulating the vaccine.

So when the lab was torn apart and she was exposed to shards of glass and a cloud of debris, including the virus, her body already had the antibodies she needed to fight off the disease.

"Was the vaccine already available to the public by then?"

She read her phone and shook her head. "No vaccine was available to the public when the lab blew up."

Nils looked at Mindy. "That confirms the timing. The lab blew up several days before we noticed the outbreak."

"The vaccine was too late, and the outbreak is now a full-blown pandemic," Mindy said.

Nils made a mental note to inform Interpol that Gavin Peak was indeed to blame for keeping the research confidential and not reporting the leak.

Nils told Sunny through the busily texting interpreter that he was grateful to hear her story, but still had one question. "Why haven't you left the hospital?"

She looked into the hallway at her fellow patients. "I took the vaccine," she said in English. "I can care for the others."

It was a simple and selfless explanation.

"When you finally get out of this hospital," Nils told her through the interpreter, "I want you to place a call to the American consulate and thank a young man there named Matthew Justice."

"Matthew Justice?" she asked with a curious look.

"He's a health and science officer who first discovered the outbreak," Nils explained. "And more than anyone else, he's been responsible for getting this pandemic under control."

"Matt Justice?"

Matt Justice had fretted all day in his hotel room, wondering what was happening next door at the golf resort.

He checked his phone every few minutes, waiting for news from Washington, Guangzhou, or the World Health Organization.

All he got was radio silence.

What the hell was happening out there?

He had just stood up to put his shoes on and walk down to the shoreline again when his phone rang.

"*Ja*, Matthew Justice?"

It was Nils Andersson.

"Are you in China yet?" Matt asked.

"Yes. Where are you?"

"I'm out of town," Matt said. "Still in China."

"Matthew. This is a real epidemic."

"Are you safe?"

"Yes," Nils said. "I'm in an army truck right now. Soldiers are escorting us around Guangzhou. But the city's in total lockdown."

Matt had trouble picturing it, considering his last memories were of an overcrowded subway system and a hectic airport.

"It's widespread and deadly," Nils went on. "We have over 25,000 dead and hundreds of thousands more possible cases."

Matt sat back down.

"Can you get into any hospitals?"

"We finally got into one."

"And what did you find?"

"We were looking for Patient Zero. Her name is Sunny, the woman you told us about from FutureGenetics who was in isolation."

"How is she?"

"Never better. It turns out she wasn't the first spreader after all. She had already been vaccinated. But does she ever have a story to tell. Matthew, I need you to connect me with some legal experts in Washington."

"I'll give you the email address of my boss from Guangzhou," Matt said. "He's in Washington now and can coordinate things on that end."

He recited Patrick Kind's email address from memory.

"Thanks," Nils said. "I'll be flying back to Geneva with the vaccine and blood samples, so I'll be out of touch."

"That's okay," Matt said. "I'm feeling out of touch myself."

"Why? Where are you?"

"Still in China, on an island off the southern coast."

"Oops. Got a tunnel."

And the signal went dead.

Matt stared at his phone. He thought of calling Nils back. There was plenty more to discuss with the WHO investigator. But Nils was a busy man.

Matt set down the phone, puzzled.

Nils had called asking for legal expertise. Just what had Patient

Zero told him?

Nils Andersson and his team had cleared out of the American School, having cleaned up the science lab as best they could.

If the students ever returned, they would never know what real life science had been conducted there.

Nils had been ping-ponging email messages with Patrick Kind, the American consul general, for an hour until they could set aside a minute and actually converse over the phone.

The troop transport truck had just emerged from one of multiple tunnels on the way to the airport when Nils' phone rang.

It was Patrick Kind, calling from Washington.

"Listen," Nils said. "We are leaving Guangzhou now with laboratory samples, and I only have a minute to talk."

"Shoot."

"Sir, the city is in shock. The epidemic is not yet under control, but local health authorities are keeping tight track of the numbers, sending out public service announcements, and beginning to dispense medication for treatment. Entire hospitals are serving as quarantine sites with police barring access and egress. And since it's China, they're throwing half the army at the problem, tracking cases, limiting movement of suspected cases, dispensing vaccines, and otherwise trying to contain the spread."

"*Can* it be contained?"

"That has yet to be seen," Nils said. "We went over strategies for prevention and treatment that may avoid more deaths. Give it a few days. If the numbers begin to hold steady, it's a sign that they have it under control."

"And what about the cause?"

"That's where things get interesting. We have reason to believe that this disaster was man-made."

There was a long pause as the diplomat absorbed the news.

Nils went on. "I have all the evidence you need to convict the president of FutureGenetics."

"What do you have on Gavin Peak?"

As the group of army vehicles noisily ground down the empty highway, Nils explained how they got into Nanfang Hospital that afternoon and what they found. He was specifically looking for a young woman that Matthew Justice had identified as Patient Zero.

"When we found her, still in isolation, I recorded her testimony. Her name is Sunny. She was a FutureGenetics employee who worked in a biosafety lab there. She told us how the company had engineered a virus and, subsequently its vaccine, purely for profit."

"They *engineered* the virus?"

"That's her testimony."

"That's all we need to convict them on 'reckless endangerment.'"

"Wait," Nils said. "There's more. The reason she was in isolation was that she had been trapped inside one of the laboratories and the company somehow blew up the lab trying to get her out. I have photographic evidence of the damaged laboratory. The result was the release of the virus in a huge cloud into the air."

"So FutureGenetics *spread* the disease?"

"Apparently so."

"And then people got sick. Can we prove the timing?"

"I have Sunny's testimony on tape, the date of Matthew Justice's visit with her in the hospital, and the dates when HPP cases first appeared."

"You know, a lab leak sounds unintentional," Patrick said. "But we can still add 'involuntary manslaughter' to the case."

"The real crime is they never told anybody," Nils said. "FutureGenetics has yet to report the lab leak to the public…"

"And yet they're selling the vaccine," Patrick finished the thought. "The sicker we get and the more we die, the more we freak out and demand a vaccine."

"That is the case."

"It's great detective work on your part," the diplomat said. "I've been anticipating some sort of case against the company and have been talking with legal experts here. At the very least, it amounts to 'profiteering.' At the most, they could go for 'genocide.'"

"That sounds about right," Nils said. "I'll send you the evidence, but my primary job is to stop what is rapidly turning into a pandemic around the world."

At that moment, they came into view of the airport.

"I have to go now," Nils said. "I'll email you the evidence from the plane."

He turned back to take one last look at Guangzhou. The innumerable dun-colored apartment blocks hung in the haze of perpetual gray skies.

He'd been in the city for less than twelve hours. And that was long enough.

That day on the links proved most enjoyable for Gavin Peak.

Mr. Pu remained the complete pushover he had been on previous rounds, but this time he posed a unique challenge to Gavin. They were partners.

And the competition was fierce. Apparently, golf ability was considered a real asset to members of the Politburo.

"How'd you like a few pointers?" Gavin had asked his competitor turned partner.

Mr. Pu had raised his thick black eyebrows as if wounded by the insult.

"I don't need help," said the offended Party chief.

"Only on your tee shot. I think it's your driver."

"These are the most expensive drivers in the world."

"Just trust me on this." And Gavin lent him his hickory sticks for a few holes.

The difference that produced in Mr. Pu's game was marked. The ball found the middle of the fairway consistently and with distance.

Zhou, who was acting as Mr. Pu's caddy, was silent about the drivers, but when it came to the approach shots and putting, she reached for the Honma Five Star golf clubs.

"I think he might benefit from the Callaways," Gavin had told her.

"Trust me," she told him with a "back off" look.

In the end, she was right. It was Mr. Pu's long putting that kept the round close.

By the eighth hole, Gavin sidled up to Zhou. "How do you know so much about golfing?"

"I don't," she said. "I just know Pu."

By the back nine, Gavin was beginning to wonder if he should borrow the man's irons and putters. But beyond that, he wondered how Zhou knew Pu so well.

By the end of the round, Gavin was sure that Zhou and Pu had long been on close personal terms. They joked and kidded in a way that left little doubt. She had been his plant within FutureGenetics. And one of her jobs had been to steer Gavin to the party secretary for favors and backing.

After all, it was Zhou who first suggested their meeting over golf when Gavin needed to buy off the press.

As dusk fell quickly on the party, the hip flasks came out, and they were toasting the bespectacled party secretary of Guangdong. He had lost the match, but shot his age, inspiring the younger men.

In the clubhouse over dinner, Zhou laughed at Mr. Pu's drunken antics.

"You're close friends with the guy, aren't you?" Gavin whispered to her.

"He was married to my aunt," she said.

Gavin had drunk enough by then that it didn't really matter to him what Zhou thought, but one of his last, most coherent, brainwaves was that her attachment to Mr. Pu was out of loyalty and adoration, whereas her relationship with Gavin was based on self-interest and mutual respect.

He had no idea which made a better foundation for a relationship.

After dinner, Gavin and Zhou took the three Chinese investors to their bungalow for that most ancient of Chinese pastimes: drinking oneself under the table.

The two central government officials kept Mr. Pu's wine glass full, even after he picked himself up off the floor twice and staggered to the bathroom. Each time, he came back paler and smelling of burgundy and half-digested dinner.

Zhou had an alarmed look when once more, Pu set his wine glass down and headed for the john. It was the third time in an hour.

Mr. Yi and General Wang were flopped on the floor with a bottle of Chinese white lightning and singing annoyingly repetitive children's songs. Already three-quarters of a fifth was consumed between the two of them.

Gavin tried to do the math, but gave up. He blamed it on his bourbon.

Finally Zhou rolled over on the carpet and rose to her hands and knees, then crawled toward the bathroom to look after Mr. Pu.

A moment later, the bungalow was filled with a hoarse cry.

Zhou staggered out of the bathroom, a hand over her mouth.

"What the hell?" Gavin muttered. As this was his bungalow, he decided to check out what was going on.

It took a full minute, but after excusing himself to several walls he eventually got to the bathroom to see what had upset her so much.

He almost lost his dinner.

Mr. Pu's form was bowed over the toilet that had been clogged and overflowed with diarrhea and vomit. His head was tilted forward and totally immersed in the bowl.

"How can he breathe?" was Gavin's first thought. Then he became dimly aware of some larger truth. Finally it hit him like a clear bolt of lightning. The guy had drowned in his own excrement.

Gavin reached out and roughly tugged on his golf partner's shoulder. The body tilted backward and crashed to the floor.

Gavin would never forget the sight of the dead man's eyes staring accusingly at him through the smeared slime on his glasses.

"Shit."

Zhou returned and crouched over Pu. She rocked him by the shoulders, but he didn't respond.

At last, she crawled away and leaned against a corner with anguish on her face.

"He's dead!" she said over and over again.

Gavin stumbled back into the living room to address Mr. Yi and General Wang.

Mr. Yi slipped a plastic bag of powder into his rear pocket and they both looked up.

"Your buddy's dead."

The two remaining Chinese investors in FutureGenetics interrupted their singing and stared at him with fixed, fascinated stares.

They didn't move from their spot on the carpet, nor did they seem emotionally affected by the news.

It took Gavin only a moment to realize that the reason they weren't emotionally affected wasn't because they were drunk. It was because they had expected Mr. Pu to die.

He pointed a finger at the two. "You killed him for his share of the business."

They just lay there, denying nothing.

They answered to nobody for the crime. They were the ministry of justice and the military. There was no higher authority.

Gavin sensed Zhou standing behind him and looking at the two partners in crime.

She must have gathered all the implications of what had happened, because it appeared to be too much to handle.

Not only was there a terrible death, but also the person who died was her patron. And what was more, he was murdered in the bungalow of Gavin Peak, her boss and lover.

She had no future in the Party or the company.

Screaming obscenities in Mandarin, she ran at the two visitors and kicked them violently. They shielded themselves, but made no move to stop or appease her.

In absolute frustration and with tears streaming down her face, she tore from the room, threw the glass door open, and ran out into the night.

Matt Justice was sitting on his balcony listening to the distant waves when he heard the cry.

It was a woman's scream from the dark outline of the Hainan Pro Golf Resort.

A minute later, he heard her running on the beach.

He had to find out what was happening.

He jumped up, ran through his hotel room, and out into the hallway.

If he ran the length of the hallway toward the shore, he could intercept her before she reached the Sheraton hotel.

His bare feet skidded down the cement stairwell out into the courtyard.

The night was filled with the evening chatter of birds, and he struggled to hear the woman's cries.

Then he heard her splashing closer. He turned in that direction and thrashed through the jungle to intercept her.

He burst out onto the sand just as she ran by.

"Stop!" he said harshly, and grabbed her by the shoulders.

In the moonlight, he recognized who she was. She was General Peak's travel companion.

It was the break he had been waiting for. General Peak's case may have just cracked wide open.

"I can help you," he said firmly. "Follow me."

She sobbed in anguish and trembled uncontrollably. Blinded by tears, she needed him to direct her through the trees.

He guided her toward the hotel and up the stairs to his floor.

"I can take care of you," he assured her. "Just stay quiet and everything will be okay."

There were no guests to worry about, but Matt was careful not to draw the attention of the hotel staff.

They made it into his room apparently unnoticed. But he had to be honest with himself. It wouldn't take long for someone to follow and find her.

By the time he locked the door, her tears had been replaced by sheer anger.

The poised assistant that he had observed before had turned into a wildly passionate woman.

He couldn't wait to hear what she had to say.

He sat her in an armchair and handed her a warm, moist facecloth to wipe away her tears.

Then he waited for her story to come out.

He had an hour, maybe all night, to get the story out of her. But that moment wouldn't last forever.

Matt was astounded as he gradually learned Zhou's story.

Mr. Pu had died at the hands of the drunken ministers of public security and the military. And their intention was to pin the murder on General Peak.

The next morning, General Peak would take the train to Sanya, where he hoped to book a flight out of the country.

"Where to?"

"It sounded like anywhere would be fine with him."

"That gives me an idea..."

CHAPTER 6

Containment

Wednesday morning, Gavin Peak awoke in Harold Priest's bungalow with the curtain open above his bed.

He fought off the dull roar of last night's drinking and wondered if Harold had any ibuprofen.

It was a moody day with a gray sky.

Gavin would rather curl up and go back to sleep, but he knew something dreadful had happened the night before, and he needed to scram.

Then he remembered the gruesome end to the night's party. He couldn't stand the sight of the dead body in his room, so he had asked to spend the night in Harold's private bungalow.

He wasn't even sure if Harold knew what had happened.

Mr. Pu's body would make an awful surprise for that morning's housekeeper.

From Harold's living room window, he watched the two Chinese investors clear out of the resort.

He would love to report them to the authorities, until he remembered that, as head of public security and the military, they *were* the authorities.

Then he remembered Zhou abandoning him and running away in the dark. Why was that?

The fog was gradually lifting.

She had lost her mentor in Mr. Pu. And her boss, Gavin, might be implicated in the murder, as it had occurred in his bungalow.

The real problem was that FutureGenetics' Chinese investors might call the authorities on Gavin.

The two men had no sooner departed via their speedy skiff than Gavin heard the wail of sirens.

He sat on the edge of the bed and listened carefully. The cop cars were drawing closer.

His shirt smelled of alcohol, but he kept it on and covered it with his blazer.

Harold came into the room just as Gavin was zipping his suitcase shut.

"Your train will depart soon. The time has come to leave."

The two Chinese officials had flown the coop and left Gavin at the scene of the crime.

At least Harold would come through for him.

Gavin's head cleared more as the police cars stopped outside the resort and he heard the sound of running feet. He shook bugs out of his shoes and slipped them on.

Without Mr. Pu's protection, he had nothing to keep the police at bay. Chinese authorities could accuse Gavin of more than murder. They could blame him for the containment leak, even pin the epidemic on him.

If Gavin ended up in Chinese court with his investors providing evidence against him, they could avoid responsibility and take over the company.

On the other hand, if Gavin could make it out of the country, he could avoid a trial and prevent being scapegoated for the deaths of thousands. He could also continue running the company and pocket his bonus pay.

From Harold's window, he monitored the policemen's movements and waited for the right moment to slip out.

They methodically stalked the bungalow where the body lay.

No doubt the tip-off had come from the men in the departing motorboat.

Gavin didn't need to stick around until the police discovered the body and started to look for him.

"This way, General." Harold escorted Gavin outside.

They stole across the dewy grass.

A hotel van waited among the police cars.

Without saying a word, Gavin threw his suitcase onto the rear seat and climbed in.

Harold joined him in the van and soon they sped down the main street toward Haikou.

Curiously when they drove through the city, it was almost as if people were afraid to leave their houses.

Gavin felt more vulnerable to scrutiny as they drove down the near-empty street.

The train station had an anonymous-looking entrance, like any other building in town. Except a high rail system swept out of the second floor and headed south over the city.

Heads bent, people rushed into the station lugging their suitcases. That eliminated one concern. It appeared that health authorities hadn't shut down train service.

Inside the station felt like an airport terminal, complete with a vast waiting area and sunny, south-facing windows with a view of arriving and departing trains.

Gavin was impressed by the high-tech design. "This is no ordinary train station. Is it some sort of monorail?"

"Ah," Harold said. "You're in for a treat. This is a high-speed elevated train direct from Haikou to Sanya. Here we like to think of ourselves as the Orlando of Hainan, and Sanya as Miami. Once there, you'll find wonderful accommodations by the sea."

The analogy seemed a stretch. But the tracks did remind Gavin of the Monorail ride at Epcot.

Harold came back from the window with a ticket to Sanya.

"Here you go, General. Have a nice trip."

Gavin studied the golf resort owner's beaming face.

"Why are you sticking your neck out for me?"

"I'm just here to help my guests," was the simple reply.

For the first time, Gavin considered Harold Priest's craven nature a blessing.

Distant police sirens impinged on Gavin's consciousness.

Harold must have heard them approaching, too.

"Got to go," Harold said, and hustled toward the exit.

"The train from Haikou to Sanya is boarding," came a pre-recorded announcement.

Gavin grabbed his suitcase and threw himself into the scrum of passengers vying to thread the security gate.

He reached the first door of the train and ducked in just as policemen barged into the waiting area.

His last glance showed Harold Priest pointing the policeman toward a different foreigner who was attempting to pass through security.

It was that tall redhead from the consulate. Matt Justice.

The guy was still tailing him!

"Shit," Gavin muttered, and stuffed himself into the train.

With luck, Harold had successfully diverted the police and they would arrest the consulate man instead.

The train's interior was modern and open like a commuter train, and there was absolutely no place for Gavin to hide. Every passenger seat was in full view.

He pushed through three full cars until he found his numbered seat.

Before sitting down, he glanced back out the large, sealed window.

Police stormed the train platform in pursuit of Matt Justice.

How long would it take before the police discovered it was the wrong man?

The platform doors hissed for several seconds and Gavin heard pandemonium on the platform. Then the doors began to shut.

When the train finally lurched forward, Gavin fell into his seat. Acceleration built and within seconds, they were suspended over the city and gliding ever faster.

He had no recourse but to throw his suitcase onto the empty seat beside him and ride it out.

It was only a matter of minutes before the policemen realized Harold's deception and threw the vestibule door open.

He lowered his head and tried to make himself look small and inconspicuous. His gaze landed on the empty seat beside him. Maybe it was the seat Harold had bought for Zhou.

As the train passed quickly over a wide river into a cultivated jungle, he thought with regret about his wild Chinese girl.

Sure, Zhou had been manipulating him to help Mr. Pu, but he admired her for it. She was forward leaning in every way. Losing her felt like losing an opportunity for personal growth.

They were entering dry, hilly scrubland.

How long did Harold say the trip would take? An hour?

Did he have that much time before the police discovered him, only to haul him off to a Chinese labor camp for the rest of his life?

Eventually, the blur of coconut palms grew tiring on his eyes. And when they revved up to 250 kilometers per hour, the collage of nearby houses and trees reminded him of his hangover.

So he closed his eyes and tried to let the gentle rocking lull him to sleep.

Matthew Justice's armpits were already hot and sticky by the time he moved out of the Sheraton.

He felt mild pity for Zhou as he left her lying asleep on his couch.

But his sympathy could only go so far. She had been in league with Mr. Pu and in love with General Peak.

Look where that had gotten her.

Now he heard police cars careening down the road toward the Hainan Pro Golf Resort. Would General Peak escape in time?

Matt had just hopped into a taxi for the train station and left the shoreline behind him when his phone rang.

"This is Patrick Kind," came the familiar voice. "Are you safe?"

"Yes, sir. I'm heading by taxi to the high-speed train to Sanya right now. I learned that General Peak might be on that train."

"Okay, great. Here's what we've developed on our end. The WHO has interviewed Sunny, the FutureGenetics patient in Nanfang Hospital, and she has verified your story that the company developed the virus on their own, then created the vaccine. However, the lab exploded before vaccines were available, and people got infected all over the city. We've got photographic evidence of the explosion, and that's why Sunny was in isolation."

"And the bastard never reported the accident," Matt said.

"Correct. So the FBI has taken possession of the evidence and asked Interpol to issue an international warrant for his arrest."

"China may be a member of Interpol," Matt said. "But I know for a fact that China's Minister of Public Security was an investor in General Peak's company, and I'm sure he'll want to keep a tight lid on that information. He certainly won't want General Peak to leave the country. Instead, he has set up General Peak and will likely put him on trial, with no defense team, here in China."

"Then you've got to get him out of the country so he can face a proper jury and we can expose the crime."

"I have an idea," Matt said. "You get the evidence, and I'll bring you the culprit."

He hung up feeling confident that things just might work out if he handled things correctly.

Now, was General Peak at the train station?

It turned out that Zhou had told the truth.

She was right that General Peak was taking the train to Sanya.

Matt caught a glimpse of the general at the station as he waited with another Caucasian man.

And Zhou was absolutely right that the police were coming to apprehend General Peak on behalf of his company's investors.

The police had picked up General Peak's trail and were storming the train station from the street below.

Matt paid for his ticket and followed the general, who climbed onto the first train car.

Then the police burst through the station door. The Caucasian man pointed wildly at Matt.

Was the guy fingering *him*?

Matt scooted through the security gate, hoping without much confidence that the police would stop there.

Of course they didn't.

He ducked into the train and kept pushing through the cars in an effort to evade the police.

Instead, they walked along the platform, following his progress step by step.

After four carriages, Matt heard the train doors hiss prior to shutting. To trip up the police, he reversed direction and ran toward the rear of the train.

A policeman shouted a command and officers ran back to intercept him.

But the doors closed before they could enter the train.

The police bellowed for the train to stop. But the train automatically began to ease out of the station.

Hands slapped against the outside of the windows in a vain attempt to stop the train.

The train picked up speed and suddenly shot out over empty space.

There was no way for the police to pursue him on the elevated tracks or follow by road at such incredible speeds. But someone would be waiting for him at the other end.

Matt grabbed the luggage rack and paused to catch his breath. He hadn't been running, but his heart raced.

Then he looked down and saw a familiar sight. The brush cut and graying hair gave him away. Just seats ahead, ducking to remain out of sight, sat General Gavin Peak.

Matt wanted to strangle the arrogant, self-absorbed, heartless bastard.

But he had a higher duty. He had to call the State Department and find a way to slip the general out of the country.

And, with police waiting for Matt, he would have to work it out before the train reached its destination.

The immediate problem was that there might be police on the train. He had to draw attention away from the general.

Even for someone with no sense of direction, it was hard to get lost on a train. He could either go north or he could go south.

He retraced his steps until he reached his assigned seat.

They were speeding just over the rooftops of the city and rapidly approaching the countryside when he finally sat down.

He waited for any policeman who had jumped aboard to nab him.

After a few minutes passed and no cops arrived, Matt felt free to contact Washington and set the gears in motion for the general's extradition.

He would need to keep his voice low, but there was lots of nervous chatter from other passengers.

When he dialed the State Department's Ops Center, a voice different than that earlier in the morning answered.

"Department of State Operations Center," a man said in a smart manner.

"This is Matthew Justice. I called before."

He could hear keys clicking in the background.

"Yes, Matthew. I have your case file. Are you still in China?"

"I am, and I need the Gulfstream that's in Hong Kong in order to evacuate."

"Where are you presently?"

"Approaching the city of Sanya on Hainan Island in southern China. I can get to the Sanya international airport within, say, two or three hours."

"Okay. Let me call, confirm the availability of the aircraft. and get a flight plan. I'll call you right back."

Matt watched the coconut palms that formed a blur out his window. He wasn't going anywhere.

Matt waited for his phone to ring and tried to ignore all the other phones ringing around him.

Under normal circumstances, the trip across Hainan would make a true getaway. He would gladly trade the permanent, stultifying atmosphere of government work or the tacky, provisional fixtures of private industry for an island adventure that only Robert Louis Stevenson could have imagined.

All Matt knew about the island was gleaned from reading about Hainan and from one previous trip he had taken over the past Christmas holiday to a Sanya resort.

Hainan was an oblong island that dripped like a ripe mango southward into the South China Sea. Only slightly smaller than Taiwan, it was made up of indigenous cultures that had long resisted the forces of history.

Hainan's east coast was developed with wall-to-wall orchards and fields, the west was not yet developed, and the central mountains were dry.

Like any actual trip to an area, the train ride down the island would prove his assumptions true, or force him to redraw his mental map of the island.

As it turned out, the details were far more complex than he had imagined. Symmetrical fields of vegetables and rice were carved out of dense forest. Man-made lakes, ditches, and ponds spilled everywhere.

The train flew like a bird just over the trees and rusty roofs of plantations.

He saw steep, verdant mountains beyond rolling grass fields, and orchards with white gravel roads winding through the trees.

Finally, he felt assured that no police were on the train. It was time to leave his seat and pay the general a visit.

"Hello, General."

Matt removed the suitcase and slid into the empty seat beside the highly lauded man who had sunk so low in his estimation.

"Remember me?"

The general jerked around with a fearful look.

"Oh. It's you." General Peak seemed confused, as if trying to dispel a nightmare. Then his eyes narrowed with irritation. "What are you doing here?"

Matt was amused by the response, but tried not to show it.

"My job is to evacuate Americans," he said airily. "And you're on my list."

"What list?"

"You know. The consulate's warden list in case of national emergencies. Friends of the consulate and all that. Patrick Kind added your name, and you're my responsibility."

"Well, that's very kind of him." The general's gravelly voice exuded warmth, while his eyes betrayed wariness.

"In fact, we have a CDC plane arriving in Sanya in the next hour to pick up passengers and evacuate them from China."

"That would be wonderful." The eyes slowly began to lose their hardness. "I was going to book a flight myself. Where is the flight headed?"

"We're bringing Americans home."

The general took a moment to look outside. Vehicles on a creaky old highway seemed at a near standstill compared with the speed of the train.

"A flight back to the States would be fine."

"Excellent."

With that, Matt stood up.

"At the end of this line, you need to take a cab straight to the airport." He reached into his wallet and handed the general a hundred yuan. "This should cover it. In the meantime, I'll leave you to your thoughts."

Just as they were passing through Wanning, an important second-tier city with a big school, a handful of high-rises, and lazy streets, Matt returned to his seat.

By the time he sat down, it was farmland again, with mountains to the east. It was a bigger island than he had expected as new mountain ranges kept popping up.

Eventually, the blur grew tiring on the eyes. Matt was just nodding off when his phone vibrated in his hands.

It was Dr. Gina Woods from the CDC.

"Matt, you're good to go. The Gulfstream is on its way from Hong Kong to pick you up. It should arrive in Sanya in less than two hours."

"That's great, except for a slight change in plans. Waiting at the airport will be an American gentleman named General Gavin Peak. I want you to treat him with the utmost respect and bring him to the nearest port of entry in the United States."

"That would be a twelve-hour flight to Anchorage," Gina said, "where the plane will stop for refueling."

"Perfect. That's as far as he needs to go."

"And how about you, Matt? Will you be on that flight?"

"No, I won't. I'm fully vaccinated and have a few more things to wrap up here."

"Take care, sir."

Matt hung up thinking, huh, nobody in the government had ever called him "sir" before.

Even though he hadn't left the train, all the phone calls made it feel like a typical day at the office.

He had one more call to make.

He opened the list of recent incoming calls just as the train entered a long, dark tunnel.

He had to wait to call Patrick Kind back.

When they emerged from the darkness, he saw a range of mountains extend down to the sea. The only sign of human activity was terracing down by the rivers.

He looked at his phone. The consul general's number had a Washington, DC prefix. Matt pushed the button to dial.

"China Desk. How may I help you?" Patrick Kind responded. So that's where the consul general hung his hat these days.

"Hello, sir. This is Matthew Justice."

"Keeping it on track, young man?"

"Yes, sir. Literally on track. But there's a new wrinkle. I need help on your end."

"Fire away."

"First, does the Justice Department still have enough evidence to apprehend and indict General Peak?"

"They assure me they do. They'll go for 'multiple homicide.'"

"Good. Because General Peak will be arriving in Anchorage on a CDC emergency evacuation plane in twelve hours."

"How did you swing that?"

"General Peak thinks the U.S. Government is rolling out the red carpet for him. The CDC doesn't know who he is, except that he's an American who needs evacuation from China."

"And we'll be waiting for him with federal marshals."

"If you can arrange it with Justice, sir."

"You bet. As soon as he sets foot on American soil, I'll have the FBI take him into custody."

Matt sighed with relief.

"Young man, you do good work."

"Thank you, sir."

"I assume you'll be on that flight?"

"Unfortunately, my work in China isn't finished."

"You know that the WHO is already in Guangzhou and several other cities in the region."

"It's more than that," Matt said. "I still have to say 'good-bye.'"

They were just entering another tunnel when he hung up.

A minute later, they came out the other side and passed from a landscape of tea terraces to a world of large white apartment houses, factories, and offices.

They pulled into the train station minutes later. As expected, a swarm of policemen waited on the platform.

Welcome to Sanya.

Matt emerged from the train first, his hands held high.

The police yanked him away from departing passengers and bent his arms painfully behind his back.

He heard the cops remark about his drenched shirt and red face, sure signs of guilt.

From the corner of his eye, he watched General Peak slip down the exit stairs. The general was getting away, but Matt was destined for the clink.

Out came the handcuffs. They felt cold and firm around his wrists. Then with a rough tug, Matt was led away.

Gavin Peak had been travelling in the CDC's Gulfstream for twelve hours with no more company than the male steward who only had fried rice meals from Hong Kong to heat up in a microwave.

The drink selection was what he might suspect of a CDC plane: no alcohol or soft drinks, only fruit juices. There was only so much guava juice one could drink before the skin turned green.

The movie selection was just as limited. There were DVDs that he could play on his private screen, but they were all David Attenborough droning on about some scorched landscape or mistreated animal.

He had visited the cockpit several times, and found the pilots equally bored. At least they had a machine to fly.

Gavin just wasn't made for confined spaces.

Golden sunlight streamed through the cabin windows late into what should have been nighttime. Such was the effect of flying northward as the small jet traced the Great Circle back to the United States.

He had drawn down the shades and tried sleep. But images of the murder in Hainan and thousands of faces in surgical masks continued to haunt him.

Even when he thought about Zhou, his co-equal in the boardroom and bedroom, it was with a touch of loss.

He wondered if he would ever get back to Guangzhou. He would miss the pregnant sky that greeted him every morning at his villa.

He looked back fondly on his climb through the village to get to Eve's house, where she had refused to take the vaccine. Silly girl.

Still, she brought a smile to his face. "Get down. Get down. And move it all around."

He had never gotten the pleasure of moving it all around with her,. His loss and hers.

But there were other women. Many Asian hotties had rubbed up against him at the American Chamber of Commerce ball and taken selfies with him. He guessed that from his perspective they should be called "themies."

But there were other cities, other countries.

From the perspective of thirty thousand feet, he let his imagination roam.

He had read about new superbugs in India, microbes that had grown resistant to antibiotics.

What if he brought Dr. Chen with him to New Delhi and they pursued their current line of attack on the India problem?

It was a vast market, with plenty of beautiful women who would die to take selfies with him.

His shoes were off and the video monitor was flickering behind his closed eyelids, when the intercom clicked several times.

He was reminded of the flight he had taken from L.A. to Guangzhou where that flight attendant from Texas had tripped in the aisle.

He had risen to the occasion and managed to diagnose the problem and stabilize her. The sound of all the passengers and crew applauding as he returned to his seat had been stirring, but unnecessary. He was a doctor. What did they expect?

Why were his actions considered noteworthy? Even the American consul general in Guangzhou had complimented him on his heroism.

What did others see in him that he didn't?

Then the pilot's voice came over the intercom.

"We'll be landing in Anchorage shortly for a brief refueling stop before we continue on to Los Angeles."

Gavin had never been to Alaska. After the south of China, Alaska sounded cold and bleak.

He lifted his window shade and let in a cool, blue glow. There was an angry sea and scattered houses as they drew close to land. There was also a dusting of snow on the ground.

Gavin involuntarily rubbed his hands together for warmth. If people weren't so enthusiastic about living there, he figured the state would have made a great penal colony.

Instantly, he longed for the watermelon-tequila drinks at poolside with tanned women soaking in the sun.

Why had he ever turned his oversexed neighbor down? What sort of puritanical streak prevented him from a momentary lapse into hedonism? Perhaps that was what others saw in him: selflessness.

And indeed as a doctor, a general, and a CEO, what characterized him was his service. He was a public servant.

With satisfaction and a tinge of vindication, he could assert to his military friends and business colleagues that they had been wrong. He had brought his military aggressiveness, his devotion to medical duty, and his single-minded pursuit of profit all to bear on the epidemic. And by any metric, the rollout of the vaccine had been a success. In fact, he would argue, only someone with all three talents could have achieved such a result.

The Gulfstream battled a fierce crosswind that created a new kind of howl over the wings. But the captain knew his stuff and set the bird down lightly on the runway.

Gavin took in the details at ground level. Scattered about in the snow were various hangars and office buildings. It was unlike most commercial airports he'd seen.

They were rocketing across what looked like a military airbase.

Then it all made sense. His status was that of an American citizen being evacuated from a disease-ridden zone aboard a U.S. Government aircraft, operated by the Centers for Disease Control and Prevention. Of course they would refuel at a military depot.

He had been hoping to walk through a jet way into a warm and welcoming terminal to get himself a hot cup of coffee. But it looked like they were rolling to a stop on an apron with camouflage-colored refueling trucks and a black Suburban standing by.

He also saw a couple of men huddled in the cold in leather jackets and blowing on their hands to keep warm.

A welcoming committee, no doubt.

Gavin slipped into his wingtip shoes and tied them tight. He was reminded of all the official functions that he had attended in Guangzhou. He enjoyed working hard, but he could easily live without the social stuff.

It was the small talk with minor celebrities who had nothing significant to say that always annoyed him. But it was small talk he prepared to share with the two men while the aircraft refueled.

Since the setting appeared entirely military, he decided to put his figurative general's hat on. After all, in China hadn't they called him the General?

The steward opened the cabin door and lowered the stairs for him.

Gavin bundled up his collar around his throat. This was going to be one cold layover. At least it would be brief.

He rose to his feet and, with a stiff-legged, rocking motion, moved forward in the cabin.

He had to duck at the doorway as he faced the cold blast of Arctic air.

Then he put on a brave smile and threw a salute to the two men waiting for him in the snow.

"Nice weather you've got for me," he told them with a smile as he carefully descended the stairway.

"Yes," one of them said. "We made it cold just for you."

Gavin grinned. These were his kind of people.

One man approached him and took him by the arm.

So polite. He didn't want his leather shoes to slide out from under him.

"General Peak?"

"That's right."

"We are Federal Marshals. You're under arrest."

Custody in the police station in Sanya was not a pleasant experience. But Matt needed to buy time for General Peak to get to the airport and successfully depart, so he kept mum about his identity.

The police looked suspiciously at his diplomatic ID and whatever else they discovered in his wallet.

Matt tracked their conversations while pretending not to understand or speak Mandarin. But the words about him and Americans in general weren't kind.

They shoved him into rank-smelling solidarity confinement, where he had plenty of time to think.

The one overriding thought, brought home by the smarting stench of the place, was that life was unfair.

General Peak had likely caused his sweetheart's death. Yet Matt had let him go.

He wondered what the FBI would do with General Peak once they had him in custody. Federal prosecutors had him dead to rights on multiple manslaughter.

Whatever sentence the court imposed, it couldn't be harsh enough.

Matt's biggest concern was that they might allow General Peak to plea bargain for a more lenient sentence in order to hire him back for his expertise in biological warfare. They might see him as some sort of evil genius in that regard.

Still Matt hoped not, and would have to trust the U.S. legal system to do the right thing.

He finally grew tired of the four filthy walls and knocked on the tiny window.

There might not be many officers left at the consulate general in Guangzhou to answer his call. But whoever remained would know him and could verify his identity and vouch for him.

"Officers," he said in his best Mandarin. "I can talk to you now."

After his release from police custody, Matthew Justice took an empty city bus back into the heart of Sanya.

They passed a single-story hospital built under banyan trees. Wearing full surgical masks, patients walked behind a chain link fence and stared out at the free world.

The bus passed an institution that suffered a different indignity. It was a tall mosque with the impassive splendor of the Middle East. But its imposing façade was marred by Chinese architectural frills.

At the bus depot, there were other buses, but few passengers. Matt consulted the schedules and found the bus for Yalong Bay.

The city receded behind him and the bus entered a long stretch of what could easily pass for a modern resort destination in Hawaii. A string of opulent hotels fronted on the sea, and an endless golf course ran along the other side of the road.

Matt checked into the Sheraton.

"You look sweaty," the receptionist said, and held a thermometer strip to his forehead.

He felt her cold hand pressed against his forehead and waited for the result.

"Sorry," she said at last. "Just checking."

Then she issued him a room key.

Matt looked around the white, pillared lobby. As in Haikou, the hotel was nearly empty.

He spent that evening on the beach, knees tucked under his chin, watching the waves roll in.

He had spent Christmas there last year, but knew his friends wouldn't be in China to join him this year.

If they were even alive.

He couldn't tell what was happening in other countries across the sea. But what he had seen in China was utterly devastating.

He sat on the patio restaurant and ordered a bowl of Thai coconut chicken and listened to the staff stacking dishes just inside.

After dinner, he checked out the gift shop. He picked up a book named *China Gate* and took it up to his room to read. The book's remarkable plot began right there on Yalong Bay.

The next morning, Matt was awakened by a telephone call from the receptionist.

"I'm sorry to bother you, sir. There is an officer from the government asking to see you."

"Which government?"

"He's from the Ministry of Foreign Affairs."

Oh God. What had he done now?

"I'll come down."

Matt hid his copy of the novel under his mattress, pulled on the same old dress shirt that had clung to his back for the past few days, and went down to meet his fate.

He expected a squad of police waiting in the lobby, but only found a young man slicking back his hair in a mirror.

"Matthew Justice?" the man asked. "I am so happy to meet you."

It took Matt a few minutes to piece together what had happened, but eventually learned that he was some sort of hero.

News of General Gavin Peak's arrest in Alaska seemed to have sparked China's interest.

To the Chinese, General Peak was someone they could pin the disaster on. And the official press would make the most of it.

"I am here to welcome you," the young officer said in conclusion. "And to warn you. There will be TV cameras and speeches."

The man was right. It turned out that both foreign and Chinese press, there to cover the Boao Forum, were stranded due to the epidemic and had little else to cover.

Over the ensuing few days, Matt received the full VIP treatment in Sanya.

He was photographed talking at every meeting. He never broke concentration. He was forced to speak to any *ad hoc* group at a moment's notice. And he tried to put people at ease.

On his final day, he walked along the endless beach of Yalong Bay, getting sweaty. It felt lonely with no vacationers in sight.

He was also developing a powerful hunger. He stopped by the gift shop for snack food. But all the shelves were empty as those stuck on the island had hoarded every last crumb.

Then the Foreign Affairs Officer took him in an official car to the airport after what looked like a recent rain.

CHAPTER 7

City of Flowers

Once Matt Justice was back in Guangzhou, it was too late for work. The consulate would be closed.

So he took a deep breath and decided to go downtown and finally take the walk that he and Eve had never managed to have.

He climbed down Orchid Mountain on his way to the city bus that would take him to the metro.

Two German children were sharing the springy seesaw, the only voices on the compound.

It might take a year for expatriates to return to the country, until he remembered the tremendous allure of the Canton Fair that planned to open its doors wide in the spring.

A woman in a tan coat greeted him as he passed the clubhouse where Eve had worked.

She looked new, and she didn't recognize him.

Matt had to wait ten minutes for the city bus to arrive. It approached the dirt turnaround and nosed up to the passenger hut where Matt stood by himself.

He got on, swiped his card, and sat down.

The engine idled and the vents pumped cold air into his face, but it was the driver's break time. The man wandered around the bus with a rag to wipe the lights, a cigarette stuck between his lips.

Eventually, the driver got back on, put on his facemask, and swung the front door shut. The brakes released with a hiss.

As they passed through the backstreet neighborhood, Matt noticed colorful shrines in the doorways of several houses. Bouquets of daisies and white roses were set around portraits of the deceased, while white candles burned in silence.

Further into town, the sidewalks were gradually returning to life. There was even a stall selling oranges, a sign of the coming winter.

As he strolled the short distance from the bus stop to the metro, people skulked around the closed restaurants like hungry dogs.

The afternoon light only reached so far, as he descended the stairs into the gloom.

His metro card was still good for another few rides.

He got on the near-empty train and took a seat.

At all the metro stops, the train picked up more people, and few got off.

As he neared his destination, Matt had to give up his seat.

Young Chinese families were chatting quietly, and heavy women in flip-flops conversed in the middle of the aisle.

On the last stop before the metro passed under the Pearl River, Matt got off.

The passengers left the platform and got strung out on a long, jagged course southward under the city toward the exit.

But when the staircase took him up to street level, he was in Zhujiang, that spanking new part of town that was built on a huge scale. He stood surrounded by the most stunning, avant-garde architecture anywhere in the world.

Guangzhou Dadao Road led out through a final gateway of geometrically interesting edifices to an open square along the river.

The modern stadium, built over the Pearl River, loomed in the dusk.

People flooded the open space. There were plenty of red flags. Police and barricades were there for crowd control.

People flowed across the wide bridge toward the stadium. There was a free concert due to take place that evening to celebrate the city's triumph over adversity, three weeks after the initial outbreak.

Matt checked out the gardens and modern skyscrapers, built for the recent Asia Games. The city looked new and interesting from that vantage point.

What was called Flower City Square felt like a mini-Central Park. Red and yellow blossoms predominated, combining the patriotic with the beautiful.

The park seemed small beside the vertical wall of buildings, but there was plenty of room for families to picnic and friends to stroll about in the cool evening.

He crossed bridges and entered a bamboo forest walk. For a moment, he blended in like a tree in the woods. He forgot that he was in a Chinese city, at Ground Zero.

Then he headed back toward town, hoping to find dinner and a taxi home.

As he walked, he checked his watch. It was late enough to reach the Atlanta folks just coming in to work.

So he dialed Dr. Gina Woods, his CDC contact who had arranged General Peak's evacuation.

"I'm calling to report on conditions in Guangzhou," he said.

"Don't worry, Matt," Gina replied. "The WHO is keeping us current with all the health data we need."

"What's happening in the U.S.?"

"We're skeptical about the vaccine, but giving doses to high-risk populations. That is generally people living or working with suspected cases. We're definitely not going to push for herd immunity."

"Still lots of cases?" Matt asked.

"Well, with public awareness campaigns, we're beginning to feel that a turnaround is within sight. The epi curve appears to have reached its peak, and that is enormously good news."

Gina paused, then said, "Speaking of news, Matt, we've been watching you on television. The Chinese have been treating you like a national hero."

"Yeah. I did a few rounds with the press."

"I must say I liked the way you handled yourself. Very impressive."

"Well, it wasn't for the right reasons."

"You were the first to alert the World Health Organization. And on top of that, you got your guy."

"Can you believe what he thought he could get away with?" Matt said. "Playing fast and loose with science. Lying to the press. Corruption at the highest levels. Only in China, huh?"

"You'd be surprised," Gina said. "No country is immune to small-mindedness, and greed knows no bounds."

It was a chilling reminder, coming from someone charged with keeping America safe.

Before dawn the next day, the consul general's Cadillac pulled up to Matt Justice's small apartment half-way up Orchid Mountain.

Inside was only the driver, and an empty back seat for Matt.

In the darkness, he rode on the overhead expressway with a feeling of humility and, with the American flag snapping sharply on the fender, a deep sense of responsibility.

In the city below, candles illuminated floral arrangements in the doorways of apartment blocks on every street.

Just as dawn was breaking, he stepped out of the car and took a deep breath. The only silver lining to the pandemic was that the economic shutdown had created near-pristine air.

He entered the consulate and was greeted with a friendly "Good morning, sir," from the Marine on duty.

Matt saluted the young man and was buzzed into the secure area.

With most employees and families evacuated from post, few were left to keep the place running.

The small staff consisted of the Marines, of course, and a handful of first-tour officers who normally issued visas. Naturally, all of that had been put on hold.

In the unused cafeteria, a quick reckoning among the officers present determined that Matt Justice was the ranking officer at post. Which made it official. He was in charge of the whole show.

He was Consul General.

Matt walked into his new office wondering if Patrick Kind would mind. Matt could get used to the place. After all, it provided a television, a refrigerator, a coffeemaker, and couches on which he could sleep if necessary.

On the phone from Geneva, Nils Andersson was the first to pierce the silence.

"Hi Nils. Tell me something I want to hear."

"I've got good news…"

"Start with that."

"The good news is that our lab confirmed that the vaccine is for that exact strain of HPP virus."

"So it should work."

"Yes, as long as the Ministry of Health and military continue to pass it out in China, and affected cities overseas continue to take it, we should see an eventual decrease in the number of cases."

"And the bad news?"

"The bad news is that we took blood from two birds while in Guangzhou–a thrush and a magpie–and both had the virus."

"Interpret that for me."

"Viruses need susceptible hosts in which to copy themselves, to reproduce. We thought that if we eradicated the virus in people, the HPP would no longer be able to replicate."

"But…"

"They found a new host. Birds have become a reservoir for HPP. So, the World Health Organization is now recommending the culling of Guangdong Province's entire bird population. That's domesticated and wild, waterfowl and poultry."

"You can't kill all the birds."

"Needless to say, there will be resistance from many quarters."

Matt could already see the environmentalists and poultry industry joining forces to fight the wholescale slaughter.

There was only one possible conclusion that he could draw. "This new disease will be with us for a long, long time."

Nils agreed. "I'm sorry, Matthew."

Matt thanked his buddy at the WHO, and wished that the world's governments would spend far more money on public health.

When Matt hung up, there was a blinking light on his phone. With the consulate's new, rudimentary organizational tree, the Marines were taking incoming calls.

It was Detachment Commander Rodriguez on the line. "Mr. Consul General? I took a call from the provincial Health Department. They say it's been three weeks and the city is releasing a number of patients from Nanfang Hospital, including someone named Sunny."

Matt stepped outside and walked toward the Cadillac. For the first time, he could see the entire city. He could also smell it, and it wasn't bad. There were actual food and earthy aromas all around him.

He took the official car from the gleaming towers of New Town north toward the outskirts of the city.

He was still struck by the absence of traffic. They rolled through town barely needing to heed the stoplights that still conducted traffic that was no longer there.

Heaps of trash littered the sidewalks, evidence of people living behind closed shutters and locked doors. Packs of dogs, the only signs of life, scavenged in the rubbish.

The magenta-colored bougainvilleas in the medians were reverting to their natural, unkempt state. And autumn leaves lay uncollected in the gutter.

Matt was still unused to the smooth ride and quiet interior of the car.

The reflective black hood gradually nosed into a neighborhood that was more familiar. Farther from the city center, he began to see pedestrians, but none of the cars that normally crammed the streets.

It was heartening to see an old woman splash water out her front door with the morning ritual of house cleaning. And a group of schoolgirls on unplanned holiday sat in a row under a tree reading aloud from their textbooks.

Finally the bold, white structure of Nanfang Hospital came into view.

The ring of police cars he had previously seen there was gone, replaced by a few dazed patients wandering free into the light of day.

He spotted Sunny at once. She wore the same green pajamas she had worn when standing in the middle of her isolation room swinging her arms with nothing to do.

He noticed that the bandages on her face and appendages were gone, and her skin looked nicely healed.

He asked the driver to stop, and walked the rest of the distance to her.

She seemed to recognize him, a small wonder after so much had happened.

"Are you okay?" he asked.

When at first she didn't respond, he prepared to apologize. Then she started to speak.

"I can talk to you," she said. "But I can't hear you."

Her diction sounded slightly muddled.

Then he remembered photographs of the laboratory where she had worked. The explosion must have rendered her deaf as it freed the man-made virus.

She looked upward into his face and held his gaze. "I would like you to do me a favor."

"Sure," he said with a shrug. "Anything."

Reading that physical gesture, she took him by the sleeve of his suit coat and pulled him through the emerging throng toward the dreaded hospital.

Patients of every size, age, and description were breathing fresh air for the first time in weeks. They were mute with awe at the deep blue sky and the sound of birds that flew freely about, having seemingly taken over the city.

Matt studied their faces. No longer wearing surgical masks and not coughing, they seemed healthier than when they had entered the hospital.

Was it the vacation from their normal lives? Their medically beefed-up immune systems? Simply the clean dose of oxygen?

One person, slightly shorter than the rest, had come to a full stop on the lip of the curb.

She wore an oversized T-shirt with a pink heart on front. Inside the heart read, "SECRET CRUSH Under one's hat!"

Her chestnut brown hair was parted to one side, but not well brushed. And she held a bridal magazine in her little hands.

He waved at her and got her attention.

She looked up. And when she saw him, her eyes sparkled with life.

Radiant, Eve was the very picture of health, like the human spirit reborn.

He ran up to her.

"You survived," he said.

"Of course, dumb ass."

He couldn't prevent himself from laughing, then grabbed her with a big, relieved hug.

They were standing face to face and he swung her off the curb. Their eyes locked in a smiling embrace. Then he pressed her against him and felt her heart beating rapidly against his.

Looking back over the city, he caught Sunny's eye. She had both hands clasped against one cheek and a broad smile on her face.

Beyond her lay the city, like a multi-faceted jewel, with every building reflecting a spark from the sun.

So many had died in the past few weeks, and so many lives had been shattered around the world. Plagues came and went as a natural process. But they shouldn't be caused by greed. And this one could come roaring back stronger than ever.

At least countries had worked together, their governments marshaling their best people to solve a global problem.

With the help and cooperation of so many, he finally saw a glimmer of hope.

About the Author

Fritz Galt is an American novelist with over thirty years of experience in the diplomatic community. He has lived abroad in Cuba, Switzerland, Yugoslavia, Taiwan, India, China, Belgium, and Mongolia. He lives with his family in Washington, DC. His bestsellers include *China Gate*, *Fatal Sting*, and *Murder in Mongolia*. For an in-depth look at Galt's work, visit fritzgalt.com.